The boy who threw the pepperoni stood above Alex, absolutely still, his eyes wide and his mouth gaping like a fish. He didn't talk. He didn't breathe. As Alex watched, the boy's skin faded away from his face and neck. He looked like Translucent Man, the see-through plastic anatomy model Alex's parents gave him for his sixth birthday. He was a full-size Translucent Man, towering over Alex—two frightened eyeballs, a mouth, and a barely chewed hot-dog chunk wedged in his windpipe cutting off the air.

Alex's stomach roiled. He swallowed hard to keep from vomiting. He squeezed his eyes shut and willed the monster to go away. But the creature still hovered, and he was just a kid, and he wasn't breathing.

# The Antidote

## by

## Susan McCormick

**The Antidote**

Cover Art by *Jennifer Greeff*

The Wild Rose Press, Inc.
PO Box 708
Adams Basin, NY 14410-0708
Visit us at www.thewildrosepress.com

Publishing History
First Edition, 2021
Library of Congress Control Number 2021900662
Trade Paperback ISBN 978-1-5092-3566-7
Digital ISBN 978-1-5092-3567-4

Published in the United States of America

# Dedication

To James and Peter,
who read endless drafts of this story

Chapter 1
Black Death

*England, 1348*

*No one in this village was safe.*

*A woman sat weeping, a still man laid out on the bed beside her. His fingertips were black, rotted away. Blood crusted at the side of his mouth. An hour before, he had been coughing, hacking, rust-tinged sputum filling his soiled handkerchief. Now he was quiet. An hour before, his breath had come heavy and harsh. Now there was none.*

*Outside the cottage, in the churchyard at the end of the lane, a pit waited. Shrouded bodies lined its bottom. Soon the man would join them.*

*A hooded figure stood beside the pit, surveying the scene with satisfaction. One of his greatest creations. Oh, he didn't invent the plague, the rats, the fleas.* Yersinia pestis *had been around for centuries. But he improved upon it. More deadly, easier to catch. The Revelstoke clan had not been able to stop him this time.*

*In a year, a third of this village would be dead. In the pit.*

Chapter 2
The Hot-Dog Kid

*Seattle, Washington, present day*

Alex had never seen a kid's skin melt away. He'd seen a lot of other things. But that day in the cafeteria was different.

Pizza day. Everyone loved pizza day. Except for Alex.

Kids crammed the middle-school lunchroom, sitting ten or twelve to a table, jostling, laughing, joking. All so easy, all so casual. Alex left the line and glanced at his usual empty table. Two guys sat there, apart, heads down. Yep. That was his table. Even on pizza day, his table was free. That's why he hated pizza day.

He might as well wear a sign around his neck: "I have no friends."

Someone bumped his elbow, and his tray lurched. Sandy Molloy. Of course. With Jack Knight, Mr. Perfect. Alex caught his apple before it rolled off. Sandy Molloy was so predictable with round fruit. Alex could catch an apple halfway to the ground by now. He put it in his mouth to hold while he maneuvered his pizza back onto the paper plate.

"Nobody eats the apples, Revelstoke." Jack tossed his in the compost bin.

Sandy tossed his, too. "He likes eating wax." He jabbed Jack in the arm and snickered.

His laugh reminded Alex of yesterday at the farmer's market. He doubted Sandy knew anything about it. Alex had bumped into Sandy's mother, and her tomatoes went flying, just like apples when Sandy was around. It was a complete accident, but ironic nonetheless. Sandy's mom was peeved enough, probably because her mom friends were there. But when they bent to pick them up, she winced. Without thinking, Alex gestured toward her abdomen. "That must really hurt." He blurted it out in front of all her friends. She'd glared at him, and no wonder. One friend snickered, sounding just like Sandy, and whispered, "Liposuction."

Ouch. He assumed her surgical scar hurt, but he knew that snicker hurt more. He hadn't said anything that idiotic in years.

Sometimes he knew things. Secrets that made everyone uncomfortable. After a few looks like Sandy's mom gave him, he had learned to keep his mouth shut. But kids still whispered. Moms still pointed.

Alex set his apple back on his tray and slunk to his uncrowded table. One guy left with barely a nod. The other didn't look up when Alex said, "Hey." He did grunt. Better than usual.

Sam the soccer superstar sat at the next table over with his teammates, some perched two to a chair. Isabel Matthews laughed at something Sam said, and her curly, dark red hair bobbed up and down. Alex craned his neck. Jack Perfect Knight slipped in next to Isabel. He would probably ask her to the Valentine Dance.

The guys at the soccer table were clever and quick and relaxed. They knew they were something special, and they knew everyone else knew, too. Alex's tablemate shoveled in pizza, head down, chewing with an open mouth. Alex glanced over his shoulder at the soccer table where Jack flicked pepperonis off his pizza with one hand and casually draped the other over the back of Isabel's chair. The kid next to Alex lifted his head and belched.

Jack's pepperoni landed near a soccer player sitting right behind Alex. The boy shoved back and stood, bashing into Alex and knocking his apple to the floor. The kid chortled and whipped the pepperoni back across the table. Alex's apple rolled lopsidedly until it nudged up against Isabel's foot. Alex faced forward and pretended it wasn't his.

Then his throat tightened. He sucked in, but he couldn't breathe. He coughed, but nothing happened. He couldn't get any air in, and he couldn't get any air out. He tried to shout. His mouth opened soundlessly.

He had to get the belching boy's attention. Alex waved his hand frantically. The boy chewed his pizza, staring at his plate, oblivious. Come on, look up! The boy wiped his chin on his sleeve, eyes down.

And then it was over. He was fine. He could breathe again. What was that? He peered around to see if anyone had noticed his panic. The kids already thought he was strange enough. He didn't need to rub it in.

Isabel's eyes followed the apple as she pushed it under the table with a purple shoe. The boys were laughing. Sam took the pepperoni and pretended to eat it. No one had noticed anything about him at all.

Then Alex saw him. And the hot dog.

The boy who threw the pepperoni stood above Alex, absolutely still, his eyes wide and his mouth gaping like a fish. He didn't talk. He didn't breathe. As Alex watched, the boy's skin faded away from his face and neck. He looked like Translucent Man, the see-through plastic anatomy model Alex's parents gave him for his sixth birthday. He was a full-size Translucent Man, towering over Alex—two frightened eyeballs, a mouth, and a barely chewed hot-dog chunk wedged in his windpipe cutting off the air.

Alex's stomach roiled. He swallowed hard to keep from vomiting. He squeezed his eyes shut and willed the monster to go away. But the creature still hovered, and he was just a kid, and he wasn't breathing.

The other kids were still laughing, teasing. No one saw what Alex saw, he was certain.

Alex hesitated, thinking of Isabel. He was about to go loony tunes, and Isabel was there to witness it.

Oh, well. He jumped up, his chair falling back with a clang. "He's choking!" he shouted. "He's choking on a hot dog!" He waved his arms and shouted it again, louder. "He's choking on a hot dog!"

He searched wildly around. No teachers. Why were there always teachers when you didn't want them but no teachers now? The room near his table was suddenly silent, everyone watching him as he danced around. There was Isabel, staring at him with all the others.

The skin reappeared on the boy with the hot dog. He was no longer translucent. His face was ashen but skin covered, his eyeballs normal and closing slowly. His lips were blue. He leaned forward on the table.

"Heimlich," Perfect Jack said. "Who knows the Heimlich?"

Alex was already in position behind him. The boy leaned back, collapsing into him. Alex put his hands one on top of the other, a fist in the boy's abdomen right above his waist and the other hand over top for extra strength. He could see the picture his mom had taped to the refrigerator years ago for the babysitters. He stared at the picture every time he got orange juice, every time he put the milk away. His dad even made him practice it once.

He pulled in and up, a thrust as hard as he could. Nothing. Nothing happened. The boy was heavy, barely able to stand on his own. Alex held him tighter and tried again, forceful and quick.

The hot dog popped out, flew across the table and doinked off Jack's forehead. Isabel shrieked. The hot dog bounced on the floor and came to rest at Sam's feet. A trail of saliva, hot-dog juice, and slime dribbled down Jack's face.

A crowd swarmed around the hot-dog boy, everyone shouting at once. He looked dazed, but he was talking. He leaned over and clapped Alex on the shoulder. "Thanks, dude," he said, his voice hoarse.

Sam slowly ran a hand across his close-cropped afro, scratching his head with a quizzical smile on his face. Alex found himself running his own hand through his bristly black hair. Sam bent his long body forward and picked up the hot dog, gingerly, between two fingers. He made his way over to Alex and the hot-dog boy, who slumped in a chair. The other kids were quiet now. Sam had that kind of presence.

"It's a hot dog." Sam placed the semi-chewed piece on the table. A few boys groaned at the sight of it. "We're all eating pizza." Sam's dark brown eyes latched on to Alex's blue ones. Sam shifted his gaze toward the table, to the hot-dog boy's spot. Hot-Dog Boy must have choked on his last bite, as there was no hot dog there, no bun, not even a ketchup smear. "We're all eating pizza," Sam said again, his voice low and steady. "How did you know it was a hot dog?"

Alex looked at Isabel, but she looked away. None of the other kids would meet his eyes, either. Sandy cupped his hand to Jack's ear with a whisper loud enough for everyone to hear. "Weirdo." Sam shot him a look, and Sandy straightened up.

Alex breathed deeply. The kids were all thinking the same thing, he knew it. Isabel was thinking it. He'd dealt with this embarrassment his whole school life.

How *had* he known it was a hot dog? There was no way he could have known. The guy had been seated behind Alex, facing the other way. When Alex sat down, the only person at Sam's table he'd paid any attention to was Isabel. Then the kid's skin fell away. Alex gagged, thinking about the eyeballs. He'd seen the boy's eyeballs and his throat dangling from his mouth. Was he crazy?

Why couldn't he just be normal? Was that so much to ask?

Everyone stared. He muttered to Sam that he must have seen the hot dog before the boy ate it. Sam shook his head and said it was a miracle.

For the rest of the day, everyone called Alex, not the other boy, the Hot-Dog Kid. Except Sandy Molloy, who made a point to shove into him and call him "Weirdo" again. And Sam. Sam called him Miracle.

Chapter 3
Translucent Man

What was going on? It couldn't be real. A hallucination.

How had Alex known it was a hot dog? He had seen the hot dog. But not before it was eaten. Not before it was stuck, lodged there in the windpipe, its pink plumpness blocking all airflow in or out.

No. People's skin did not melt away. Not in the world of normal kids.

Yeah, well, he wasn't normal.

This was not the first strange incident. But he had never *seen* things before. When he announced to the second-grade class that Noah was absent because of head lice, the words popped into his head. And right out of his mouth, no censoring involved. It didn't happen often. He'd never told his parents. Noah had not been pleased. Noah's mom had not been pleased. Noah was one more boy who never came to Alex's house.

Today he'd seen someone's skin dissolve. He certainly was not going to tell his parents now. It was way too crazy.

He ran home after school, so keyed up he covered the two miles down the hill and along the lake without stopping. His parents would be at the hospital for several more hours. He had the house to himself.

He rummaged around on the bottom shelf of his bookcase, shoving things this way and that. Erector set, microscope, chemistry set, all toys from his childhood. Most were from the educational toy store, his parents' favorite place. Good toys to play with for a boy who didn't have friends.

Finally Alex found him. Translucent Man. Or Translucie, when Alex was six. Alex pulled him out of the box, sat on the bed, and held him up close. He used to love Translucent Man, with his muscles and wire-like nerves and blood vessels running up and down his arms and legs. His belly was hollow, and all the organs were crammed inside, each one removable yet all fitting together perfectly.

Alex fingered the plastic windpipe, that all-important conduit of air. It was called a trachea, he saw from the box, a ridged hollow tube from the nose and mouth to the lungs. He'd never paid any attention to it before. He was too busy pulling out the heart or stuffing all those intestines back in. Now he saw that even Translucent Man's trachea was not clear, it was pink. You wouldn't be able to see a hot dog in there if Translucie had choked on it. What had happened in the cafeteria?

There had been a book. Alex threw Translucent Man on his bed and ran back to the bookcase. There it was, an accompanying guide to the human body, with each organ system explained in language suitable "for children ages eight to ten." Why couldn't there be a version for twelve-year-olds? Wouldn't matter anyway. No instruction manual was going to cover someone's skin disappearing.

No one else had seen it. Isabel would have done more than shriek if she'd seen what he'd seen. Had he really seen it? Was it a trick of the lights? A trick of the mind? Did he figure out the kid was choking because he'd just felt that same choking sensation and his imagination filled in the rest? But then he would have seen pizza and not a hot dog.

He tossed Translucent Man's book on the floor. His parents were doctors, and their study was full of medical journals. These were magazines for doctors, with new studies or experiments about diseases and their treatments. *Heart. Annals of Internal Medicine.* And that Mercedes-Benz of journals, as his father called it, the *New England Journal of Medicine* or *NEJM.* Alex sometimes read them for fun when he was bored. His father used to show him interesting pictures from his journals, like an x-ray of a stomach stretched to ten times its usual size in someone who was a hot-dog-eating-contest winner. Why didn't those contest guys ever get hot dogs stuck in their tracheas? And what did their stomachs look like with all those hot dogs jammed in there? Alex would know if their skin fell away like Hot-Dog Boy's.

It had not happened. It wasn't possible. There had to be a logical explanation.

Alex considered the journals lined up on the bookcase in the study. Journal after journal. And books, too. New books that looked like they had never been opened and some very old books that smelled like chemicals and dust. Somewhere in here had to be the answer to what he had seen.

Chapter 4
Dysentery

*Oregon Trail, 1852*

*The family was small to begin with, Ma and Pa, two girls, and a baby boy. Their wagon traveled in a group with six others. Across the Great Plains, hot and dusty, fifteen miles on a good day, Ma and Pa walking to keep the wagon lighter for the oxen.*

*"My stomach hurts," Mary Jo said to her sister.*

*"Don't tell Ma," Kate whispered. "She didn't have any breakfast 'cept coffee. She let you have her biscuit. She'll be plum upset if she thinks that biscuit made your belly ache."*

*The passing man on the horse nodded at the wagon train, then drew a red handkerchief out of his satchel to wipe his brow. They camped together the night before, drawing water from a shallow well, contaminated, he knew, with* Vibrio cholerae. *He knew because* Vibrio *was his creation. He drank from his own canteen.*

*By the next day, this small family would be dead. Cholera. They didn't know the disease could be prevented with soap and water, washing hands. That drinking a simple solution of water, sugar, and salt would save them. Those Revelstokes did, but those Revelstokes weren't here. Diarrhea and dehydration would take this family and half of the wagon train and others like it along the trail west.*

Chapter 5
The Explanation

Alex didn't learn much from the journals at first. He started with vision and brains. He found articles about pink eye and disgusting inner eyelid bumps you could get if you wore contact lenses too long without proper cleaning. Ewww. He found articles about seizures and headaches. But nothing remotely related to hallucinating a hot dog.

Then he found it. An article about the capacity of the brain, how people use only a tiny fraction of their brains, but in times of stress, the brain can do much more. If a person thinks they are about to die, they feel time slow down, but that's because the brain uses everything to save itself, registering every little thing it sees in case it is important to the person's survival. So they remember tons more stuff than they would normally have seen in those few seconds.

Maybe his brain, seeing the boy choke, remembered that it had seen the actual cause of the choking while Hot-Dog Boy was still eating it. Maybe when he gazed at Isabel's blue hair ribbon, he unconsciously glimpsed the hot dog.

It was the perfect explanation.

See. No need to concern Mom and Dad about this at all.

It also explained how he knew Sebastian had strep throat in third grade. Or about Jack's problem with constipation. His brain was paying attention.

It's not like he wanted to know these things. These personal details were icky. The kids called him creepy, weird. He liked to think of himself as different. He was different, all right. The Fish House alone made him different enough.

Alex lived in a city, Seattle, but in a house in a park on the edge of the city, on the edge of the water, on the edge of the world as far as he was concerned. No one ventured anywhere near his house. All the runners and moms with baby strollers stayed on the flat, paved trail along the lake, which circled the park and provided views north to Mount Baker and south to Mount Rainier, an enormous beast of a volcano-mountain, covered in glaciers made of snow and awe. A huge, forested hill rose in the middle of the park, with trees as big around as orca whales and twisty, unmarked trails that might go anywhere. That's where Alex lived.

The kids at school didn't understand how he lived in a park. Yet another bizarro element to his life. So what? He was happy to have an entire park for a backyard. When he was young, he didn't understand why they lived there, either. He just knew his dad was in charge of the fish. Even though he was a doctor. Now he knew that Dad was an expert in salmon hatcheries. He studied it in graduate school before he decided to be a doctor. The city wanted to reestablish the salmon population in the stream in the park, and Dad wanted a year off work. When Alex was a baby, his mom returned to work as a doctor, but his dad stayed home all day, taking care of the salmon and taking care of him. When Dad went back to the hospital, they stayed in the house in the park so he could watch over the fish.

The kids at school called it The Fish House. In first grade, he made the mistake of telling Jack about his dad's two jobs. Jack told Sandy Molloy, of course, who teased him that he smelled like fish. "Fish Boy from The Fish House." Not that anyone had ever been there. No one ever came over. The moms always had some excuse or other. But Sandy labeled it The Fish House, and the kids never let it go.

That wasn't all. Sandy never missed an opportunity for a laugh. Alex's black hair stuck up in the front. He'd slick it down with water in the morning, and by the time he got to school, it would be pointing straight up again. "Spiky hair, spiky hair." Plus, Alex said "urinate" instead of "pee" and "I feel nauseated" instead of "I have to barf." So much for having doctors for parents. He'd said each of these only once, but did Sandy ever let him forget? Nope.

It didn't help that his middle name was Asclepius. Sandy heard his full name called out on the first day of kindergarten, Alexander Asclepius Revelstoke, and he laughed so hard the whole class joined in. Miss Teeter put a stop to it, but Sandy kept on when her back was turned. "Asclepius. Asclepius. What kind of name is Asclepius?" Never mind that Sandy's real name was Alfred. Nobody dared tease Sandy Molloy.

Alex asked his mother about his name, and she threw up her hands. "It's a family name. Your father felt strongly about it."

His father told him it was Alex's grandfather's name. And his grandfather before that. It meant first doctor, blessed by the gods. That didn't matter to Sandy.

"Weirdo Asclepius Fish Boy from the Fish House. Weirdo Asclepius Fish Boy from the Fish House."

In second grade, the teacher banned all birthday treats due to a classmate with a peanut allergy. Alex knew it was Sandy Molloy. He'd seen it in his mind, but he had the good sense to keep his mouth shut until Sandy himself told the news.

Well, Alexander Asclepius Revelstoke now knew why he could see these things. His brain was operating at full capacity, working overtime. Take that, Alfred Molloy.

## Chapter 6
## La Grippe

*France, 1918*

*The train was full of soldiers. The Great War was over. The men were going home.*

*The Great War. The War to End All Wars. What euphemisms. War had always been and always would be. Battle lines drawn throughout time. For what reason? Forgotten in history.*

*Man would go on killing fellow man. More war would follow. But this war was his.*

*The Revelstokes were his only foe. They had not succeeded this time. His spoils lay out before him.*

*Half the men on this train were sick. Some would not survive the short ride to the coast. Battle injuries had taken their toll. But his disease would take just as many.*

*He could see them now, feverish, coughing, bloody noses, pneumonia setting in. Men around them tried to move away, but there was nowhere to go on the crowded train. They would soon be on a ship, bound for home. More would fall to his contagion. Then home, to their families, to their wives. His illness, his Spanish flu, spread the world over. One-third of all souls would feel his infection.*

*This war was his.*

Chapter 7
The Clog

In science class the next day, Alex maneuvered himself into a seat at the table next to Isabel. Mr. Beaker talked at the class, warning against something, predicting disaster.

His name wasn't really Mr. Beaker. Sebastian and Wolfgang Nguyen, twins from Alex's elementary school, loved math and science and gave all the teachers new names so the kids could talk about them in code. Even Alex knew the names, though he'd never said more than a few words to the twins. He had to think before he spoke to a teacher to make sure he didn't call someone, namely the principal, Mr. Tangential to his face. The guy did go off on tangents when he spoke. But he was really Mr. Tanner. Ms. Parallel was Ms. Pearl. Mr. Beaker was Mr. Baker. Mr. Cylinder was Mr. Sylvester.

Alex only half listened as Mr. Beaker droned on. Blah, blah, blah. Isabel measured and poured and mixed, the tip of her tongue sticking out while she concentrated. She'd done the same thing that morning, spinning the lock on her locker. Alex saw her from down the hall. He had made up his mind. He was going to do this. He had his line prepared, quick, simple. "Would you like to go to the dance with me?"

She had seen him coming and waited by her locker. She gave a quick nod and a smile, her curls bobbing around her face. Then there was Jack, sauntering up from the other side. Alex heard the whole thing.

"Valentine Dance?" Smooth Jack said. "Go together?"

"Okay. Great," she said.

Yeah, great. Alex was dreaming, anyway, if he thought she would go to the dance with him.

Isabel glanced over from her science bench now, caught him staring, and dropped her head. He probably looked demented. Brown corduroy pants suddenly blocked his view. Mr. Beaker tapped his desk and stared pointedly at Alex's empty flask. Alex got to work mixing himself.

The class was transforming liquid and powder into a delightful Green Goo, a non-Newtonian fluid, whatever that meant. Mr. Beaker had the molecules drawn out on the board, lots of OHs and Bs, and he prattled on about cross-linking polymer chains. All the kids knew was they added some sciency type of alcohol to borax and food coloring and created a gooey mess they could stretch slowly like a rubber band or break in two if they stretched it quickly or bounce if they angled it just right. Better than gelatin, firmer than tofu, more durable than either, they could pour it and tear it and squish it, and it stayed all oozy and shiny and wonderful.

Isabel's goo was a slimy mess, a mass of mush. Alex leaned sideways to tell her more borax, but she held her hand out to Jack at the next table over, her goo oozing between her fingers like green porridge. Sandy

Molloy motioned to his firm goo pile the size of a top hat and laughed at her. Jack elbowed him in the ribs.

"More borax," Jack said to Isabel, and he even came over and wiped her goo back into the beaker and helped her add it.

Mr. Beaker told them they'd love the goo. That they could do anything with it unless it involved throwing or hair. And no ingesting. And absolutely, capital "A" Absolutely, Absolutely No Putting Goo Down the Drain.

That was the warning. Those were the rules. Old school, old pipes, indestructible goo. He said it four times and wrote it on the blackboard. No Putting Green Goo Down the Drain. He said it had never happened before, and it wasn't going to happen today.

But it did. And it was Sandy Molloy who did it. He said it was an accident. He said he didn't hear. As everyone else cleaned up bits of jelly-goo and headed for the trash cans as directed, Sandy sidled over to the empty row of sinks and pitched his in. When it didn't slip down easily, the numskull pushed with his fingers until the huge glob dropped out of sight.

Then Sandy turned on the water. He frowned. This couldn't be good. The guy was usually impervious. The water stayed put, rising higher and higher and not draining at all. Sandy peered around, grabbed the plunger they used when the old sinks were slow, and gave some hearty thrusts. The water didn't budge. Not only that, a strange noise came from the pipe under the sink, a clang and a bang and a whoosh.

Mr. Beaker's head whipped around at the sound. He stood with his eyes on the sink, his mouth ajar.

"Who put Green Goo down the drain?"

Sandy stood immobile, one hand on the plunger, one hand on the faucet as if it were glued there.

"Turn off the water! Everyone, turn off the water!"

Students washing hands snapped to attention at the tone of his voice and tightened the taps. The pipe noise continued, louder, and people stepped instinctively toward the center of the room. Alex saw a pipe shudder. He stepped around the table to Isabel, but she moved toward Perfect Jack.

"Okay. Stay calm," Mr. Beaker said, but he was anything but. He strode to the door and pressed the red intercom button, the one meant for emergencies because it broadcast to the entire school.

"Attention." He licked his lips. "Attention. Turn off all faucets. Do not, I repeat, do not flush the toilets." He lifted his finger off the intercom. A toilet flushed, the whooshing sound unmistakable. Mr. Beaker made a small noise, like an injured animal.

"It's all connected." He shook his head. "Bad design. Stand away from the sinks."

At that moment, the sinks turned into fountains, with water and who knew what else spraying toward the ceiling.

The class howled and huddled together in the middle of the room. Isabel and Jack and Alex all crouched in a heap. Then it happened again, another shower of watery brown.

"Ewww!" Isabel cried.

The water came from every sink but Sandy's. Clear water still filled his sink, unchanged. Sandy himself loitered by the door, ready to slip out. Mr. Beaker seized his collar and pulled him back.

"Not so fast, Molloy. I'll deal with you in time. Right now, GO GET MR. SYLVESTER!"

Sandy bolted out the door and was back before the sinks erupted again, Mr. Cylinder in tow. Sandy was panting, but Mr. Cylinder was bent over, hands on knees, wheezing and coughing. He'd lugged a huge, heavy case full of wrenches and piping.

The pipe banged again. Everyone hunched in, but this time the spray was much smaller.

"Never thought I'd see this on my watch." Mr. Cylinder scowled at Mr. Beaker. "In all my years, we've never had a problem, not in all my years." Mr. Cylinder was old. No one knew how old, but he was wrinkled and leathery from too much smoking behind the dumpster.

Mr. Beaker glared at Sandy Molloy. Sandy inspected the floor.

Mr. Cylinder worked quickly, or as quickly as he could with the heavy case and the awkward angles. The students gathered around, but not too close, mesmerized by the turn the day had taken. Sebastian and Wolfgang later said it was the best science class they'd ever had, right up until it was the worst. Alex tripped over Jack's foot trying to see and careened to the front of the crowd, stumbling past Isabel as he did.

"You." Mr. Cylinder stuck a thick finger into Alex's ribcage. "Pass me the wrenches. I'll have to start here, then move to the main drain cleanout where this goo has blocked the entire system." Mr. Cylinder scooted under the sink as best he could and snatched wrenches out of Alex's hands, throwing them back at him until he found the right size. His hands were surprisingly strong for such an old man. Alex had to take care not to drop them, but Mr. Cylinder twirled them around in his hand as if they were pencils.

Mr. Cylinder lay on his back, working his magic with the pipes and the wrenches. He had to twist hard to get the fitting to move, and they could see his eyes bulge along with his biceps. He yanked the P trap open, and the goo slopped out.

"This. Does. Not. Belong. In. Pipes." He spat it out, pitching Green Goo onto the floor with each word. The P trap was finally empty. He flipped it upside down and gave a final slap. Then he laid his head back and closed his eyes. The class waited. He seemed to be holding his breath. They seemed to be holding their breath.

Mr. Cylinder thrust the P trap into Alex's hand. "Take it." Alex couldn't catch it in time, and it clattered to the floor.

Alex's chest hurt. He couldn't breathe. He stayed there, leaning over, eyes squeezed shut, hand in a fist at his chest it hurt so much.

Mr. Cylinder's hand made a fist. He held it over his chest.

"Hurts," Mr. Cylinder said. "Can't breathe."

Alex gasped, trying to force air into his heavy chest.

"Heart attack," Mr. Cylinder whispered.

Alex squinted at Mr. Cylinder. And he almost vomited.

Mr. Cylinder's face was fine. He had beads of sweat on his forehead. But he had no body. A red heart squirmed where his uniform nametag should be. No nametag. No uniform. No skin, no nothing but a heart, bigger and boggier than Translucent Man's, pumping slowly. Then the heart muscles fell away and exposed the blood vessels, coming and going to the atria and the ventricles.

Not again, not again, please don't let this happen again. It's not real. It's a brain trick. The pain in Alex's chest eased.

"Heart," Mr. Cylinder pleaded.

Alex sprang out from under the sink. "Call nine-one-one!" he shouted. "He's having a heart attack."

Mr. Beaker was on the floor in a flash, bringing Alex tumbling down with him. Mr. Beaker, Alex, and Mr. Cylinder's heart all together under the sink. Alex could tell that Mr. Beaker couldn't see the bloody mess.

Alex saw the clot now, a tiny bit of gunk blocking Mr. Cylinder's heart artery the same way the Green Goo gunked up the school pipes. Blocking the blood flow to the heart and making that most important muscle ischemic, injured from lack of oxygen. His mom the heart doctor had drilled this into him. If too much time went by, the muscle would be irreversibly damaged, a dead area, useless, making the whole heart weaker in the job to pump blood to the body. Even worse, right now the ischemia could cause the heart's pacemakers to go wild, to set off a crazy heart rhythm, a beat so fast or chaotic that no blood would pump. If that happened, Mr. Cylinder would die.

Mr. Cylinder's heart looked a little wiggly. Not oomph, oomph, oomph like a bellows.

Mr. Beaker eased Mr. Cylinder out of the small space. "Sebastian, call the office. Tell them nine-one-one. Everybody back. Stand back. Give him some space."

Alex tried to remember what else his mom said. What were you supposed to do when someone had a heart attack? He couldn't think. His brain was too full of Mr. Cylinder's insides.

"Aspirin," Jack said. "My grandpa had a heart attack, and while we waited for the ambulance, they told us to have him chew an aspirin."

"Good thinking." Mr. Beaker rushed to his desk. Isabel trailed him and brought the bottle back to Mr. Cylinder. She couldn't get it open, but Save the Day Jack was on it, opening the bottle and offering Mr. Cylinder the aspirin in the palm of his hand.

"Chew it up," Jack said. "That's what they made my grandpa do."

"Ick," said Sandy. Isabel frowned at him, and he shut up.

Mr. Cylinder chewed slowly. His face was pasty and sweaty. Mr. Cylinder's heart jiggled like a sack of worms. The steady rhythm faded into a frenzy of extra beats. Alex narrowed his eyes to blur his sight because there was nothing he could do. He was right here with the guy, but he was utterly helpless.

The moments dragged. No one spoke. Mr. Cylinder's breathing was fast and shallow. Alex peeked again. His heart was, thankfully, protected under clothes. His body was back.

The paramedics finally arrived. It seemed like an hour. Alex heard later they were there in eight minutes. They gave Mr. Cylinder oxygen and nitroglycerin and said the aspirin was a smart idea. Alex saw Isabel beam up at Jack. The paramedics hooked Mr. Cylinder up to their heart monitors to watch for the dangerous rhythm. They put him on a gurney, leaving the open pipe and the goo behind. The ambulance whisked Mr. Cylinder away, maybe to the hospital where Alex's mother worked. Maybe she would work on him. Maybe she could explain what was happening to Alex.

# Chapter 8
## Measles

*Boston, 1919*

*The child wiped his runny nose and watery eyes, then clapped his hands as the song ended. He paused to make a wish, coughed, then blew, spittle spattering the three yellow candles and the cake.*

*The man nodded and stepped back, wiping his hands three times with his red handkerchief.*

*Thirty people gathered close, tiny hands grabbing for cake, older hands more patient.*

*The clown set down his juggling balls and happily accepted the last piece.*

*Thirty people here, thirty people there. He was satisfied. This disease was one for the ages, with every single person on earth caught up at some point in their life, usually as a tot. Measles would infect them all. Many would succumb, and if not to death, then to deafness or blindness or brain impairment.*

*The child's fever came that night, a high fever, higher than his mother had felt in any of her children. Within three days, a red, splotchy rash covered the child, his face, his entire body. The next day, his cough changed, deepened, worsened. Within a week, he was dead.*

*Within three weeks, every child at the birthday party fell ill, save one. Within two months, one other child was dead. Four had painful, oozing ears that would never heal and never hear. One had convulsions and her brain stayed the brain of a child.*

*The clown died as well.*

Chapter 9
The Tunnel in the Mountain

Alex's mom was a cardiologist, a heart doctor. Alex knew what might happen to Mr. Cylinder. His mom did cardiac catheterizations, or "caths" as she called them, to hunt for a blockage in the blood vessels to the heart. Just like Alex had seen. Arteries could get gunked up with plaque, a buildup of cholesterol due to that forbidden high-fat diet his mom always rankled against. Then she would thread a tiny balloon through a blood vessel in the leg and up to the blocked heart vessel and blow up the balloon to smush the plaque. Or she could leave behind a stent, a hollow tube, to hold the vessel open and let the blood through like a tunnel in a mountain.

His mom had talked about heart caths since Alex was little. "Straight to the heart," she'd say with a smile as she cut into her steak and stabbed a piece with her fork. Later they gave up steak and all red meat, though Alex and his dad still went to Bill's Burgers if his mom worked late on Saturdays. "Mom doesn't need to know about this," Dad would say, code for "Mom would go ballistic if she knew you'd eaten a double-patty burger, fries, and a chocolate shake."

Alex once read an article about how much fat and calories were in fast food. A lot. His mom helpfully showed it to him in the *New England Journal of*

*Medicine*, where Alex found the article about brain capacity.

No amount of brain capacity could make someone's skin melt away. It had happened twice. It wasn't a hallucination. No amount of brain capacity could show a hot dog or a heart clot. Even the *NEJM* didn't cover that.

More proof that he was not normal. "Different" didn't begin to describe how weird he was. Sandy Molloy was right.

His mom couldn't help him. His mom would only freak out.

Alex's dad was a doctor, too, and his dad, Grandpa Asclepius, and his dad and his dad, all the way back forever. Grandpa was an old-time doctor, a family doctor, in a tiny remote town in the mountains of Canada. Grandpa Asclepius could do anything—treat asthma and diabetes, deliver babies, set broken bones.

Alex hadn't seen Grandpa Asclepius in years, but he still remembered the stories. Once Dad gashed his hand when he took Grandpa's knife to gut a fish on his own. "If you're old enough to use a knife, you're old enough to stitch this up yourself," Grandpa told him. Grandpa made Dad open the suture packet and get out the needle, which looked enormous to Dad, curved and wicked, before Grandma Bea said, "Enough, Asclepius," and Grandpa took over.

That was years ago, when Grandma Bea was around and before Grandpa got sick. Alex hadn't seen him since then.

Alex's dad was an internal medicine doctor. He took care of all parts of the body. Mom knew about hearts. Dad knew about everything else.

So he went to his dad with his story about the Hot-Dog Kid and Mr. Cylinder. He didn't mention eyeballs or wiggly heart sacs. Without these minor details, his story sounded plausible, not "weirdo" in the slightest. In Alex's family, around the dinner table, his mom and dad talked about medicine all the time, describing interesting cases from their day and sometimes asking advice.

"You'll never guess what I saw today," Mom would say. "Takotsubo cardiomyopathy."

"No way," Dad would say. Then he'd explain to Alex that it was actually possible to die of fright or to die of a broken heart, that the heart could get stunned and even stop in a strong emotional situation.

Alex thought he might have experienced Takotsubo cardiomyopathy himself that very day in science class. That might account for the no-skin trick of the light.

As Alex described what had happened, minus the Translucent Man details, he realized that he had grown up in medicine, heard stories of ailments as a little kid, ate dinner with diseases bantered about as idly as, "what a rainy day this is." Plus, he read the *New England Journal of Medicine*. The *New England Journal of Medicine*, for gosh sakes! No wonder he could visualize things perfectly, imagining the inside of the body exactly, especially since he and Translucie were such good friends.

Much calmer, Alex finished his tale. Maybe he was normal after all. He grinned at his dad, who turned his head away. "I guess you and Mom taught me well."

Dad didn't say anything.

"Remember that pop-up book you gave me, *Your Heart and How it Works*? I read that every night for six months. The pop-ups were permanently popped out by the time I was done."

"Yes," his dad said slowly. "I remember that."

"Mom's always going on about 'chest pain this and blood clot that.' Of course I know all about heart attacks."

His dad regarded him, blue eyes to blue eyes. "Of course. But, Alex, Mom doesn't need to know about this."

Alex was surprised but a little relieved.

"Just yet," Dad said. "Mom doesn't need to know about this just yet."

Chapter 10
The Man at the Bus Stop

Alex headed to the library the next day to search for books on the brain. The Hot-Dog Kid might have been a hallucination, but now it had happened twice. Somehow, his brain had been able to recreate what Hot-Dog Kid and Mr. Cylinder were experiencing. He needed to know more about the brain's potential and the tricks it could play. He needed a logical, scientific reason behind what he'd seen, for his own sanity.

He waited for the bus home, protected against the drizzle by the covered glass enclosure of the bus stop. He thought about his dad's words. He thought about the Hot-Dog Kid and Mr. Cylinder and Bill's Burgers and the time his dad dropped the Thanksgiving turkey on the floor and then scooped it right back onto the platter, plus all the other things they didn't tell his mom. Why did Dad lump chest pain, Mom's favorite subject, in with fatty foods and kitchen sanitation?

A man watched him from the corner of the bus stop. He was fit-looking, with a crew cut, blue jeans, and a black tee shirt. He wiped his hands three times with a red handkerchief he took from his pocket, a handkerchief so large and out of place it might belong to a magician.

Alex nodded, and the man nodded back. Alex flipped a page in the book on top of the stack in his arms, and the whole pile collapsed, books falling everywhere. What a klutz. They both bent to collect them, and the man reached for the closest book. Also the only book not from the neurological section and embarrassingly titled *So You Think You Might Be Crazy*. Maybe the guy hadn't seen it. The man handed it back without a word, but Alex thought he saw a smirk.

Alex's body shot back. His mind turned black, all black like coal, murky like the ocean bottom, like the worst of the night. He hit the glass of the bus stop. So hard, the wind got knocked out of him and he couldn't breathe. He leaned there, gasping. He shook his head to clear his mind.

An icicle of fear gripped Alex's chest, tight and frigid and terrifying. He opened his eyes and closed them immediately. The man's outline had faded, and the swirling blackness was his face, his body. It was happening again.

Alex could see inside this man and he saw something horrific, black and dark. This fit-looking man, this smirking magician, must be very sick.

Alex slowly knelt to get his books. He didn't see the man glare down at him in loathing and recognition from eyes that did not look sick.

Chapter 11
To See

*Seattle, present day*

*He had waited twelve years for this day. Proof that he was free of the Revelstokes, proof that he was not.*

*He was not free.*

*But he would be soon, more free than in decades.*

*This last Revelstoke was coming of age. He had the gift. He was starting to see.*

*This had to be delicate. This had to be careful. This was his last chance.*

*This child was the key.*

*First, he needed to know what the last Revelstoke could do. And if he had what he wanted.*

*Then he needed this last Revelstoke to set him free.*

Chapter 12
The Bees

The man with the red handkerchief never boarded the bus. When it came, he stepped back as if it wasn't his, but only one bus came to that stop. Alex was only too happy to get on without him, without his black illness.

Were these sick people everywhere? Did people just look normal on the outside and it wasn't until you peeled away their layers that you saw the diseases underneath? Or was Alex insane and making it all up in his mind?

Alex eyed the brain books in his lap. As if the answer would be in one of these. Who was he kidding? He was the one who was sick—sick in the head.

The drizzle had stopped when he stepped off the bus. His shoulder ached from hitting the bus stop. He walked along the lake loop trail toward home, shifting the heavy books back and forth.

He passed a woman tying her shoe. She had skin. Her face and her arms were all there. A teenage runner sprinted by him, legs pumping but intact. When would it happen again? His heart pounded as he looked around, but no one else was in sight.

An island sat across a narrow strip of lake, and Alex saw a thin plume of blue smoke, like the start of a fire but blue instead of black. It dissipated quickly, but almost as quickly a dark cloud formed against the gray sky, a tiny black cloud growing larger by the minute, a noisy black cloud, a buzzing black cloud.

No, no, no, no. Nothing but bees buzzed like this cloud. He was allergic to bees. They made his face swell up so you couldn't see his eyes. His dad said the next time it might mess with his breathing, like Sandy Molloy and the peanuts. Alex never left the house in the summer without his epinephrine pen. But this was February. There were no bees in February.

Just offshore now, the dark cloud of activity droned louder and louder, closer and closer. He thought he could actually see the individual bees. Not a few. Not dozens. Hundreds. Thousands of bees swarming toward him, like in *Winnie the Pooh and the Honey Tree*.

He ran, and they followed. A pack of stinging danger. He swerved into the woods. They raced in behind him, the din like an airplane engine. He threw his library books at them, over his shoulder one by one. As if that would do anything. Ridiculous. He dropped the whole stack and ran faster. The mass stayed with him. It would be bad enough if this horde caught him, but with his allergy, without his epinephrine pen, it would be certain death.

Desperate, he ran as fast as he could. He could not outrun bees. He was too scared to look back. Their roar filled the air. They had to be close.

He would never reach home. Home was too far. But he knew this forest. He was near a hiding spot, his "tree house" on the ground. Fallen trees all came together to make a shelter he could crawl under, with boughs and bigleaf maple leaves and pine needles stacked high on top to make a roof. Two more corners.

He knew every tree root waiting to trip him, every hole that might twist an ankle. He dashed and he jumped and he dodged. The buzzing grew louder and louder.

The bees caught up to him, surrounding his face, his arms, all around his body. Bees brushed his cheeks. They flitted in his hair. He forced his arms to stay down, to not swat them away or they would sting.

There it was! Sanctuary. He dove in. The needlelike branches swept off the bees and closed in behind him, sealing him off. He landed in a ball and rolled to a stop. He held his breath. A muffled humming overhead. Then silence. Blissful, unthreatening silence.

His heart stopped pounding. He sat up and shook off the leaves. He brushed his arms to get the dirt off. And he brushed off a bee. A single bee. A solitary menace.

One bee could kill him.

Alex jumped up. His head hit the roof of branches. The bee swirled around lazily, circling his body. Alex stood absolutely still, not even breathing. The bee landed on his hand, gliding to a stop as if it were a runway. Alex gritted his teeth to keep from screaming. The bee sat there. Alex's hand quivered from holding so still. The bee did not budge.

Alex's eyes were riveted on the bee and burned from not blinking. He locked his knees to keep from falling. He couldn't stand there much longer without moving.

Was this it? Alone in the woods, hidden by tree branches where no one would find his dead body?

The bee took off. No sting, no pinch, no pain. The bee flew around his head, the buzz in his ears amplified by his fear. It flew in a larger circle, a big slow tour around the shelter. Then the bee flew out, leaving him alone. Safe.

Chapter 13
Valentine

What was going on? He'd seen skin melt away. He'd slammed against the side of the bus stop so hard his shoulder still hurt. Thousands of bees chased him from the lake in February. He couldn't explain any of it. How much of it had really happened? He had to get a grip.

It didn't help that the next day was Valentine's Day. Never a good day. Not for Alex. Not for most boys. Not for most girls. Definitely not for sixth graders.

In kindergarten through fourth grade, the teachers made them write out valentines for everyone in the class. Everyone received the same number, but it didn't take brains to see that some kids' valentines were bigger or fancier or came with chocolate hearts attached.

Isabel Matthews always got the prettiest, biggest hearts to match her dark red curls. Even in elementary school, Alex chose her valentine carefully, giving her "Be Mine" instead of "You're a Champ!" Jack Perfect Knight always cleaned up, with chocolate hearts and homemade cookies.

In fifth grade, the teachers let them give valentines to whomever they wanted, no quota, no rules. They said they were old enough now to make wise choices about their valentine selectees. Not true, Alex thought, as he compared his tiny stack to Jack's or even Sandy Molloy's. Wolfgang and Sebastian, the twins, had fewer than he did, but they shared everything, so their pile looked large.

Sixth grade, middle school, was the worst because kids gave valentines willy-nilly, with no teacher guidance whatsoever. And there was the dance. A dance! Eleven- and twelve-year-olds mixing in with the seventh and eighth graders at a Valentine Dance held during the last two periods of the afternoon. Isabel and Jack. Alex wanted to skip school just for this reason, but his mom could see through any "I'm not feeling well" excuse except death itself.

The dance was worse than Alex envisioned. The PTA decorated the gym with red balloons and streamers and cardboard hearts with Cupid's arrows going through. Geez. Chaperone moms and teachers stood in clusters. Alex saw Mrs. Nguyen try to shoo the twins to the dance floor. They looked as mortified as Alex felt. Music played, all the wrong songs, and boys sat on the bleachers or stood against the wall. The girls' volleyball team stuck together and busied themselves pouring red punch. A girl broke off from a dancing group and ran off to the bathroom in tears. Isabel and Jack stood in a corner and talked, but even they seemed ill at ease.

The bell finally rang. Students fled the gym, clearing the school faster than on the last day before Winter Break.

Alex skipped the bus and walked home, happy to have the cool drizzle on his face after the stuffy, tense air in the gym. He wore a waterproof jacket over his fleece. Red fleece for Valentine's Day, which earned him an extra excused tardy in homeroom. School spirit bribes.

He paused at the park edge and searched the lake for black clouds, bees, buzzing. Yesterday was a freak event. No way it could happen again. Still…

He'd collected his library books last night, on guard against signs of danger. Today everything again seemed normal, but his eyes lingered on the lake. He was skittish. Anyone would be.

He started up the hill toward home. The woods were drier than the loop trail, with only a few drops of rain seeping through the thick tree canopy. Alex slowed down and breathed deeply. Rain, pine, and dirt. Some of his favorite scents. He relaxed, letting go of the stupid dance, the bees. This was his forest.

The old growth forest was a smaller version of the huge rain forests out on the coast, the Hoh and Queets and Quinault Rain Forests in Olympic National Park where some of the world's biggest trees stood. A ranger there told Alex that because of the cool climate, a toppled tree could last centuries, not like a tropical rain forest where things disintegrate quickly. A dead tree could become "a nurse log," providing nutrients for new trees that grew on top as it crumbled. The smell of decay permeated the air, an earthy, solid smell Alex loved.

He passed one of his special places, a fort in the tree trunk of a snag, a huge, old, dead tree whose center had been opened up by lightning decades, maybe even centuries before, the woody carcass big enough to sit in and stretch his legs. He poked his head in now but decided to keep moving. The woods also had a cave, dark and smelly with sludgy puddles. Ick. One summer a rock shifted inside and crushed a boy's leg, and the whole area was blocked off with signs saying, "Off Limits." Alex hadn't been there in years, but he'd never liked it anyway. Around a few more corners was his tree house on the ground. He slowed and stared at the opening, barely discernible due to the overlapping branches with their long pine needles. His legs shook. Those bees had been right here.

On the ground next to the path, he spotted a banana slug, a slow, wet creature the size of a skinny hot dog. It excreted a coating of slime as it picked up debris to protect itself, leaving a long mucousy trail behind. Just like the hot-dog trail on Jack's forehead. Alex shook his head to get rid of the image. That was the day his life had changed. That was the day he started seeing things.

All the other images flooded in, the eyeballs, the flaccid heart. Oh, boy. Think of something else! The stupid Valentine Dance sprang to mind. No, not that. Something else. He strained to hear the quietness of the forest, the noises muted by the giant trees with their thick bark. Rustling and creaking and whistling, all soft and muffled. Much better than thinking about Jack's forehead. Or eyeballs.

Then he heard it. He knew the sounds of his forest, and this was not one of them. It was steady and low, but it wasn't the trees or the wind. Louder as he moved forward, he crept slower and slower.

Who knew what this might be?

The noise was rhythmic and lulling. Alex was almost on top of it before he realized what it was. Breathing.

Breathing from something alive, something large. He glanced around. His own breath was loud and fast, but this breathing was louder. Whatever it was, it was close. So close its breath filled the air, foul and fetid.

He stood still. What was it? Where was it? He slowed his breathing so he could hear. Where could he hide? His hollowed-out tree and his tree fort on the ground were near, hopefully close enough in case he needed them. The breathing continued, loud and raspy.

Then Alex saw him. A dog. A dog stood on the other side of a giant nurse log, hidden by a leafy branch, shivering. He was a huge dog, with a big square head and long, floppy ears. He was multicolored, black, brown, and tan. Alex had never seen anything like him on the dog show on TV after the Macy's Thanksgiving Day Parade. Not a purebred, that was for sure.

The dog's head flailed around, his eyes wild. He skittered away as Alex climbed over the log. The dog limped along, his head and shoulder bobbing with each slow step. He glanced back and tried to trot. He tripped on a tree root and pitched over, his rump flying up in the air. Alex edged closer. The dog knew he was beat and lay on the ground, his head turned away.

Careful, careful, don't scare him more.

"It's okay, boy. Don't be afraid." Alex knelt toward the dog. No wonder the dog was limping. The pad of his back foot was shredded, bloody and matted with pine needles and dirt. The flesh was raw, cut in so many places the individual paw pads were not clear.

"Ah, fella. How'd you do this?" Alex placed his hand on the dog's back and the skin flinched. The dog didn't move, so Alex kept his hand there on the soft fur and then slowly, gently, petted the dog's back.

The dog lay there, breathing heavily. Then his leg blurred. The blood, the mud, the ragged tissue all disappeared. Alex saw far into the foot. Several chunks of green glass lodged deep in the pad, covered over with granulation tissue that had grown in around the injury, the dog's own attempt to heal.

Every time he walked, though, every time he put weight on the foot, the glass shifted, causing a new tear, never healing.

"You poor guy. We have to get you home to my mom and dad. They can take that glass out. They can fix your foot."

The dog looked away, defeated, Alex could tell. He put his big head on the wet ground and sighed.

"It's okay," Alex said again. "I can get you there."

He took off his outer jacket and folded it in half. He nudged it under the dog's body. Then he rolled the big dog on his side and onto the jacket. So far, so good. As long as the dog didn't move. He kept one hand on the dog, keeping him on his side. He scooted around to the other side and pulled and unfolded the jacket until it lay flat on the ground. Then he gently rolled the dog back down. Now the dog lay in the middle of the jacket.

Alex had seen this done at the hospital, waiting for his mom. The nurses called it a "draw sheet," and it looked like a neat trick.

"Okay, here we go." Alex crouched and grasped the top of the jacket. He leaned back and pulled. Nothing. The makeshift gurney didn't move. So much for that idea.

"Wow. You're heavy, fella." The dog fixed his eyes on Alex. Those big, brown eyes. Now they seemed disappointed. What was it about dogs' eyes?

Alex tried again, leaning and pulling with all his strength. Nothing. Zero. Zip. The jacket did not budge even an inch.

"Okay, okay," Alex said, thinking fast. "I have another idea."

Now he took off his red fleece jacket and wrapped it around the sore leg. The fur and the muscles fell away again, revealing a milky pocket of pus. Alex squinched his eyes until the grisly wound blurred. He tied the jacket tightly around the dog's waist, tucking the see-through leg up under the dog's belly in the sling. Out of sight.

"Come on, fella, come on," Alex encouraged. The dog shifted his weight, then gingerly stood. Three legs supported his weight. The jacket secured the injured leg under his body. He took one step, then a little hop, then more steps. The three legs worked fine, almost as good as four. Alex and the dog hobbled along, to the edge of the woods, into the clearing, almost home.

A dog! He had no collar, no tags, no sign that he belonged to anyone anymore. What if Alex could keep this dog? He looked like a good dog. A dog who trusted him. A dog who would love him. A dog was what had been missing from Alex's life.

He'd name him Valentine. The name popped into his head and it seemed to fit. Today was Valentine's Day, after all. Even though Alex never liked Valentine's Day. But this dog resembled a gigantic Valentine, wrapped as he was in a red fleece bow. His Valentine.

There was no way his parents would let him keep this dog.

The dog panted faster and slowed down. Alex slowed with him. Anything to spend a few more minutes with his Valentine before his parents said no.

As he and the dog trudged along, Alex realized where the name came from. The word was carved over the front door of the hospital, the door he had gone through more times than he could count, every time he went to see his parents after work.

Tempus, Sanitas, Valentia. Time, Health, Strength. The dog's name meant Strength.

Chapter 14
The Belch

Alex and the dog stumbled up the front stairs. The dog hopped, but Alex could see how tired he was. And thin. Who knew how long he had been in the woods.

His mom was home, just as he'd hoped. She was home early because she and Dad were going out for Valentine's Day, and she was dressing up. She had a soft spot for Valentine's Day and that morning had already given him a heart-shaped box of chocolates. She hardly ever gave him candy. Bad for the teeth and the pancreas, she would say, because too much sugar hurt the pancreas and caused diabetes. Mom was always one to kill the fun.

She had his dinner on the table, a veritable Valentine's feast of heart-clogging fatty foods like lasagna and garlic mashed potatoes and a red velvet cupcake with a cinnamon heart on top.

"Happy Valentine's Day," she called from the kitchen as he walked in. She came out with an apron on and a tray of cookies in her hand. An apron. His mother never wore an apron.

She stopped as soon as she saw the dog, who huddled behind Alex's leg as if he were hiding. His mom didn't say anything. The hand with the cookie tray was stopped in time, the cookie smell filling the air.

The dog couldn't stand it any longer and bolted out, surprisingly quick for a dog with three legs. He bumped the tray with his big nose, cookies flew in the air, his mom screamed, and the dog gobbled up the cookies as they fell.

Then, before Alex could do anything, the dog leaped toward the table, front paws up, weight supported on one leg as if he had been doing it his whole life, his big head in the lasagna until it was gone, too, along with the cupcake and the tiny red heart.

Then he burped, a huge belch, that bad breath now mixed with cookie and lasagna and cinnamon.

Alex was stunned. His mother looked catatonic. The dog plopped at his feet and flopped on his side so his bad leg was up. He gazed up at Alex. He belched again. Those big, brown eyes looked happy. His dog, Valentine, looked happy.

Chapter 15
I Can See Disease

Alex's mom did not look happy.

"What is this?" she whispered. Her whisper voice sounded scarier than her shouting voice, though that sounded pretty bad, too.

"This is Valentine. I found him in the woods. He's hurt. You have to help him."

"He doesn't look hurt," his mom whispered.

"He is, he's hurt, it's his paw, you have to help him."

"He ate my cookies."

"He's hungry. He's hurt."

"He ate your dinner."

"I don't need it. It looked pretty fatty, anyway. It's bad for my heart," Alex said.

"I made you that dinner," Mom whispered.

Technically, she hadn't made it, Alex knew. She'd picked it up at the grocery store deli and the cupcake shop. And the cookies were from a premade bake-and-serve package in the refrigerator. Alex didn't mention this.

"I know. It looked delicious. Thank you. But he was hungry. He probably hasn't eaten in days. See how thin he is?"

They studied the dog, who beamed at Alex contentedly.

Don't belch, don't belch. Alex knew his mom could only take so much.

But he did belch, and then he threw up, and the cookies and the lasagna and the cupcake all came out all over the Oriental rug. His mom's prize rug that his parents bought in China before Alex was born.

His mother would never let him keep the dog now, now that he had eaten her special treats, swallowed them whole, and then barfed them up all over her memory of her carefree traveling days. He loved this dog already but there was no chance of him staying. Not anymore.

It took him a moment to realize that his mom was down on her knees, apron and all, stroking the dog, gently pushing on his stomach and unhooking the fleece sling. She saw the paw and she clicked her tongue, like she did when Alex got a splinter.

"He's starving," she said. "He ate too fast. All that fat. No wonder he vomited. He's dehydrated, too. See these mucous membranes?" She lifted his jowl with her finger. "And this foot. What happened to his foot, do you think?"

Alex couldn't believe it. His mom had turned to doctor mode. Maybe she hadn't noticed the carpet.

"Roll the carpet back, Alex. We have to get him out of this mess."

She knew about the carpet and she didn't care! Alex dropped down and started rolling the carpet, gently nudging the dog to the side. His mom took off her apron and wiped the fur around his face.

Alex had to give it to her. His mom knew her way around vomit.

"Look at this paw. Poor thing." She tried to lift his leg, but the dog jerked and scrabbled around trying to get away.

"Oh, my, this isn't going to be easy. He doesn't want to hold still. Must be pretty painful."

Alex lay his arm across the dog and held tight to keep him from moving. The dog was strong, and his three good legs pushed in all directions, his eyes frantic.

Alex relaxed his grip, leaving just one hand on the dog's back. The dog relaxed and Alex moved his hand around to the soft area of his belly that had no fur, petting lightly, humming under his breath. The dog stayed put.

"That seems to be working," his mom said. "Now let's see if I can get in here." She slowly lifted the paw and the dog balked.

Alex started to sing, softly, slowly. "Tummy rub, tummy rub, tummy rub." He kept his hand moving back and forth across the dog's belly, back and forth. "Tummy rub, tummy rub, tummy rub."

Alex's mom smiled at him. The dog's eyes were almost closed, his face peaceful. She tried again. This time the dog didn't move.

His mom felt along the bottom of the paw. "This looks pretty bad. I wonder how he did it."

"He stepped on glass," Alex said.

"Hmm. You might be right." She palpated some more. "It could be glass. It could be a lot of things. Maybe he caught it on a fence."

"No, it's glass," Alex said. "It's that thick green glass like old soda bottles. You have to get it out. I think it's infected."

He could see the glass, green and sharp, he could see the pus, a thick white pudding of trouble.

"I don't know, Alex. I think we should clean it up and soak it, then maybe we can see better."

"It's right there!" Alex said, too loud. He pointed to the glass bits, to the pus.

His mom set down the paw and stared at him. Her voice was back to a whisper, the scary whisper again.

"Alex, what can you see?"

Then he knew. Then he saw. The paw was bloody. It was shredded. But it was covered in beefy red tissue. There was no glass, no pus. Not visible anyway. He had seen through, Translucent Dog this time.

He kept his eyes on the dog. He didn't want to acknowledge her question. He could feel her eyes bore into him until finally he had to meet her gaze.

He looked at her and she looked at him and he knew that she knew. She knew that he could see what was underneath, the disease hidden under the skin.

He could see disease.

And he knew that this was one of those things he should not have told his mother.

Chapter 16
The Marble

Alex's mom took care of the dog's paw quickly, efficiently, soaking and cutting and extracting and leaving in a wick to treat the infection collection. Alex kept up his "tummy rub" song and his petting. She bandaged the foot and strapped the leg back up in a sling, much like Alex had done. She didn't say much except, "Bring me gauze" and "Hold that toe."

This wasn't good.

When Dad came home, they didn't go out for Valentine's Day dinner. They didn't eat dinner at all, as far as Alex could tell. They sent him to bed, and he went because the dog went, lying on the floor near his bed.

The dog fell asleep quickly, with an occasional whimper as he shifted around. Alex lay in bed wide awake. Valentine's nose twitched and his eyes fluttered in his sleep. Alex strained to hear what his parents were saying, sometimes in low voices, sometimes shouting.

He could only hear pieces. None of it made sense.

"How long have you known?"

"Your father wasn't strong enough."

"We'll lose him."

"Think what could happen."

"You told me he was dead."

"He's just a boy."

"We can't protect him."

"If we know, ILL will know."

Had they said ill? Will? Bill? What were they talking about?

The next day his mother announced she had changed her week's schedule. She would be home in the afternoon when he got home, and she wanted him to take the bus and no more walking home alone.

The day after that his parents told him they were not going skiing for the upcoming President's Day week. His school had four days off, but they were not going to Crystal Mountain like they always did to ski and snowshoe and sled in the shadow of Mount Rainier. Instead they were going to visit Grandpa Asclepius, Dad's dad, in the middle of the mountains in Canada. They almost never made the trip in the winter because the roads were so bad and sometimes closed for days because of avalanche risk.

They almost never made the trip at all. It had been years since Alex had seen him. After Grandma Bea died, Grandpa got really sick. Even before that he had been sick. He had heart disease, lung disease, lots of disease. His mom said it was because he used to smoke.

"Whoever heard of a doctor that smoked?" she said.

"It was a different time," Dad said. "Everybody smoked then. They didn't know."

Then Grandma Bea died, and Grandpa got throat cancer and almost died himself. His voice was different now, a gravelly whisper after the surgery, but he didn't die. He retired from medicine and stopped coming to visit, and Alex and his family stopped making the trip north.

"He's too sick," his mom would say. Even Dad never went to see him. Alex hadn't wondered why, hadn't thought about his grandpa much at all. Until now.

What was going on? Alex tried to ask questions, but his parents weren't talking. The dinner table was eerily quiet. The only bright spot was Valentine.

Dad took him to a vet, who pronounced him thin but on the road to recovery. The vet noted his halitosis, or bad breath, but said he didn't see any dental cares (cavities, Dad translated) or gingivitis (gum inflammation) as a cause. He told them to brush his teeth daily, and he gave them the name of some doggy breath mints but said he didn't hold out much hope, given the severity of the problem.

Most importantly, from Alex's point of view, the dog had no microchip, no way to trace the previous owners. Alex couldn't even pretend to be sorry. They put up signs, "Dog Found," with Valentine's picture, but that week, at least, no one responded. It was as if the dog had dropped from heaven.

They bundled in the car for the long drive north. Two hours to the border, then a line of cars waiting to cross into Canada for the long weekend. Alex could see cars full of kids and skis and families and snowboards. Going to Whistler, going to Sun Peaks, going to White Pass. Alex loved skiing. His family only skied once a year during this vacation at Crystal Mountain. He would race down the hill, so fast it felt like flying. He wore the dorky helmet for his mom, but at least it cushioned the noise, like he was in his own private world.

They wouldn't ski this vacation, for a reason still unclear to Alex. They were going to Grandpa's, and though mountains circled his house, the skiing there was for experts only, double black diamond, not for the faint of heart. His dad used to ski like that, but a bum knee kept him from anything but the blue slopes now.

Once they were in Canada, the cars thinned out and they traveled alone on some stretches of the road. Four to five more hours, if the roads were clear. To Revelstoke. Where his family had lived going back to his great, great, great, he didn't know how many greats grandfather. All doctors. Just like Grandpa. Just like Dad.

Could they all see what was underneath? Injuries? Disease? He didn't think his dad could. When Alex was three, he jumped off the porch and hurt his leg. His dad said it was okay, and Alex walked around on it all day before it was so painful he asked to be carried. They went to the ER that night, and it was broken and he got a lime-green cast he wore for six weeks. Dad felt horrible, but it made a great story when people went all gaga about both his parents being doctors.

Anyway, he didn't think his dad could see disease. But he suspected Grandpa Asclepius could.

When he was four, he swallowed a marble. He never told anyone because his mom always told him not to put things in his mouth, that he'd choke or get a bowel obstruction. He didn't know what a bowel obstruction was, and he didn't care.

They were on one of their visits to see Grandpa Asclepius and Grandma Bea, who gave him a bag of marbles and showed him how to play, drawing a circle and setting the marbles in a cross. Best of all, though,

Alex loved the way the marbles felt in his mouth, and he swished them around with his tongue, clicking them against his teeth. Then he swallowed one. It went right down so he knew he hadn't choked. But boy was he worried about bowel obstruction. Whatever that was.

He tried to ask his mom. "So what is bowel obstruction, anyway?"

She just laughed and ruffled his hair and said, "Don't be silly."

He worried all that day and the next, waiting for something horrible to happen. Then his grandfather took him in his arms, and he relaxed, marble or not, and his grandpa whispered, "The marble's past the danger area. You don't have to worry about it anymore. It will pass out on its own."

And it had, the next day, with a clink into the toilet bowl. He flushed it down without even considering a plumbing obstruction. He was so happy to see the marble out of him. He figured his grandma and grandpa didn't want it back.

Alex always thought Grandpa had seen him swallow the marble. Or counted the marbles and knew one was missing. Or heard Alex ask his mom about bowel obstruction and figured it out on his own.

But now Alex knew. His grandfather could see disease, too.

And, after years of avoidance, Alex's family was driving pell-mell north to see him.

## Chapter 17
### ILL

They arrived long after dark. Valentine sat in the back with Alex, taking up most of the seat. He was belted in with a dog seat belt Alex bought when he got the breath mints, extra-large size. He predicted his mom's exact words.

"What if we had an accident," she said. "That dog would become a one-hundred-pound projectile." He didn't want any excuse for her to leave the dog behind in a kennel.

The dog didn't mind the seat belt, and he took to the long car ride as if it were just another day lying around with Alex. He didn't move much anyway, with his bad paw. But in less than a week, it was healing well, and Alex bet he'd be up and running in no time.

They turned off the main road and onto the dirt lane that led through the woods to a large clearing where Grandpa's cabin stood. Alex hadn't been there in years, not since he was little, yet he remembered it instantly.

Valentine was sleeping, but he woke as soon as they arrived, straining against the belt and whining.

"Sounds like he has to go to the bathroom," his dad said. "Perfect timing."

"He's such a good dog," his mom said. Alex couldn't understand why she was so taken with

Valentine, especially after the carpet incident. She never once mentioned it.

Valentine barked, a sharp, quick bark. His ears were back, and he pushed his big head right up against the window. In the few days he'd had him, Alex had never seen him like this, even when he really had to pee. Even when gallons came out.

As soon as Dad opened the door, the dog tried to jump out, but he was still belted in. Alex unhooked the buckle while his dad untangled the belt from Valentine's legs.

"Hold on, old boy, don't want you to hurt another foot," his dad said.

Once free, Valentine bolted out, moving with surprising quickness, barely a limp, to the steps and up to the porch.

A shadow rose from a bench with a rustling. Valentine stood so close that in the dark they looked like one being. When Alex got to the porch, he could see Valentine leaning heavily on his grandpa, or maybe it was Grandpa leaning on Valentine.

They didn't move. Alex mounted the stairs and joined them.

"My boy, my boy." His grandpa opened his arms, bringing Alex into their fold. For a second, an icy chill of terror gripped Alex's chest like it had with the man in the bus stop. The fear disappeared as soon as it came and he felt himself relax, like when he was younger. He realized how tense he'd been, they'd all been. In his grandfather's arms, the tension fell away. It always did.

"It will be all right," his grandfather whispered in his scratchy, hoarse voice. "But it will not be easy."

Not the reassurance he was hoping for.

Then his parents were there, and their little group broke up, and the strain returned. His parents and his grandfather hugged, and his dad strode ahead to switch on the lights. His grandfather straggled behind, and the dog stayed right with him.

Grandpa's house was more of a cabin, made of logs, but warm and bright with big windows and a spectacular view of the mountainside. There was no need for curtains because there were no neighbors. For the first time Alex thought those windows looked sinister, huge and wide and opening up their inner world to the blackness outside.

Grandpa breathed heavily from the short walk. He coughed a few times into a handkerchief, started to say something, then had a coughing fit so severe his eyes teared. Alex's dad looked away. His mom rubbed at her eyes like she was going to cry. The dog leaned in harder.

His grandpa seemed smaller than Alex remembered, shorter and slimmer. He still had thick black hair, though, and those blue Revelstoke eyes.

He waved them into seats around the fire. He had an enormous fireplace surrounded by large, smooth rocks, and a big, dark wood mantel. It was covered with photographs, old photos of Grandpa and Grandma Bea and Dad when he was young. Alex had never seen those before. Maybe they hadn't been there or maybe he'd been too short.

Grandpa had been waiting for them, and he had sliced apples and cheese and bread on the table by the fire. His mom must have had the same thought because she grabbed for the food, but Alex had already lifted it onto the mantel and out of reach of the dog.

Valentine didn't make a move for the cheese. He stayed right next to Grandpa.

"Better leave it on the mantel, just in case," his mom said.

Valentine's big mouth exhaled right into Grandpa's face. His mom tried to push the dog's head away. "He has such bad breath."

"Hmm, I don't notice." His grandpa put his face closer to the dog's. Even Alex would never put his face that close. "It doesn't bother me," Grandpa said.

Valentine settled down then, laying his hefty body at Grandpa's feet. The room was quiet again. Alex could hear his grandpa wheezing.

Then Grandpa whispered, "What have you told him? What does he know?"

"It's late," his mother said. "Can't it wait until tomorrow?"

"No!" Alex shouted, and his grandfather spoke, too.

Even though Alex shouted and his grandfather whispered, Alex still heard his words.

"ILL won't be waiting."

## Chapter 18
## Evil

"ILL!" Alex's mother's voice was shrill. She pleaded with his father. "All this time. All this time you told me ILL was dead!"

His mom was freaking him out.

"Not dead." His father averted his eyes. "Indisposed."

"As good as dead! You promised me!"

Alex's grandfather shifted in his chair and fixed his eyes on Alex. "It is time," he said. He inhaled slowly and coughed, finally breaking his intense gaze. Alex's parents sat stiffly. His mother gripped the sofa so hard her fingers looked like claws.

"Revelstokes can see disease, can diagnose illness, without labs or x-rays. And not just disease. Injury, illness, anything wrong with the body. We can see inside the body, right to the problem, sometimes detecting the problem before the patient even knows he is sick."

Grandpa said they were doctors going way back, as far as anyone could remember, using their gift to figure out what was wrong and using their medical school training to fix it when they could. "Some things are harder to cure, of course, like cancer, but if we find it early enough, we have a fighting chance."

Alex was right. His dad didn't have the gift. Alex's grandfather did, Grandpa Asclepius, and his father before that, Great Grandpa Asc. The gift skipped around, no pattern. Grandpa's grandpa didn't have it.

"And now Alex has it," his mom spat out, as if the words were a bad disease themselves.

"I couldn't tell. I didn't know. I looked for signs," his father said.

Alex's throat tightened at his father's next words. "I thought we were safe."

"You couldn't know," his grandfather whispered. "The gift is not clear until boyhood is gone."

"He's still a boy," his mom said softly. "He's too young for this."

"You have the gift." His grandfather leaned toward Alex. "It is a wonderful gift, and you can help so many."

"Help?" His mom took a fast gulp of air and had a coughing fit herself. His dad put his arm around her on the sofa. Her coughs subsided, and she buried her face in his shoulder, crying.

Then she lifted her head and spoke in her scary whisper voice. "How did you 'help' Bea?"

Grandpa's face slackened. He dropped back in the deep chair, eyes closed. Valentine pushed himself up and rested his head in Grandpa's lap. Alex wished he could do something, too.

They all looked so miserable, his mom with tears falling down her cheeks, his dad biting his lip to keep from crying himself, his grandfather slumped in his chair.

"Tell me," Alex said. "Tell me what's going on."

His dad stood and came to him. He crouched down, eye level, blue eyes to blue eyes.

"It's ILL," he said.

"Ill? What's ill?"

"I-L-L—we call him ILL, all in capital letters to emphasize his power. ILL is a man, a being, an essence."

"Evil," said his mom. "ILL is evil."

Alex shivered and moved closer to the fire. His mom was scaring him, but he could see she was even more scared herself.

"Yes, evil," said his dad. "ILL is evil."

"And disease and temptation and danger and addiction. Anything that can make us sick, ILL might have had a hand in," his grandfather whispered.

"But not everything," his dad said.

"No, not everything," his grandfather said. "Some diseases are his, and some diseases just are. There are bacteria and viruses and cancer cells and cholesterol plaque. They all play a role. ILL can manipulate these as well. Changing the nicotine content in tobacco plants to increase the addictive potential of smoking, which causes cancer, for instance."

"And some diseases are all ILL," his father said.

"Yes." His grandfather nodded vigorously. "Take polio. ILL was behind it. A terrible disease. It existed for thousands of years causing little problem, but in the twentieth century something changed. ILL transformed the disease. The infectious virus suddenly caused epidemics, spreading quickly from person to person, thousands upon thousands of people affected. Paralyzed, crippled, dead. Until Jonas Salk and the vaccines in the 1950s, no one was safe."

"Every time there was an outbreak of something new, we had to wonder if ILL was involved." His dad raised his voice. "Going back centuries, through all millennia. Plague. Cholera. Spanish flu. Smallpox. The only clue we had was that when ILL created a new disease, he came after Revelstokes."

Alex's mother jumped. At the exact same moment, so did his grandfather, a small movement, almost imperceptible. Alex saw his odd expression. His grandfather opened his mouth to speak, then closed it. A moment later he did speak, slowly. Alex knew he was leaving something out.

"Yes. The only clue." What was he hiding? Was there another clue besides terrorizing kin? Grandpa continued, speaking normally. "Revelstokes could get in his way. We could thwart him. Only Revelstokes have this power."

"Small illnesses, major disease, epidemics, ILL could cause all of these," his father said. "But there are also whole diseases that do not exist, will never exist, because of Revelstokes."

"Revelstokes have changed history by stopping some of ILL's horrors. And ILL does not control everything," his grandfather said. "But enough. There would still be disease without ILL. But not nearly as much."

His mother sucked in her breath. Alex strained to hear her words. "But not now. He's not able to do this now. He's as good as dead. He has no power. That's what you told me. Right?" She sounded so desperate.

"You are correct," his grandfather said. "Recent diseases are not his. AIDS, Ebola. ILL did not cause these. His power is much diminished. Not like before."

His mother reached her arm around Alex's shoulder and drew him closer to her, farther from his grandpa.

"He is manacled. Shackled," his grandfather said. "It took all my father's powers to do it."

"It was after polio," his father said.

"Revelstokes could not stop polio." His grandfather leaned toward Alex. "But my father stopped ILL. My father told me he would stop ILL or die trying."

Alex's father spoke softly. "And he did both."

Chapter 19
Grandma Bea

Alex's father put his hand on Grandpa's shoulder. "Grandpa Asc died long before I was born. I never knew your dad."

Alex's Grandpa Asclepius didn't say anything.

After a moment, his mother said, "Then it's over. Grandpa Asc destroyed him. ILL is impotent."

"No. Not completely." His grandfather sighed. "He doesn't have the power for his huge creations anymore. But he can still hurt. One by one, he can hurt."

One by one? That didn't sound good.

Grandpa Asclepius was silent. Alex's mom cleared her throat. "Not Bea? You're not saying he hurt Bea?"

"Grandma?" Alex lifted his eyes to Grandma Bea's smiling picture above the fireplace. Grandma Bea, who always had a bandage with a puppy on it for when he skinned his knee. Grandma Bea, who loved swings and never tired of taking him to the park. Grandma Bea, who donated her own scarf for his first snowman. Had ILL hurt Grandma Bea?

His grandfather sagged into his chair. "Bea. My Bea."

"Mom." Dad's voice was soft, too. "What happened to Mom?"

Alex's grandfather took a deep breath. For once he didn't cough. "ILL didn't cause the burn. It was a minor

69

burn. Minor. It was right after I saved that family. Family of six, mom, dad, and four kids, all boys, tiny kids, oldest one was eight. They'd gone mushroom hunting in the woods, and the three-year-old broke his arm jumping off a tall stump trying to be like his older brothers. The dad called to ask if I could see him at their house, so I took my bag and headed over. He'd broken his arm, all right, so I put him in a splint, and they invited me to stay to dinner. The mom had made a huge quiche with all the mushrooms."

Grandpa paused and panted to catch his breath.

"We all sat down to eat, and she passed me that mushroom quiche, and it was as if I could see through it, and what I saw were the mushrooms, the poison mushrooms, *Amanita phalloides*."

Alex's mom gasped.

"I never heard this story," his dad said.

"I've had a lot of time to think about this," his grandfather whispered. "I'm convinced this is what happened to Bea. I made ILL angry."

What were they talking about?

His dad must have seen how perplexed he was. "*Amanita phalloides*. Death cap. Poison mushrooms. The family picked poison mushrooms by accident. It can happen if you aren't an expert mushroom hunter, a mycologist. There are a few cases every year. It hurts the liver, and without a liver transplant, it's usually fatal. And it's almost impossible to get a transplant in time. Not to mention six transplants."

"The family would have died." His mom put her hand to her mouth. "You saved them all."

"Yes, my gift saved them all."

"How did you see the mushrooms?" his dad asked. "They hadn't eaten them yet. They didn't have any disease."

His grandpa was quiet for a moment. "I don't know," he finally whispered. "I have heard that some Revelstokes have extra gifts. I don't know," he said again. "But I think that's why ILL was so upset. He knew about me, of course, but I was a minor player. Not much power, not much skill. A trivial amount of gift. This was something new, this ability to see disease before it even took hold. I might have other powers. He didn't know. I didn't know."

His grandfather stopped. Alex could see him struggling, his mouth all twisted, but it didn't seem to be his breathing. Poor Grandpa. Finally he started again.

"I never will know. I never went any farther, I never tried… Right after that, right after that…"

"Mom?" Dad said.

"Yes," his grandfather whispered.

"But Grandpa's shackles? How could ILL hurt Mom? ILL had Grandpa's shackles blocking his power."

"I know. It happened right here." He gestured to the fireplace, and his voice grew stronger. "Bea added a log, and a shower of sparks touched her sleeve and it caught fire. She got it out immediately. The burn on her arm seemed minor. We ran cold water over it and washed it and put on an antibiotic burn cream, and after a day or so it was healing well."

He paused, breathing slow and deep now. "Then I saw something. I think I saw something. I'll never be sure. As we cleaned it one day, a wisp of blue smoke formed over her arm, then a tiny cloud the size of an egg, then it fell on her arm and was gone. I asked her about it, and she hadn't seen it, so I was never certain. But she got sick."

Alex sat fully upright. What had his grandfather said? Blue smoke?

His grandfather continued. "The burn became infected. Nothing we tried could stop it, not antibiotics, not even surgery when it came to that. A superbug, they called it in the city hospital. But I knew what it was. It was ILL."

"And Bea died. And right after that you got cancer," his mom whispered.

"Yes. Right after that I got cancer." His grandpa patted the dog's head, still in his lap.

"You told us not to visit," his dad said.

"ILL beat me. Even without his powers. I knew it was him. He gave Bea the infection, and he gave me cancer. Oh, it was the cigarettes, too, don't get me wrong, the cigarettes for the heart problems and the lung disease and the throat cancer. But it was ILL, too."

He coughed again, a rough, hacking cough. "Why did we all smoke? ILL had a hand in that, too."

Alex's mom shook her head.

"Oh, yes," his grandpa whispered. "I know it's a lot to think about. This was all long, long ago. Those potent cigarettes sent smoking addiction through the roof. And not just smoking. He popularized a sweetener that was sweeter, more intense, and cheaper than sugar itself. One company tries it, then all the other companies follow suit. ILL didn't have to do anything more. He exploited our weaknesses. Fat, too. Everything we craved was ever more available, ever more delicious. Larger portion sizes, higher sugar content, increased fat. They will make it if it sells. And it does. Now we have extra-large soda drinks and super high-fat foods and all the other temptations that cause ill health."

He turned to Alex. "Take sweets. It isn't normal for our bodies to crave so much sugar. The more we eat, the more we adapt, the more we crave. ILL didn't create cravings. He just made the temptations harder to resist. But I digress."

Grandpa panted again. His words came out slowly. "Even with the Revelstoke shackles, ILL got Bea. He tried to get me. I had to keep you safe. I had to keep you all safe. And you have been."

His grandfather was speaking so slowly Alex thought he was done. His words were so soft, Alex may have been the only one to hear.

"Until now."

Chapter 20
Lepra

*Hellas (Greece), 300 BC*

*His mother was snatched away from him. One day she was there and the next she was gone, taken by men sent with a decree. He screamed and cried and grabbed at one man's leg with his toddler arms. He tripped another, and the man cursed and hurled him into the corner. His grandmother and his grandfather and his brother stood by, unspeaking, and let her go. His mother.*

*They never told him why. When he asked them, they turned their eyes to the side and mumbled and couldn't look back. He stopped asking. He stopped talking at all. His brother carried on, carried on as if they had never had a mother. Given up by her own parents without a fight.*

*He lived in that house where he used to have a mother. He never knew his father, a soldier, they said. He lived in that house with his grandfather and his grandmother and his brother. But he lived alone. He didn't speak to them. He didn't look at them. He didn't have a family.*

*He made up stories about his mother. When he was six, he thought she was a fairy and could fly to him when he needed her. When he was ten, she was a goddess, called back to take her rightful place. When he was twelve, his brother told him the ugly truth.*

*Leprosy. Banned from the city, made to live on the fringe, outcast, for fear she would pass it to others. Left to die. Slowly.*

*The whole family would be banned if they hadn't let her go. That was nothing to him.*

*He tried to find her, leaving the city walls, searching in the rubble of society outside. Beggars and vagabonds, convicts and murderers, the sick and the dying. All thrown together in a heap of humanity scrabbling to survive. But not the lepers. Even the lepers were not fit to live with these, forced to live farther out, alone with their unspeakable disease.*

*He finally found them. His mother had long ago succumbed, remembered only by an old leper with no ears and no feet. The man was not Greek, but one brought back from the conquered land. The old man told him his mother was different, stoic, unfazed by the toll of leprosy on her body, curious even. And, finally, peaceful in death. She spoke of him, her little angel, her left-behind child who tried to save her, too young to know about her shameful illness.*

*The old man reached under his rag clothes and brought out a large cloth, clean and shimmery, alive in its radiance.*

*"I have watched for one like you," he said. "One worthy of my work. I have waited. Centuries. I am satisfied with what I accomplished. I am ready to leave this world. I have allowed this disease to take me. I knew you would come for your mother and that you would find me." He handed the youth the cloth, then he leaned back and breathed his last.*

*The boy returned to the city and resumed his quiet life. The cloth from the leper stayed hidden in the shed.*

*Then he saw the light patch. One started on his arm, a lightening of the skin until it was a circle of white moon above his wrist. Then another on his leg. Then his trunk. Then bumps, on his arms, on his feet.*

*Nothing hurt. He was numb. Even the cooking kettle falling on his toe caused no pain. His toe turned red, then white with pus, then black. Then there was no toe.*

*More bumps appeared. More light patches. All covered with his clothes. No one to know.*

*Until his brother spied him undressing in the shed. Saw his mangled feet, his skin with ulcers and pustules.*

*His brother stood silent, as on the day his mother was taken. His brother was as silent as he himself had been all those years.*

*It all came out at once, the years of silence, the years alone. He dove into his brother and the two went down as one, coiled around each other with arms and legs entwined. The old leper's cloth lay in the barrel, but they crashed into the cask and its contents spilled out, the cloth pressed into the dirt under their thrashing mass. His body heaved, and his strength against his brother was infinite. No pain. Numb.*

*It happened in seconds, but the change was immense. His brother lay curled, feet deformed, toes gone, body covered in crusted sores.*

*He gave his brother the leprosy, and he was free. He gave others more through the years, plague, smallpox, polio, influenza. Each time, he felt his power grow. But never so much as the day with his brother.*

*The cloth from the leper stayed with him always.*

Chapter 21
All That is Left

"My gift is small," Alex's grandfather whispered. "ILL knew it, too. I found my gift when I was older than you, but ILL was right there to see what I could do. Nothing, that's what. I'm embarrassed to say that I left a friend in need. He died of polio. I am still ashamed when I think of it all these years later. I am a country doctor with a knack for diagnosis, and that is all. What harm could I cause ILL way up here in a tiny town in the mountains? I diagnose my patients, they are grateful, but little changed in the world, in ILL's world of evil and disease. Until the mushrooms, I didn't even consider that I could do anything else. Years ago, generations ago, ancient Revelstokes ago, it wasn't like this. Revelstokes were spread across the oceans. Some had gifts stronger than others. Revelstokes could see disease, but some Revelstokes could do much more."

"More? What more?" Alex's mom asked.

Alex's head was already about to explode. Now there was more?

His dad shook his head. "We only know through stories. Events get distorted over the years. Skills are forgotten. Two generations might go by with no one having the gift, so people start to doubt it ever existed."

His grandfather nodded. "We know they had gifts great enough to fight back, to fight disease. Track ILL's new creations and stop their spread beyond the first few patients. Great enough to battle ILL. And battle they did, until most of the Revelstokes were gone. Through time, the family got smaller and smaller. For hundreds of years, our family here in Revelstoke was all that was left."

Alex could see what was coming.

Alex's grandpa assessed him. "Now you, my boy. You are all that is left."

No. This couldn't be. Alex's stomach felt like it had when he saw the wiggly heart.

His grandfather's voice was soft and raspy. "You have the gift. You have started to use it. This will not go unnoticed. ILL will test you, to see how strong your gift is, to see how strong you are."

Now Alex's own heart felt wiggly.

"Enough. Enough." His mother put up her hands. "I never fully understood all this, and maybe I didn't really believe it. One thing I know is that when you two first told me about ILL, before we were even married"—his mom stared pointedly at his father— "you two both assured me ILL was a thing of the past. Unable to harm. Shackled."

"ILL as we knew him is no more. But he is still out there. He must work one person at a time now. He cannot harm on a large scale. But he can still harm."

He mother sat upright. "This is not at all what I imagined. What I was led to believe. Tell me about the shackles."

Alex's grandfather nodded. He stroked the dog, and when he spoke his voice was stronger. "ILL has a weakness," he said.

Chapter 22
The Shackles

*Revelstoke, Canada. 1961*

*This Revelstoke was clever. The one they called "Asc." Noble, righteous, unafraid. Twice the man his son was.*

*He knew the son had the Revelstoke curse. He had witnessed the revelation when the youth came of age. A child at his school fell from the slide and lay there, stunned. The Revelstoke teen looked into his eyes, and his face confirmed the family curse. He knew the bone was broken. He did not need his father's x-ray machine.*

*But this youth was not his father.*

*He had tested him years ago.*

*His superior polio creation had been everywhere. The mountains of Canada were not immune. Every summer brought fear. Don't go to the pools, to the theaters, to any crowded place where his polio lurked. No one knew it was a virus. No one knew how it spread. The world was terrified. Until that Jonas Salk and his vaccine, summers were a special time.*

*It was an easy matter to infect the young Revelstoke's friend. When he had trouble swallowing, the Revelstoke looked in his eyes and saw the weakened nerves of the esophagus. He would know the nerves to the diaphragm would follow. The lad would soon have trouble breathing.*

*And what did young Revelstoke do?*

*The Revelstoke fled. He said nothing to his friend. He was afraid. Afraid to tell the boy he would die. Afraid to stay by his side and contract the disease himself.*

*He did not pass the test. This Revelstoke was inconsequential.*

*But his father was not. The man they called "Asc" marched right to the sick boy's house and broke the news to his family and tried to get the boy to the city where they had a breathing machine, an iron lung. To no avail. The polio was quick. The Revelstoke could not save him.*

*But the Revelstoke father had courage. He had tenacity.*

*Now, years later, he and this Revelstoke "Asc" would meet.*

*The Revelstoke's patient was very sick, an old man with a mild skin infection that blossomed, first a redness and then a tiny blister and then a boil. It grew despite penicillin, it grew despite the new antibiotic, methicillin.*

*Methicillin was a problem. The medicine men were always trying, inventing new drugs to make his job harder. Methicillin could treat bacteria that penicillin could not. A great new antibiotic, they said. A cure-all.*

*Not for this man. His boil grew into an abscess that would not heal, even after that Revelstoke lanced it and drained the pus out. The infection spread to his blood and his heart and his lungs. He was febrile and chilled and broke a tooth with his teeth chattering.*

*This was a bacterium to be harnessed.*

*He traveled to the man's tiny shack, one room with no windows and one small half door. No electricity, just candles and a potbelly stove for heat in that cold, snowy winter. A room of death, with all that coughed up infection everywhere. The Revelstoke visited in vain. His medicines did not work.*

*An infection like this, unresponsive to the old medicine and the new, unhealing, worsening... In time, on its own without his help, it would spread. But right now, right here, he could stoke a worldwide epidemic of infection with no cure.*

*When he arrived in that dismal place, the Revelstoke "Asc" was sick as well. He had contracted the virulent disease. He knew there was no cure, he could barely walk, but still he was there. Why wouldn't the Revelstoke give up? Two men dying in that tiny, dark shack, one on the bed, one kneeling on the floor.*

*They were of no concern to him.*

*The Revelstoke saw him and knew him and shouted but could do no more.*

*He took out his black cloth, shaking it loose into a huge flag of shimmering glory. He swirled it in the air, capturing the bacteria, capturing the cause of this incurable illness.*

*Then the Revelstoke was up. He must have used his last strength. He grasped an edge and wrested part of the cloth away.*

*No matter. There were more, endless, a rope of black, continuing on regardless of how much the Revelstoke pulled. He cackled at him, laughing at his desperate, feeble attempt.*

*And then...and then...*

81

*The cursed Revelstoke thrust the cloth into the fire of the potbelly stove. The Revelstoke yanked it out in an arc of flame. A thin curve of orange blaze hung between them, suspended momentarily in time.*

*The moment ended. Fire reached across the black to touch the red.*

*For millennia, the cloth had survived.*

*Now the black cloth burned. Only a tiny bit remained unscathed.*

*The Revelstoke shackles took hold.*

Chapter 23
The Weakness

Alex's grandfather spoke without coughing. "ILL's power to harm lies in a black cloth, magical material with an energy to create or transform disease. To destroy the cloth is to destroy his power. Revelstokes cannot search out ILL. ILL appears on his own terms. Opportunity is rare. Generations go by without a face-to-face encounter."

Maybe they would get lucky like those generations. Nothing face-to-face.

"Your Great Grandpa Asc met him," Alex's father said. Alex closed his eyes and shook his head.

"Yes. Your Great Grandpa Asc, my father, had a patient who was very sick, and ILL wanted what he had. Years later, reports came of methicillin-resistant *Staph aureus*, in Britain and finally in the United States and here in Canada. Now it is everywhere. Bea's arm…"

He stopped talking and took some slow breaths. No one spoke.

He went on. "My father didn't know it, but this was the first case of a resistant organism to the new antibiotic. But ILL knew. When he appeared, a huge figure, larger than life, my father saw a chance, a once-in-a-lifetime opportunity to save humanity. My father told me all this later that night. He was able to get that cloth and burn it. ILL stomped the fire out, but his body shrank down, smaller and smaller, to the size of a normal man. My father tried to reach him, but ILL was gone in an instant, out of that death shack. His cloth was ashes. Only a tiny bit remained unscathed."

"The shackles," Alex's mother said.

"Yes, the shackles," his grandfather said. "My father destroyed most of the magical cloth and ILL lost his power. That strain of *Staph aureus* bacterium died with my father. ILL never made another epidemic. He can only wreak havoc one person at a time, nothing contagious, nothing that can spread, no diseases on a large scale. He is weakened."

Weakened. Alex leaned back and let his breath out.

His grandfather turned toward his dad. "My father only lived one more day. I think it was the happiest day of his life."

Chapter 24
Part of ILL

Alex's mind buzzed. He'd never be able to sleep. Grandpa pried Valentine off his leg and sent the two of them to bed. He gave Alex a hug like he'd done when he was small, a relaxing hug that left him calm and secure. Alex fell asleep as soon as he lay down. By the time he woke, sun streamed through the windows, and the dog was gone.

He found Grandpa at the big window in the living room, gazing out at the snow. Valentine leaned into him.

"Why does he lean on you?"

"Your dog is very smart," his grandfather said. "He has a gift, too, a special gift. Animals are way ahead of us on this. Dogs, cats, dolphins. Even birds to some extent. They can all sense disease."

Valentine? His dog had powers, too? "What disease is he sensing?"

"Come see for yourself." His grandfather drew Alex to him, staring right into his eyes.

"Every Revelstoke is different," Grandpa said. "I see disease by looking in people's eyes. My father only had to look a person up and down, like today's whole-body CT scanners. Do you know what you have to do?"

Alex froze. The icicle grabbed his chest again. The terror rushed in. He struggled to breathe through what seemed like a straw, struggled to breathe through a throat on fire with pain. His grandfather's skin melted away to reveal his throat and lungs, the lungs shrunken and gray but not nearly as ominous as the dark lump pushing in under Grandpa's chin.

This was not happening, not with his grandpa.

Grandpa pulled him into one of his big, relaxing hugs. His skin returned and he smiled down at Alex. Alex's mind cleared. He could breathe normally again.

"Is that what it feels like for you?" Alex said, "Like you're breathing through a straw?"

"Ah, you have an extra gift. You can feel disease as well as see it. My father told me about this. It will make you an excellent doctor. You'll have empathy, the ability to put yourself in the shoes of another, to really know what it feels like for them."

Feel disease? Seeing was bad enough.

"So you know how I breathe. I suppose it does feel like I'm sucking through a straw, never enough air, always too much work." His grandpa paused and took several long breaths, inhaling deeply and exhaling through pursed lips. Alex had seen him breathe like this before.

"Smoking is terrible. COPD—chronic obstructive pulmonary disease—comes from years of smoking. What did we know? Cigarettes were all over. Everybody smoked, cowboys, politicians, movie stars, doctors. It seemed so glamorous." He hacked, the cough racking his body. "There's nothing glamorous about this.

"ILL is a patient man. A few puffs and you're hooked. It may take years, but smoking will get you in the end—heart disease, stroke, COPD, cancer, you name it."

"Your cancer's back, isn't it?" Alex knew it was back. He had felt the pain. He had seen the lump under his grandpa's chin.

"Yes. That is your dog's special gift. He knew I had cancer. And he makes me feel strong. I haven't felt this strong in months. But there's not much more to be done for the cancer. I wouldn't want to do more anyway. Look at me. I can barely breathe. I've had a good life. I have some time left, and then I'll be with my Bea."

His grandfather took a few shallow breaths, ragged and wheezy.

"That's something I never considered when I was young," he said softly. "ILL and Revelstokes—this has been a battle for all ages. I am a Revelstoke. I expected ILL to come after me. But the innocents…Bea. He made her sick because of me. And my friend, Jim, with the polio. That is something I will live with forever."

Alex didn't know what to say. He leaned in on his grandpa's free side. Valentine leaned on the other.

"We Revelstokes can see disease," his grandfather finally said. "I know what I've got. I don't want to live on and on, not like this." He wheezed in and out. "There was a time when we could do so much more…" His grandfather coughed and braced himself with a hand on Alex's shoulder. "Long ago, Revelstokes—"

Alex didn't hear him. He was fighting to breathe, fighting the pain in his throat, in his grandpa's throat, fighting the terror, more than the terror of not being able to breathe.

His grandpa took him in his arms, and he could breathe again. The pain was gone. He relaxed against his grandpa's thin body.

"You have to be able to control it," his grandfather said. "You have to figure out how you do it, so you can control this gift rather than it controlling you."

"It's not a 'gift!'" Alex hissed. What was this thing? "I don't know how it works. It just happens. I see horrible things. I feel it. And it hurts."

His grandfather tightened his hug.

Alex had to ask. He had to know. That icicle of fear was the worst part. "Why do I feel so afraid?"

"Ah. You have this, too." His grandfather pulled him around and gazed deep in his eyes. His grandfather's eyes were blue and gentle and strong. For a second, though, Alex saw a flicker of unease.

"Some Revelstokes have more gifts than others. You embody the disease, ILL's disease. You feel afraid because you don't know if you can get rid of it, rid of the disease, rid of him. You feel what ILL created, and you feel ILL. Part of ILL is in you for a second in time, and ILL is very, very scary."

Chapter 25
The Vendetta

*Hellas (Greece), 275 BC*

*He'd heard rumors of Asclepius. A healing man. With sons who were healing men.*

*Then he saw his brother. He had not seen him since the day in the shed. He knew him immediately. They had always looked alike.*

*He should be crippled. He should be dead. He was whole, and he was living just as those around him.*

*His brother was alive.*

*His brother had married, had children, had happiness, had health.*

*The healing powers of the healing men were to blame. The healing men became the Revelstokes. The Revelstokes became his private vendetta.*

Chapter 26
Like Bea

"Can you believe I was a doctor who smoked?" His grandpa laughed, then coughed, then choked. Alex sat with him on the front porch and gazed out over the clearing and the trees covered in snow to the huge mountains, craggier than the mountains around Seattle. The sky was clear, and the air was fresh and cold. Breathing it in made Alex's lungs hurt. His grandpa loved it out here, so Alex stayed put, bundled in a wool blanket over his winter coat. Valentine lay between their legs, sleeping.

"Everything was different in those days. Everybody smoked. ILL must have been in his heyday. There are all kinds of diseases that ILL can cause, and you're an unlucky innocent if you fall in his path, but there's also disease that ILL set loose through a cascade of more and more temptation. We cause disease ourselves through our own cravings. It's up to each one of us to fight them on our own. But cigarettes, oh, how people craved cigarettes!"

Grandpa surveyed the mountains and took a deep breath. Alex tucked his cold feet under the dog. Grandpa continued. "ILL took something addictive and made them almost irresistible. This was before we knew about smoking and health risks. Then along came C. Everett Koop, the US Surgeon General in the 1980s, and new laws and warnings on cigarette packs. I thought that might be the end of cigarettes, the final demise of that addiction. People tried to stop, and the only new people smoking were the rebellious types, the 'you can't tell me what to do' types. Getting back at the establishment, teenagers getting back at their parents, trying to be cool." He laughed and hacked and coughed. "Pretty cool, huh?"

Alex smiled wanly.

"I underestimated big business. Despite the health risks, we still have cigarettes, we even have e-cigarettes." His grandfather coughed again.

The dog sat up and panted in their faces. Alex pushed his fragrant head gently away. "Sorry," he said to his grandfather. "His breath is awful."

His grandfather breathed deeply. "Rejoice in his bad breath. I cannot smell it. Your dog can detect my cancer. He makes me stronger when he is near. His breath is different for me. Those with cancer cannot smell this dog's breath."

Lucky Grandpa. The dog seemed to smile. A fresh wave of noxious breath wafted over to Alex, who coughed and smiled back.

"ILL has lots of tricks up his sleeve," his grandpa continued. "We got extra-large sugary sodas and supersized portions. Twelve ounces of soda has one hundred fifty to two hundred calories. It adds up every day. Not to mention the sugar. Forty to fifty grams. High fructose corn syrup. Straight to the pancreas. If it's a large drink, that's thirty-two ounces, three hundred seventy to five hundred thirty calories, over one hundred grams of sugar. Then they made extreme sizes and bigger than extreme sizes. Outrageous. Type

II diabetes and obesity soared. A double whammy. Two diseases. A dream come true for ILL. As bad as smoking." He hacked again, setting off a spasm of coughing. "Well, maybe not as bad as smoking."

He shook his head. "Now we have 'Would you like chips with that' and enormous sugar-laden muffins with chocolate chips."

"I like those muffins with chocolate chips," Alex said.

"Exactly. You see what we're up against. You see how tasty they are. That's what we're fighting, we doctors trying to keep people healthy, we Revelstokes who know about ILL and cravings."

"Mom doesn't even let Dad and me eat red meat."

"A woman ahead of her time," Grandpa said. "A good influence. Once in a while is okay. Though I can't think when I last had a steak. Or a hot dog."

Alex shuddered, remembering the hot dog stuck in Hot-Dog Kid's throat. That made him think of Mr. Cylinder and his wiggly heart and the man at the bus stop with the red handkerchief and the black insides. Alex's mouth went dry. He remembered hitting the side of the bus stop and not being able to breathe.

"I think I've seen him," he said softly.

"What?" His grandfather's whole body jerked toward him.

"I think I've seen ILL. He looks like a normal man, but I know he's sick."

His grandfather spoke slowly, hoarsely. "He is sick. Very sick. But not like you think. Tell me what happened."

"He had an unusual handkerchief. He looked fit and healthy, but his insides were nothing but black darkness. Somehow, I got thrown all the way across the bus stop."

His grandfather's mouth dropped open, and his breathing grew more labored.

"So. He has already found you." It seemed to take all his energy to speak. After a long pause, he continued. "That was him. His form has changed. But that was ILL. ILL is all disease—what you saw, that blackness, that darkness, that was evil itself. That was ILL."

He paused again. Now his words were barely audible. "He saw what happened. He knows you have the gift. He knows you have power, probably more power than any recent Revelstoke." His grandfather was shaking.

"Revelstokes help people. We figure out what's wrong so they can get better. In that bus stop you saw what happens when all that helping goodness meets so much disease. That was the force of centuries of Revelstoke good coming up against ancient evil itself." His coughing was violent now, raw and harsh.

Valentine rose to his feet, and his grandpa leaned forward against the dog to brace himself. He spat out his words, louder now, between the coughs. "You have to use your power. You have to fight back. You don't want to be like me. You don't want to be like Bea."

Chapter 27

It's Best Not to Know Your Classmates Wet the Bed

Be like Bea. Alex did not want to be like Bea. He did not want to be like any of them. Not his sick grandfather, living alone in the mountains afraid to have his family visit, not his parents, afraid to leave their son alone. Not even himself, with this cursed gift that made him different from the other boys, a weirdo like Sandy Molloy said.

He stood and left the porch. His grandfather stayed, braced against the dog, who sat stiff and strong like a sentry.

As soon as he was in the house, Alex raced to his room, slammed the door, and tumbled onto the bed. Why did he have to be a Revelstoke? Why did he have to have this gift? His father didn't. ILL didn't care about his father. His father was normal.

Alex wasn't normal. He'd never been normal. Now he knew he never would be.

Everyone knew it. No one ever invited him over to their house. No one ever came to The Fish House in the woods.

Hardly surprising. Look what happened with Michael Dalton.

Michael was a sporty kid, good at lacrosse and basketball and soccer. He knew all the sports stats and watched Mariners baseball games on television and went to Sounders soccer games with his dad. He was funny and loud and likeable. He was invited to all the birthday parties. But he never went to sleepovers.

When the twins, Wolfgang and Sebastian Nguyen, turned eight, they had a big party and invited all the boys in the class, including Alex. It was the first party he'd been to in years. Their father was a music teacher and named them after Wolfgang Amadeus Mozart and Johann Sebastian Bach. They were the shortest kids in the class, had been since kindergarten, and when they turned eight, they looked like they were six. They had a trampoline in the backyard, and they could bounce higher than anyone, and they could flip forward and backwards and land on their feet.

The party had a real band of their father's music friends and fried chicken and buns from the best chicken place around. There were cookies and watermelon and ice cream and cake.

Alex sat on the ground eating watermelon with Michael. Alex's mom said no trampolines. That was the problem with having doctors for parents. His mom said trampolines caused too many Emergency Department visits, with broken arms or broken legs or broken heads. Alex had planned on bouncing as soon as she was out of sight, but she also told Mrs. Nguyen, who gave him a huge hunk of watermelon and parked him in the corner with Michael, who had a twisted ankle from soccer. Unfortunately, Sandy Molloy sauntered by at the same time, saying "Fish Boy's Mama doesn't want him bouncy bouncing. He might get hurty wurty."

Alex sat there miserably. A sharp pain stung his neck, and he swiveled toward Michael. Michael spat, and another watermelon seed shot Alex's way. Michael had a plate full of watermelon, and he ate another slice, shooting off seeds as he did.

"Let's see how far we can spit them," Michael said. Juice dripped off his chin. He spat another seed, this one toward the boys on the trampoline. He spat another, farther this time. Alex's seeds were next to him on his paper plate. He picked up the plate and tried to spit one, too, but his fizzled in half the distance of Michael's.

"I bet I could hit them." Michael waved his watermelon slice toward the kids on the trampoline.

"No way," Alex said, but Michael tried anyway, spitting seed after seed, faster and faster. He never got anywhere close, but they laughed so hard Michael's eyes started watering. Then he jumped up, knocking Alex's plate and sending watermelon seeds flying all over. Michael searched around frantically.

Alex felt the sudden urge to go to the bathroom, and he could tell by the wet spot on Michael's pants that he needed a bathroom, too. "It's over there," Alex said, and they scrambled to the house. Michael took a long time to come out, and when he did, his cheeks were red.

Alex didn't mean to say it. It just came out. "I guess that's why you aren't staying for the sleepover. It must be embarrassing to wet the bed."

Michael's red cheeks turned pale. Alex clapped his hand over his mouth. How did he know Michael wet the bed? He couldn't believe he'd said that. Michael started to cry, silently. Tears mixed with the dried watermelon juice on his chin.

"I won't tell anyone," Alex said.

Michael wiped his eyes with his sleeve. "I'm eight. No one wets the bed when they're eight. No one."

"Well, actually," Alex said, "Sandy Molloy wets the bed. He wears pull up diapers at night."

Michael's mouth twitched. Alex thought he might cry again. Instead, Michael smiled, then flashed his huge grin.

They never spoke about it again. In fact, Michael never spoke to him about anything again. But Alex noticed that he did start going to sleepovers.

## Chapter 28
## Fat on Fat

*Washington State Fairgrounds, 2005*

*The man washed his hands three times. On the wooden table, he placed a red handkerchief and a sealed bowl. He carefully took off the lid, making sure it sat on the handkerchief and not on the table top itself. He brought out a second, smaller sealed bowl, and sprinkled the wheat germ onto the yogurt. Not purchased here. Carried with him.*

*He surveyed the fairgrounds, noting the food stands with glee. Triple-fat double-fudge ice cream. Deep-fried snack cakes. Chocolate-covered bacon. He could not have dreamed this up himself. Humankind would eat itself to death. With a little help. It had not been hard. The more they ate, the more they wanted. Sugary cereal for breakfast? Why not put sugar on that? Sweet tea not sweet enough? Make it sweeter.*

*Once someone concocted something delectable, everyone clamored for it. Then more, more, more. Bigger, fattier, sugarier. It had a life of its own.*

*His arm jerked as a grubby child pushed into him, his sticky hands momentarily clutching the red handkerchief and touching his bowl.*

*"Sorry," the kid said, barely glancing at him.*

*Disgusted, the man swept up his bowls and tossed them into the garbage can in an elegant arc. He readied a similar arc of blue smoke to follow the child but stopped himself just in time.*

*"I want the fried butter," the tyke said to his mother. "Can I have it? I want to try it."*

*His mother laughed. "What will they think of next? Yes, you can try it. I'll try some, too. It actually sounds interesting."*

*He need not waste his precious energy. This child would destroy himself.*

Chapter 29
The Test

Gift. Some gift.

After what happened with Michael and the bed wetting, Alex became the "quiet" kid, "shy," his report cards said. Easier to not speak much, lest he divulge some unfortunate intimate detail, some secret. All because he was a Revelstoke.

If he'd died in the woods with the bees, no one would have noticed. Just his parents. Not like if Sam the soccer star died. Or Isabel. They would be missed. They'd have candles and stuffed teddy bears and crying galore.

What were those bees? There are no bees in February. This had to be a test from ILL. Alex broke out in a clammy sweat. He was breathing almost as hard as his grandpa. He might have died. How many more tests would there be?

He did not want this Revelstoke curse.

He avoided his grandfather the rest of the day. That also meant avoiding Valentine because the dog stuck to his grandfather's side. Alex sat by the fireplace, pretending to watch the flames. He fiddled with a cylinder of long fireplace matches and pulled one out. The match was long and thick. He pressed it against the striker and the match exploded in a flame so unexpectedly large he dropped it immediately, and it was lost in the fire.

His father found him by the fireplace and stood next to him without saying anything for a while. Then he cleared his throat and spoke, staring straight into the fire himself.

"Your mom, well, your mom never understood this whole aspect of my family. In fact, she didn't really believe it, never truly believed it until you found that dog. I don't have the gift, so she never had proof before. And some of the stories are pretty fantastical."

His dad still didn't look at him.

"She certainly didn't believe in ILL. That is my fault. I never fully explained."

Alex turned to face him.

"Now your mom's gone overboard. She's worried sick about you, not thinking straight. So it's best if you ask any questions to me and leave your mom out of this."

His dad stood and left, leaving Alex alone by the fire.

Everyone was silent at dinner. His parents seemed tired of talking, tired of pretending life was normal. Dinner was fast and bed was early.

Same thing the next morning. All quiet, all tense. Valentine lay under the table, hoping for dropped tidbits. Alex curled his bare toes around the dog's warm fur. It would be nice to be a dog, oblivious, waiting for snacks from the sky.

A knock at the door startled them all. His mom actually jumped.

Alex didn't know what he expected. A fit man with a red handkerchief? He exhaled quickly when the door opened, relieved. A mother and a child stood on the porch, the child's hand clutched in the mother's. The mother's face was red, her brow furrowed, and her nostrils flaring. The little girl's face was pale and frightened, peeking up at her mother, then quickly averting her eyes. She tried to detach her hand from her mother's grip, to no avail.

"Dr. Revelstoke, I know you're retired," the mother said as soon as the door opened. "I'm sorry to bother you. But she swallowed something, I know she did, and I just need to know if I have to drive all the way to the city or if she will be okay."

His grandfather stood there a moment, a strange expression on his face. Then he spoke. "It's no bother, Imogene. I seem to remember you swallowing a thing or two when you were her age." The girl looked up at that.

The mother, Imogene, clenched her jaw. She shook the girl's hand. "Tell him. Tell him what you swallowed."

The girl stood there, her mouth tight shut.

"I know she swallowed something, I know she did, but she won't tell me what."

The little girl shook her head once, her mouth still shut.

"Mary Beth," his grandfather said quietly. "Your mama will promise me that no matter what you swallowed, she will not be angry with you." He looked right at the mother, Imogene, straight in her eyes, but he spoke to the girl. "She only wants to make sure you're all right. Sometimes she's so worried she gets angry, but not today."

The girl tilted her head toward him but stayed silent.

His grandfather continued, still fixing on the mother's eyes. "Even if she has to drive you two hours to the city hospital, she would do anything to keep you safe. She loves you more than anything."

Imogene's grip on the girl's hand loosened. Alex could see her shoulders drop and her face relax. She nodded, tears in her eyes.

"Mary Beth," his grandpa said. "Your mama only wants you to be all right. Did you swallow something?"

The girl's mouth slackened. She was about to speak. Alex held his breath.

Then the girl shook her head. Alex breathed out heavily.

"Tell me what you swallowed!" her mother screamed. The girl broke her hand free and slipped toward Alex's grandfather.

The mother shouted, "Do something, Dr. Revelstoke!"

His grandfather stepped back. He put his arm around Alex's shoulder and gently pushed him forward.

"Alex," he said. "What did she swallow?"

Alex was startled. How did he know? He couldn't conjure this up out of thin air. The visions always just came to him, whether he wanted them or not. And mostly he did not. He did not want to see this little girl's skin melt away.

His grandfather searched his face with those imploring Revelstoke eyes. Then Alex knew. Not what she swallowed. In fact, he no longer cared what she swallowed. He squinched his eyes shut and refused to think about the girl. His grandfather was luring him in, trying to get him to use his gift. Tricking him into wanting to care. Well, he didn't. He didn't care. He didn't want to be a Revelstoke. Let his grandfather, the true Revelstoke, let his parents, the doctors, figure it out. Leave him alone.

He set his mouth as tight as the girl's. He opened his eyes and saw his grandfather's pleading blue eyes locked on his. Alex shook his head just like the girl.

Imogene let out a sharp breath. She looked from him to his grandpa. "Dr. Revelstoke?" she said.

His grandfather broke his stare. He sighed. Then he slowly knelt. Alex thought for a moment that he knelt in defeat. Then he realized what he was doing.

His grandfather knelt in front of the girl and gazed into her eyes. Directly in the eyes. Then he took her hand and looked up at her mother. "She swallowed a battery. The little disc kind. It is stuck at the bottom of her esophagus and can be very dangerous because it can burn into the lining. Right now it is fine. You need to drive to the hospital in the city and they can take it out with a scope. I will call to let them know you are coming. If you wait too long, she could get very sick."

The mother's eyes widened.

"You have good instincts, Imogene. You knew she swallowed something. Now remember your promise."

He turned back to the girl again. "Your mama loves you. That's why she brought you here. She will not be angry at you if you tell her these things. You can always tell your mama."

Then they were gone, leaving his grandfather regarding Alex warily. Alex tried to look anywhere but back at him.

His mom glanced from one to the other, puzzled.

"What just happened?" she asked. "What did Alex have to do with this?"

"That was a test," his grandfather said.

She put her arm around Alex's shoulders and drew him toward her. "A test? A test!" Her voice was angry. "Don't you think he's been through enough? All this Revelstoke talk. All this ILL talk. He's only twelve! He's too young for this. And then you give him a test!" she said shrilly.

His dad put a hand on her shoulder. "I don't think it's quite like that," he said quietly.

His grandfather gazed at the three of them, standing there together, his blue eyes now full of grief.

"That was not a test from me," he whispered in his low voice. He raised his hand and pointed toward the trees by the driveway. Flapping in the wind, caught on a branch, was a red cloth. A handkerchief-sized square.

"That was a test from ILL."

Chapter 30
The Antidote

They left the next day after another stressful meal, Alex's mom a mass of bloodshot eyes and tears, his father pale and thin-lipped, his dog a whimpering mess straining against his leash to stay put beside his grandfather. Alex sat in the back of the silent car with a mind swirling with fear and images of the little girl with the battery.

He gazed out the window and saw billboards with six-foot hamburgers and eight-foot cartons of French fries, glistening with fat and salt. They looked so good, they looked so bad. Another showed a happy family at a picnic, each child lifting a giant cookie, the mom smiling adoringly. The next one showed a sad white-haired woman with her hand to her head and read, "Do you know the signs of stroke? FAST—Face drooping, Arm weakness, Speech difficulty, Time to call 9-1-1. Time makes a difference. Act FAST."

It was too much for him. Disease was everywhere. Temptation was everywhere. ILL was everywhere. Alex's head hurt. He felt like the white-haired lady on the billboard.

His mother had begged his grandfather to let them stay. But it was clear to look at Grandpa Asclepius that he had no magic trick of protection. His father had seized the red handkerchief and hurled it into the fire.

106

ILL had visited this tiny town in the mountains, had tainted the log cabin in the woods. Grandma Bea's picture smiled at them from the mantel, a reminder that this place was no safer than Seattle.

His father tried to reassure his mom, and he must have succeeded. Or maybe it was grandpa's words. "ILL has found him here. ILL will find him anywhere." In any case, they were going home. It didn't matter where they were. ILL was here, ILL was there.

His grandfather pulled him aside in his study as his parents packed the car.

"You are a Revelstoke. You have gifts you haven't yet found. ILL is shackled. You can fight him. You can finish what my father started." His grandfather paused and breathed deeply. "Revelstokes cannot find ILL. ILL must find you. Make it easy. Stay with your usual routine. Go to school. Take your standard routes. You want him to find you."

Alex opened his mouth to protest but his grandfather held up his hand. He had the cylinder of strange fireplace matches, and he tucked them inside Alex's jacket, their pressure pushing against his chest.

"Be ready. With fire, you can destroy his cloth, destroy all his power. You can end this."

Alex wanted to scream at him. But his throat was tight, and he couldn't speak, let alone yell.

"You have so much ability. You will help so many. You have to find your powers and control them. To see disease, I look into people's eyes, not just the eyes, but the pupils, deep into the blackness of the eyes. Then out of the blackness I see their body all laid out for me. I see the problem."

Alex didn't want to see the problem. He didn't want this power.

"You need to figure out how you do it. How you see disease. Then you need to figure out what else you can do."

His grandpa opened the closet and pulled out his ancient doctor bag, a squat leather case with two handles on top. "I have something for you." He set the bag on the desk. He rummaged through the case, bringing out a stethoscope and a tuning fork and a hammer to test for reflexes at the knee.

Then he brought out a vial, an old glass vial with a glass top and a wax seal. There was a tiny amount of purple liquid at the bottom. He tilted the vial and the liquid changed to golden and then back to purple again.

"My father gave this to me the day he died. There is very little left." He held the vial up to the light and gently swirled. The golden liquid shimmered and glowed, momentarily brightening the room. "Enough for one use. It's an antidote. Against ILL's ill. Or any ill. It will heal anything. This is all that is left. Saved through the generations. My father could have used it for himself. As he lay dying, he gave this vial to me."

The vial emanated a soft golden light, mesmerizing Alex.

"A Revelstoke must release it. It will be powerless for anyone else. You must be the one to decide." His grandfather abruptly brought the vial down. It turned deep purple, and Alex's grandpa's face turned dark as well. "I have never used it. Not for my patients. Not for Bea."

His face cleared. His blue eyes were full of pain. "When Bea was sick, I wanted to use it," he said, his voice gravelly but steady. "But I knew about you, I thought you might have the gift. You were so little, and I couldn't protect you myself." He swirled the vial. "But this might."

He paused, his eyes still locked on Alex's.

"I know you do not want this. I know you do not want any of this. But you are the last Revelstoke. ILL will come for you. You need to be ready."

Alex's head swooned, and he gripped the desk. He swallowed hard to keep the tense, awful breakfast from rising up.

His grandpa gently pried Alex's fingers from the desk and placed the vial in his palm. Alex closed his hand around it, feeling its warmth. The vial vibrated as if it were alive.

"You can use it only once," Grandpa Asclepius said, his voice husky. "Use it well."

Chapter 31
One Left

*Revelstoke, Canada, present day*

*This kid, this Revelstoke spawn, held his future in his scrawny body. The last Revelstoke.*

*The Revelstoke war had raged through all eternity, and now it came to this.*

*One left. Time to end this Revelstoke reign. This boy's time on earth was limited.*

Chapter 32
Miracle

By the time they got home, Alex was determined to reject his Revelstoke gift. To ignore it. To push it out of his mind and pretend this curse of birth did not exist.

He retrieved the long matches and the vial from his duffle bag and stuffed them in the bottom of his sock drawer. Then shoved his gym shorts on top. And his balled-up school sweatshirt. Then he took them out of the sock drawer and pulled his desk chair over to the closet and put them as far back on the top shelf as he could reach, behind his box of plastic dinosaurs that he'd loved as a kid but now were dusty and forgotten. And an old game of dominoes. He shoved his gym shorts and sweatshirt on top. There. Gone. He slammed the closet door so hard that Valentine appeared from wherever he had been sleeping.

Alex sat on the floor with the dog's head even with his and wrapped his arms around his furry neck. Valentine's neck was thick and solid and comforting. It was one thing to know your classmate had urinary difficulties and quite another to know that an evil force was responsible for much disease and that you were next.

They had been gone a long weekend. Four days that bridged worrying about his dog's paw to worrying about every cough and sniffle and sick person out there. Tomorrow was school.

Tomorrow he would see teachers who only needed to get kids from early man to modern China to do their jobs well, see kids whose whole world was soccer and the next math test. And here he was, a Revelstoke, with a gift. Well, he didn't want it.

On his desk he saw the stack of books on the brain from the library. When he thought he could explain things with science. Ha! That was the day he met ILL at the bus stop. The day the bees chased him. He'd gone back to the woods that night to get these books. And now here they sat, a connection between his former normal life and today.

The day he met ILL…

His heart pounded. He stood slowly and inched toward the stack, as if the books would attack him. He lifted the first one and opened the cover. Nothing but the pages of a book. He lifted the second. Alex's heart beat so fast he put a shaking hand on his chest hoping to slow it. He opened the book. A small square of red cloth fluttered out and drifted lazily to the floor. Valentine barked, deep, menacing barks Alex had not heard before. The red square lay on the floor as if it were nothing. Not absolute proof that the bees were from ILL.

Alex snatched the cloth from the floor. He pushed the chair back over to the closet and pulled the matches and the vial out from their hiding place. He cast the fabric into their space and piled on top anything within reach.

Valentine stopped barking. Alex climbed down and stood in the center of the room breathing in and out so hard that Valentine forced his body under his hand like he wanted to calm him. Alex let his fingers rest there for a moment, feeling Valentine's soft fur and strong back. Then he zipped the matches into his backpack. He shoved the vial in his pocket without looking at it. He felt it there, a sickening warmth warning him that his life was at stake. All their lives were at stake.

He didn't want this. He couldn't do this. He would not engage.

Don't change anything, his grandfather had said. Go to school. It didn't matter, Alex told himself the next morning. Nothing was going to happen. He didn't want to be a Revelstoke. ILL had nothing to fear from him.

How his dad convinced his mom he had no idea. She almost didn't let him go, her hands on his arm in a vise grip. His father whispered in her ear and her hold relaxed.

For an instant, Alex wished her hands were still there.

Heading up the school steps, Alex was surprised things seemed so normal, so ordinary. Kids swarmed in all directions, sweat and perfume mixed in the air with shouts and laughter. First period was a school assembly. Alex saw Isabel as he filed into the gym, but he couldn't find her once they were seated in the bleachers. His class was in the front row, which was good because the gym was stuffy and hot, and up high in the bleachers it would be worse. He was perspiring enough sitting here waiting, waiting.

No. Forget about it.

He craned his neck to try to see Isabel, but he couldn't pick her out from the other hundreds of students crammed into the gym. Just as well. She'd probably be with Jack. He wished he were Jack, sitting next to Isabel without a care in the world.

Alex touched the bulge in his backpack where the matches hid. The vial pressed against his leg, a constant reminder.

Mr. Tangential, the principal, stood on the stage. He welcomed them back and encouraged them to keep focused for the annual state testing that would happen soon. No absences. Good breakfasts. Lots of sleep. Yada yada.

Alex couldn't believe he was sitting here listening to the virtues of a healthy breakfast when the King of Unhealth was after him, maybe waiting somewhere right outside those school walls. Hot and cramped as he was, he felt some degree of safety within the school. Likely unfounded. ILL could be here as well as out there.

His spirit was here, at least. Vending machines right down the hall sold honey buns and sodas. And all that other stuff his mom called empty calories, of no sound nutritional value—chips and packaged cupcakes and Chocolate Dingaloos. Whatever those were.

Up there on the stage, Mr. Tangential himself looked like he partook in honey buns and Chocolate Dingaloos. His red neck was tight in his shirt collar and his suit jacket strained to button over his belly. The vending machine was right near his office, after all.

Alex gazed warily around the gym. ILL couldn't be in here, could he? There was a poster at one end Alex had never noticed. It showed a group of sweaty boys, each with a bottle in his hand, some holding them, some drinking, deep refreshing drinks. The bottles didn't have water. They had soda. An advertisement for soda right there in the gym!

It actually looked pretty good, this cold soda the boys in the poster guzzled. The gym was stifling.

A sharp crack sounded. Some students covered their heads like in their drills for intruders and gunshots. Alex's head shot up and he scanned the gym. Was this it?

A few teachers stood and made moves out of the bleachers toward the floor. Then Alex saw why. Up on stage, Mr. Tangential lay flat on his back.

The microphone must have dropped on the floor, making the noise. Alex was close, right there in the first row. Without thinking, he rose and jogged to the stage. Mr. Tangential was breathing fine, but sweat covered his face. Alex reached for his hand, which was warm and clammy. He felt for a pulse. His mom taught him how to do that years ago. Mr. Tangential's pulse was weak but steady and grew stronger as Alex held his wrist.

Alex was hot before, but now he was sweltering, hot and sweaty and thirsty and lightheaded. Mr. Tangential's wrist slipped out of his hand. The wrist suddenly had no flesh. A bony hand flopped on a bony arm.

Mr. Tangential was a skeleton, quite skinny without his suit and flab. Blood vessels coursed over the bones, blueish and reddish flowing this way and that, now with a brisk whoosh of movement out of the heart and toward his head.

Mr. Tangential started to move. Teachers were all around.

"He fainted," Alex said. "From the heat."

"I fainted," Mr. Tangential said. "From the heat."

"Looks like you fainted," said Mr. Beaker. "Probably from the heat."

"It's called syncope," Alex said. He'd read about it when he read about brains.

"Synco-what?" Mr. Beaker said.

"Syncopation," Ms. Parallel, the music teacher, said.

"No. Syncope," Alex said. "It means fainting."

They brought Mr. Tangential water and dismissed the school back to the classrooms. Alex spotted Isabel in the top bleacher, and he thought she might be smiling at him. As if he could tell from that far away. In his dreams.

On his way out, Alex's eyes searched around for the telltale red handkerchief. He saw nothing, nothing out of the ordinary, nothing suggesting evil.

The loudspeaker crackled with an announcement half an hour later saying Mr. Tanner was fine, the nurse had seen him and that he had fainted, or had syncopation, from the heat, and it was important to stay hydrated when the air inside was so warm, and Mr. Sylvester would look into getting the heat turned down.

"Syncope!" Alex groaned to himself.

Finally it was last period. Alex had relaxed inside the school, and now one period separated him from the outside where ILL might be.

Gym. Alex didn't like gym because all the guys changed in the locker room together and it was uncomfortable. Alex changed quickly in the corner, head down and eyes averted.

He wasn't the only one. Tom, the boy who always left the lunch table early, changed in the opposite corner. Tom had a limp that Alex knew was from a serious scooter mishap when he was young. Alex never looked at Tom, and Tom never looked at Alex. They never talked at the lunch table, and they certainly never talked in the locker room.

Wolfgang and Sebastian were in the class, too. They didn't seem to mind the locker room at all. They jabbered nonstop, whooping it up and lingering on the bench.

Out in the gym, the stage was gone, and the basketball hoops were down. The room was still too warm, so Mr. Cylinder must have had no luck with the heat. Mr. Sphere, the gym teacher, divided them into teams and they started in, chugging up and down the court, sweating and dripping. Mr. Sphere often lectured about sportsmanship and geniality, but a lot went on that Mr. Sphere never noticed. Elbows and fingernails and knees. Mr. Sphere sat on the bottom bleacher, blissfully fanning himself with the attendance list. He was a large man with a larger afro and a low, loud voice that carried across the gym. He had a whistle around his neck, but he never blew it. Every so often he checked his watch, or shouted out, "What's the score?" but otherwise he was oblivious.

Tall Sam was good at basketball as well as soccer. He could dribble and dart and twist and spin. He could send up beautiful shots that curved through the air before swishing through the basket. He could jump higher than any of them to get the ball on the rebound.

He leaped up now, launching off one foot and gliding into the air with an arm raised overhead. He caught the ball and landed gracefully and turned to look for someone to take his pass. Tom stood in his usual place outside the three-point line. He didn't move much because of his leg. He raised his arms to show he was free.

Then Sam crumpled to the floor, as gracefully as he jumped, except in the opposite direction. He didn't say anything. He just lay there.

Alex was halfway down the court and by the time he came over, Sam was surrounded by the class, and Mr. Sphere crouched next to him.

"Give him some space," Mr. Sphere said in his low, booming voice. "Back up. What happened here? Did he get hit?"

"No, no, he just fainted," Tom said.

"Like Mr. Tanner," Sebastian said.

"Maybe it's syncopation," chimed in Wolfgang with a smile. Alex knew he was musical enough to know syncopation from syncope.

"Syncope," Mr. Sphere said. Apparently, he knew, too. "It's hot as can be in here. Get him some water. Stand back. Give him some air."

Alex pushed to the front. Sam lay there, still and gray. Alex knelt beside him, pushing as best he could against the heft of Mr. Sphere to get closer. He picked up Sam's limp arm and felt for a pulse.

No pulse. He couldn't feel anything, not the faintest hint of a pulse. What he could feel was his own heart racing, so fast and so uncoordinatedly out of control that it hurt.

He dreaded looking, but he knew he had to. He moved his eyes from Sam's arm to his chest. His skin was gone. His muscles were there, and his ribcage, and then that was gone, too. And there was Sam's heart. Not racing at all. Barely moving. Quivering. With an

118

unusual and abnormal thickening of the muscle of one ventricle, nothing like the heart in Alex's old pop-up book, *Your Heart and How it Works*.

Then Alex's own heart heaved. Just like that. From racing in his chest to nothing. A million tiny fibrillations useless for blood flow.

Nothing lasts a long time.

And then a light radiated above them, a bright, welcoming light hanging over him, hanging over Sam.

Alex shook his head. He dropped Sam's hand. Only seconds had gone by. Sam hadn't moved. Mr. Sphere lifted a cup to Sam's lips to get him to drink some water. Alex knocked it out of his hand and screamed, "AED!"

This got Mr. Sphere's attention. He shoved Alex aside and grabbed Sam's wrist himself. He felt his neck, searching for a pulse there.

"No pulse!" shouted Alex. "We need the AED!"

"Get the AED!" Mr. Sphere shouted, his huge voice rocketing off the walls, and boys scattered across the gym. Mr. Sphere pulled up Sam's shirt, now back in place where it belonged. He pushed down on his chest, counting off the compressions as he did. "Call nine-one-one!" he shouted between counts.

The AED, the automated external defibrillator, was something everyone in school knew about. After the incident with Mr. Cylinder, the school purchased three of them and placed them all around. Teachers drilled into them the need for an AED to get the heart pumping again if someone had a heart attack. The someone they thought about was always Mr. Cylinder. The school bought the AEDs for Mr. Cylinder.

But here was Sam. Star soccer player. Star everything player. The typical victim, Alex knew, of hypertrophic cardiomyopathy, which caused sudden cardiac arrest. His mom talked endlessly about this disease, about the need for some way to screen. Part of the heart was too thick, blocking blood flow out. No blood flow, no life.

Sudden cardiac arrest could happen in young athletes with bad luck. Or with bad genes because it was often inherited. If the doctors knew someone had it, they usually restricted their exercise because the obstruction was worse when the heart strained to pump more blood to the muscles. It could hit just like this, without warning. Boom. Sudden cardiac arrest.

Tom took over compressions. Mr. Sphere had the AED pads in his hands. He tried to tear the package to get them out, but his hands were shaking. He finally ripped it open and two pads tumbled out. He flipped the package over to study the drawing to see where to put them. Alex grabbed the pads and pushed them onto Sam's chest. His parents made him practice this, too, like the Heimlich. They had an AED in their car.

Alex saw Sam's exposed heart again, his still heart with the AED pads floating above where his ribs and skin should be. The AED's flat, unexcited computer-generated voice said, "Stop CPR. Analyzing. Shock advised. Charging. Stand clear."

"Stand clear!" Mr. Sphere shouted, taking charge again, moving everyone back.

The AED fired with a small click. Sam's body jumped a little. Tom started compressions again.

"Stop CPR. Analyzing. Shock advised. Charging. Stand clear," the voice said.

"Stand clear!" Mr. Sphere shouted, his arms out to make sure no one was close.

Sam's body jumped again. His heart twitched and twitched again, and faintly, slowly, started to pump.

"Analyzing," said the machine. "No shock advised. Check for pulse."

A heartbeat showed on the little monitor. A steady heartbeat, speeding up as Alex watched. More than that, he could see Sam, turning his head and licking his lips.

"Sam, don't move. Just lie there." Mr. Sphere's loud voice was now a hoarse whisper. Sweat dripped off his face and onto Sam.

Sam opened his eyes and looked at Mr. Sphere, then at Alex standing behind him.

"Miracle," Sam said, eyes on Alex.

The paramedics arrived, and Mr. Sphere cleared the gym and told them to wait in the locker room. Alex lingered, like he had earlier in that same gym, making sure there was no red handkerchief. There was none. ILL wasn't here.

Mr. Sphere met them in the locker room to say Sam was wide awake and talking and looked okay and would go to the hospital to see what had happened.

Alex already knew. Sam had sudden cardiac arrest. Alex helped save him. But Sam's star days were over.

Chapter 33
The Blue-Haired Girl

Directly after school, Alex headed to the library two blocks away, eyes darting left and right the whole way. He needed books, needed something to take his mind off Sam, off ILL, off the miserable curse of being a Revelstoke.

The librarian, Ms. Parker, sat in her usual place behind the wide reference desk. He liked Ms. Parker and was glad to see her because she'd been away for a while and he hadn't known if she would return. When he was younger, she used to save new books for him to check out first, before the other kids. She knew he would read them fast and have them back to her in no time.

She always gave him a friendly hello whenever he came in. While she was gone, a stout, stern woman sat behind the desk, greeting him with a frown as if she expected trouble and noise. Ms. Parker never minded a little noise. In fact, she sometimes laughed quite loudly herself, then she'd put her finger to her lips to suggest silence, then she'd burst out laughing even harder.

Now she peered intently at her computer screen. Her face glowed from the light on the screen, and there must have been something yellow there because her face glowed yellow. Especially her eyes. Even when she turned away from the computer to smile at him and give him a wave.

Though he hadn't seen her in a while, he didn't want to talk to her today because she always asked him how he was like she meant it, and he always felt obliged to answer. What could he possibly say? So he gave her a quick nod and a wave and darted past, headed for the Fantasy/Sci Fi section with books about monsters and creatures and evil and heroes and hope. With impossible situations and battles and bravery and smart, beautiful girls. He could use a smart, beautiful girl to help him fight his battle. Which he was not going to fight. He was going to hide.

And then a beautiful girl appeared. Not Isabel. This girl did not look anything like Isabel.

He took a book from the bookshelf just as the girl took a book on her side and there they were, gaping at each other across the void. She was close to his height, and he looked directly in her eyes. Her coloring was the opposite of his. He had blue eyes and black hair that stood up in the wrong places. She had sad black eyes and blue hair that was flat and smooth and curved in under her tiny, delicate chin.

She put her book back and blocked his view. Alex wandered around the bookshelf, but she was gone. There was no one there. He glanced around, trying not to be too obvious. No one anywhere. Alex was alone with Ms. Parker.

Where had she gone? The library wasn't large. One big room with the stacks, which he could easily see by striding up the ends of them, the bathroom, currently with its door open, and Ms. Parker's private office. That was it.

Maybe she wasn't even real.

His shook his head hard as if that would clear all the weird things going on. He scanned his book at the self-checkout near the door and left quickly, before Ms. Parker could catch his eye.

The air was frigid and the low clouds meant rain, but the glass protection of the bus stop was not inviting. In fact, it looked sinister. Alex felt for the matches and the vial. ILL had found him at the bus stop. Now it was empty. But even the bus stop sported advertisements. "24 oz for the price of 12," with a huge plastic cup full of soda, and "Let us do the cooking," with a microwavable cheese-goo-ooze dish that didn't even have a name. Alex bent his head into the wind and stepped back to the street.

He trudged home, happy to find he'd beaten his mother. She'd be mad, but he had to get out. His grandpa had told him to follow his same routines. Well, this was not his same routine. He was headed to a hiding spot.

Valentine was thrilled to go along. He left his mom a note, grabbed his jacket from the peg in the hall, and set out for his hollowed-out crag. He hadn't been there since summer. That made it safe. At least he told himself it did as he crawled in. The rain didn't penetrate inside his tree trunk. The earth was dry, and the air was warm and cedar scented. After a while, the air smelled like Valentine's stinky breath, but it was still preferable to the stuffy, strained air of home. He spent all afternoon there, lost in his book, in someone else's troubles, someone else's danger.

The next day at school he relaxed, as period after period passed without mishap. At home his mom was waiting for him, and her anxiety filled the house.

"I'm going to the library."

His mom's eyes flicked around the room and her jaw tightened. "Honey, wouldn't you rather stay here?"

Forever? I can't stay here forever, he wanted to say. Instead, he shook his head and said he needed something for school. He kept quiet about what Grandpa had said. Stick to routine, take your standard routes. What did it matter? Who was to say ILL wasn't right here in the woods? In the Fish House itself?

No, no, no. Not possible. Alex was not going to fight ILL. He was not going to engage. He was not the Revelstoke Great Grandpa Asc was, or even Grandpa Asclepius. ILL could certainly see that.

"Take the dog, he's restless," his mom said. Alex knew she meant take the dog to stand guard. She hovered while he gathered his library books and hooked the leash to the dog. Good thing his mom didn't know what he found in the book. If she knew that red square was in her house... Well, she didn't know.

She opened the door and stood aside as they escaped. When he looked back from the edge of the clearing, she was there on the porch, still watching. He gave a half wave and plunged into the woods.

He and Valentine emerged on the other side into an unexpectedly bright February day. He sped along the lake, wary of the open water, then headed up the hill to the library. The dog trotted along beside him, his limp barely noticeable.

Alex's back muscles clenched as he craned to see behind every bush and around every corner.

"Mr. Revelstoke!"

Alex jumped. The voice was deep and booming. Alex's heartbeat thudded in his chest and in his ears, fast and hard. He whipped left and right. Valentine yelped as Alex yanked his leash. Where was he? Where was ILL?

"Mr. Revelstoke!"

Alex spun. The gym teacher, Mr. Sphere, lumbered up the street from behind. Alex exhaled, relief making his knees weak. His heart slowed. Certainly ILL would not appear in front of a man so large.

Stop it, Alex told himself. ILL is not coming. He does not want you because you do not want to be a Revelstoke. You are not a threat to him.

"What a beast of a dog," Mr. Sphere bellowed, leaning his big body down and taking Valentine's head in his hands. He gently shook the furry head back and forth, talking what sounded like baby talk. Which seemed strange from such a giant man.

"Whew. Bad breath, though." Mr. Sphere straightened. Alex nodded in agreement.

"Can you sit, fella?" Mr. Sphere brought his hand over Valentine's nose, and the dog obliged him by sitting. "Good dog," Mr. Sphere said, avoiding Valentine's head and patting his back.

Mr. Sphere turned to Alex. "Mr. Revelstoke, I am glad to run into you."

"Alex," Alex said.

"Well, Alex, that was quick thinking yesterday with Sam. You might just have saved his life."

"Th—thank you," Alex stammered. Mr. Sphere smiled, nodded, and walked on.

Alex continued to the library, raising his face to the uncommon afternoon sun. He was glad to be out of the house and away from his mother, but even more he was hoping to see the girl. He tied Valentine's leash to the bicycle rack outside the library, under the shade of a large pine tree. He opened the library door, and there she was.

Black eyes. Blue hair perfectly framing her perfect face. Her sad, perfect face. This time she didn't vanish. She was real. Except for her blue hair.

"Hey," he said.

"Hey," she said.

"I'm Alex."

"I know."

He didn't bother to ask her how. He just stood there, gawking like a doofus.

"Are you done with those?" She gestured toward the books in his hand.

"Yes." He dumped the books in the return box, happy to be free of the reminder of the day with the bees. He nodded to Ms. Parker, who gave him a funny smile. The girl turned and walked toward the back of the library. She didn't glance back to see if he was following, but he was definitely following.

"Where'd you go yesterday?" he said.

"I disappeared."

"Where?"

"Nowhere."

"Why?" he said.

"Because I can. Because I want to. Because I don't want to be here."

Well, he didn't want to be here, either. He didn't want to be anywhere, not with his grandfather, not at the Fish House.

"Where do you want to be?" he said.

"Home." She twisted her head away. He didn't know what to do, so he waited.

"There is no home," she said. "I don't have a home anymore."

"Everyone has a home."

"Not me. Not now. My home disappeared."

She sat on the floor and covered her face. Alex stood there awkwardly. Should he stand here? Sit next to her? He was halfway to the floor when she looked up, so he stayed put in a crouch.

"Your home disappeared?" Alex said. "Like a fire?"

"No," she said. "Not a fire."

She didn't say anything else. Maybe she didn't want so many questions. He kept his mouth shut. She reminded him of someone, the way she spoke, the shape of her face. She seemed familiar, but he'd never met this girl before.

"Anyway, I feel safe here," she said.

It all came back to him. How unsafe he was, how unsafe they all were, how vulnerable. ILL. He wanted to tell her, but how could he tell her, this sad, scared girl? He didn't even know her. He couldn't tell anyone. He could hardly talk to his parents about it. Certainly not his mom.

The light in the library shifted. Alex could see a dark cloud outside the big picture window. He jumped up. Dark forces were out there, outside this warm place. The wind kicked up, brushing tree branches against the glass. Weather in Seattle could change quickly, especially in the winter, and this beautiful blue day was turning stormy.

"I'd better get going before it pours." Alex nodded toward the window.

"I knew this sunshine couldn't last," she said. Alex detected the hint of a smile, the first smile he'd seen from her. "I think this was my first sunny day since coming to Seattle. It's not like this in California."

"I like the rain," he said. "But I have to go. My dog's out there."

"Where?" said the girl.

"Right there, under the tree."

"I don't see a dog," she said.

Alex dashed to the big window. He could see the entire lawn, the bicycle rack, the bus stop. Where was Valentine? He raced to the door, pushing hard to get it to open against the wind. The lawn was empty. No dog.

Not completely empty, though. Caught under the bicycle rack, flapping in the wind, was a red handkerchief.

Chapter 34
Pain

Alex ran down the hill toward the lake, calling Valentine's name. The name he'd had for less than two weeks. Alex didn't even know his real name, his past. Maybe he'd gone off to his old life. Maybe his owner came along and recognized him.

But the red handkerchief. It had definitely not been there when Alex fastened Valentine to the rack. No one used handkerchiefs anymore. Now it was all tissues and hand sanitizer. No one carried around a handkerchief. Except ILL.

Did ILL have his dog? Did ILL have Valentine? Sweet, trusting Valentine? That poor dog was just getting better, just healing. What would ILL do to him?

Alex stopped at the bottom of the hill to catch his breath. The wind swirled his hair and cut through his thin jacket. It had been so warm and beautiful earlier, everything had seemed warm and beautiful. Now he was right back in it, in it with ILL.

He turned toward home, down the winding road along the lake, green and tree-lined, usually peaceful but now whipped into a frenzy of wildly waving branches with leaves and pine needles flying through the air.

He shouted out, "Valentine! Valentine!" but the wind caught his words and swallowed them.

He ran a little farther. His lungs burned from the running and the wind. He staggered along, all the way to the park. Yelling, screaming, "Valentine, Valentine!" No answering bark. No dog.

He leaned forward against a tree, gasping for breath. What a fool he was. He thought he could decide himself to ignore ILL. Forget about him, squelch his own Revelstoke curse, stifle any inklings of disease he might glean from those around him. But ILL was forcing him to confront him, to fight. ILL had his dog.

It was starting. He had no choice.

His grandfather wanted Alex to defeat ILL, to finally rid the world of this ancient evil. ILL wanted the same thing, to finally rid himself of this nemesis family. Alex was the last Revelstoke. ILL was here.

Destroy the black cloth. He gripped his backpack that held the matches. He had to get close enough to ILL to destroy the black cloth.

A hand grasped his shoulder. Alex wheeled around, his arms shooting up, ready to strike.

"No! It's me!" The blue-haired girl stood there, her hands flying to her face for protection.

Alex dropped his arms with the backpack, dropped his whole body back against the tree. He was on edge, anxious and jittery.

"I can help you look for your dog," she said. "Maybe he was afraid of the wind."

Alex shook his head.

"You tell me where to look and I can help."

Alex shook his head again. What could she do? What could anyone do? Even his grandfather had been beaten.

"Tell me," she said. "Tell me how to help."

He told her. He told her about Revelstokes. About ILL.

She stood there silently. The wind lashed at the trees. A few big drops of rain started to fall. Then more. Big, heavy drops that soaked them both in minutes.

Alex picked up the backpack. Why had he told her? He was sorry as soon as the words were out. He looked out at the lake, pelted by the large raindrops.

"Your dog will be soaked," she said, matter-of-factly. "Let's find your dog."

She didn't believe him. He could tell. She thought he was a raving lunatic.

"Let's look in the woods." Alex avoided her gaze and started walking. "I want to look where I found him."

Once in the forest, the thick trees blocked the storm and dampened the wind. The tree canopy caught most of the water high above them, and the rain was only a drizzle. He could talk without shouting.

"I found him here." Alex showed her the nurse log, the ancient fallen tree on its side, massive and long, with fully grown trees lined up on top, their roots splayed around the nurse log like thick wax dripping down. He climbed over, and she detoured off the path to get around. No dog.

Alex told her how he saw the glass in Valentine's paw. "I named him Valentine not even knowing it meant 'strength.' What a name."

The girl was quiet, poking around in the leaves. He shouldn't have mentioned seeing through the paw. What an idiot! She wouldn't understand any of this. He had to say something normal.

"What's your name?" Alex asked.

"Penelope."

"Penelope is a nice name," he said, trying to keep the conversation going.

"Penelope was Odysseus's wife. She waited for him for twenty years while he was away at war. People said he was dead. But she had faith."

"That's one of my favorite stories, *The Odyssey*." It was true. He didn't bring up *The Iliad*, Homer's other poem, which mentioned his namesake, Asclepius.

"Mine, too," she said sadly. "My parents used to read me the poem when I was little at night before bedtime, and my dad tried to explain the hard parts." She bit her lip. "No more." She kicked at the leaves.

Alex didn't say anything.

"My parents are dead," Penelope said.

"What?"

"My parents are dead, and that's why I'm in Seattle." She covered her face with her hands, so her words were muffled. "I wanted to ride shotgun. You know, in the front seat next to my mom. She never let me, not like my dad. She was such a scaredy-cat. She never let me do anything. Thanks to her I was belted safely in the back. I would have died, too, if I hadn't been in the back.

"We were driving to get my dad at the airport. We were really late because my dance class ran over and then we had a flat tire and had to wait for road assistance to fix it. Mom tried to reach Dad, but just got his message box."

She sat on the ground and started to cry. Alex knelt next to her. He couldn't think of anything to say.

"We heard about the plane crash on the radio. No obvious survivors. Then Mom's phone rang, and the speaker phone started talking. Of course she had it on speaker phone. She would never drive without two hands on the steering wheel. She could hear and I could hear. 'Please pick up any white phone when you get to the airport, and you will be met by airline personnel.' We both knew what that meant. Dad's plane.

"Mom looked straight ahead, but she couldn't see. Couldn't see the corner, couldn't see the tree. She was in shock and she crashed. The policeman said she was in shock."

Penelope rocked forward, back and forth, her thin shoulders shaking. Alex put his hand on her back. She felt warm. She stopped rocking and sat still.

"So my dad and my mom died on the same day. Now I'm here. I couldn't come on an airplane. I was too scared. I had to come on a train."

"I like trains." What a dumb thing to say. It just popped out. She didn't seem to hear.

"And I have this silly blue hair." A glint in her eyes suggested a smile. "I don't even remember dyeing it. I was in shock, too, for a while."

"I like your silly blue hair." And he did. It was an especially appealing color. He looked into her eyes, still tear-stained. "That's terrible about your parents. I don't know what I would do."

She sat without saying anything. Alex sat next to her thinking about his parents. Her mom and dad were dead. He couldn't believe he'd told her about ILL.

Penelope broke the silence. "If there wasn't an ILL, would there still be disease?"

She sounded like she believed him.

"Yes," he said slowly. "ILL caused a lot of disease. Not everything. Some diseases just are. Some people are sick, and it has nothing to do with ILL."

"And some people have accidents." Penelope spoke softly.

"Yes." He said it just as softly. Then he gestured around. "I think we should look through these woods. I think Valentine might be here. But…" He had to warn her. She had no idea what she was getting herself into. Neither did he. "You don't have to come with me. I don't know what might happen."

"It's okay." She said it without any emotion at all. "It doesn't matter to me. ILL can't hurt me anyway. There's nothing left to hurt."

What was she saying?

"My parents are dead. If I were dead, we'd be together."

She said it as if it were a simple fact.

"What if it doesn't work that way?" Alex said. She couldn't really be thinking this.

"I wouldn't know. I'd be dead." She flipped her hair and smiled, and he couldn't tell if she was serious or not.

Alex had never known anyone like this. Of course, he hadn't known that many kids at all. Not well. But he didn't think they were like this.

They came to the clearing where the bee stung him when he was little, when his eyes swelled up and they found out he was allergic. The sky was dark and low, but the rain had stopped. On the far side of the meadow, where the sky was darkest, a blue swirl appeared like a tiny tornado. It grew bigger and floated toward them, a cloud of blue smoke drifting across the field.

Oh, no, not again! This was how the bees started. Alex grabbed Penelope's hand and ran. She had seen the unusual cloud, too. The long, wet grass slowed them down. They made it to the woods where they could run faster on the dirt path. The cloud was still there, elongated now along the narrow trail.

"What is that?" Penelope shouted, panting.

"I don't know. But it doesn't look good."

They ran up a little hill and down a little hill. They jumped over fallen logs and trampled through deep piles of leaves. The cloud stayed right with them.

They were almost to the hollowed-out tree. They could hide in there, like he hid from the bees. He could see the tree. Just a little further. The blob was gaining on them. Closer and closer until it was right on top of them. Warmth surged through Alex's body. The cloud emerged on the other side, just for an instant. Then it was gone.

The tree! He pulled Penelope in and they collapsed, huffing and gasping. His adrenaline was flowing. At first, he didn't notice anything else. As he calmed down, though, he felt it and he knew.

Sharp pain pierced his lower right abdomen. Every little movement made it worse. He was hot and sweaty. He wanted to vomit. Suddenly he was icy, chilled, terrified.

Then it happened. One side of his jacket was gone, his shirt, his skin. He looked down and saw his insides. His *insides*. He closed his eyes and screamed, but he only made a squeak. By now, he'd seen exposed body parts. But seeing his was different. These were his vulnerable organs flapping in the breeze.

Don't look, don't look! His eyes peeked down anyway. The lure of the fascinating awfulness was too much.

No shirt. No skin. Intestines in a tidy swarm, slithering like a fat pinky-orange snake. On the edge of the mass was a swollen, red tube, a tiny, fat worm that swelled even while he watched.

He heaved sideways to get his head outside the tree and vomited.

"Ewww. Disgusting."

She meant the vomit. She couldn't see the truly disgusting innards that he could see.

Penelope was giddy, laughing, but in a hysterical way. "That blue cloud chased us, and it went right through you! Right through you!"

"I know." Alex couldn't take his eyes off his appendix, swollen and inflamed. "Do you know what appendicitis is?"

"Sure I do. I had my appendix out when I was ten. They showed me pictures and told me all about it. It hurt like the devil."

"I know, I know." He swallowed hard, trying to control his nausea.

She finally saw him. "Oh, boy. You don't look good."

He vomited again. Pain shot through him.

"Oh, boy," she said again. "Oh, boy. Do you think you have appendicitis?"

He shifted slightly to see if he could get more comfortable. He was hot again, boiling, even without his shirt and with his insides exposed. Every move was agony.

"Okay. Okay. Don't panic." Her voice sounded panicked. "When this happened to me, it took a while to hurt really bad, but once it did, they said it was an emergency, and I had to go to surgery right away or it would burst, and then I'd get an even worse infection, and then it would be really serious."

"You're not making this any better." He gritted his teeth.

"Okay. Right. And I might die," she added.

"I understand." He could barely get the words out. "I know about appendicitis. You don't need to go into all the gory details."

"Got it," she said. "The cloud...does this have to do with the blue cloud?"

He couldn't answer her. The throbbing was so bad he couldn't move at all. He sat perfectly still, eyes closed.

"They gave me drugs in an IV in my arm to stop the pain," she said.

"Great. Don't tell me that," he said, his face screwed up from his own pain.

"We have to get you to the hospital to have surgery."

"No. I can't go anywhere. There has to be another way."

He knew what was going to happen. It was happening right before his eyes. The pressure inside the little worm-like organ was building up so much that it would explode. Perforate. Pus would ooze out into that glistening abdomen and infection would set in. Peritonitis. From the look and feel of it, his appendix was ready to burst.

The pain was worse, a searing pain like a fire burning right in his belly. He was breathing so fast his lips tingled.

In his pocket, he had the antidote his grandfather had given him. The antidote he didn't want. The antidote against ILL's ill. The one-time-use antidote, saved for generations, eked out waiting for the right time. Now? Was now the right time? His fingers grasped for it, felt the warm tube.

Penelope grabbed his hands, and the vial dropped back in his pocket. "Look at me!" she shouted, but he could barely hear her. She stuck her face in his face. "Breathe slower! You're hyperventilating. Breathe slower!"

He leaned against the tree hollow. His heart raced. He fumbled for the vial again, and once he found it, he clenched his fingers so it wouldn't drop.

Don't panic. Easy to say, but all he could see was his appendix about to pop. Think! Penelope was right. He tried to breathe slowly, evenly, concentrating on his breathing to take his mind off the pain. His dad had shown him how when he broke his leg, and he used it whenever he needed to distract himself. Long, deep breaths that made his stomach rise before his chest. Breathe in, breathe out, one. Breathe in, breathe out, two. Slow and steady. Up to four, then repeat. Think about your breathing, concentrate on your breathing.

Each breath pushed a knife into his abdomen. The breathing didn't make the pain any better. He counted to four over and over, panic rising again. Breathe in, breathe out, two. Breathe in, breathe out, three. He hurt so much he couldn't think. He was going to die here if he didn't use the antidote.

He hugged his sides with his elbows to try to splint against the fiery pain, hands in front of his body clasped tightly around the antidote, avoiding the open gash where his intestines were. He tried to envision his breaths taking the inflammation and the pain out of his body. If he had a body.

Alex wished the breathing would work like it had when he was little. He breathed in the cedar, fresh and green and spicy. The base of his neck tingled, then his back. Breathe in, breathe out. He breathed in the decaying leaves, earthy and musty. Breathe in, breathe out.

"Look!" Penelope cried.

Pink vapor emanated from his nose and mouth. He sat up with excitement, then fell right back because the pain was still there. Though maybe not quite as bad. He vomited again, his stomach empty except for a small amount of burning fluid.

Calm down. Keep breathing. Slow and steady. Breathe in, breathe out, one. He could see the pink, amorphous mist seeping out, but he tried to ignore it and breathe. He closed his eyes. He kept breathing, getting to four and starting again and again.

"Alex, Alex?" Penelope said. "Is it any better?"

Alex stopped his deliberate breathing and opened his eyes. The pink vapor was gone. His nausea was gone. His pain was only a soreness now. It had been so severe, the memory made his brain hurt. He stole a look down and his shirt was back, his intestines tucked safely away where he couldn't see them. His hands were tight fists. He still clutched the antidote. He carefully put the vial back in his pocket.

"What was all that?" Penelope said. "Alex, what just happened?"

"ILL," Alex said. "That was ILL."

Penelope sat there with her mouth open, black eyes wide. Now she believed him.

Alex was utterly exhausted. This was ILL shackled? What had he been able to do before?

"I can't fight him. It's too hard. It's too painful. All I want is my dog back."

"Baloney," she said. "Look at you. A giant cloud of darkness attacked you. You fought off appendicitis just by breathing. You beat it with your brains, by staying calm, with your mind. Mind over matter. You can do this."

"Maybe," he said. "Maybe."

"You have to fight him. Isn't that what your grandpa said?"

"I don't know how. Even if I wanted to. He's here, but where? He's attacking me, but how do I attack back? I can't give him appendicitis. I can't get his black cloth." Alex's side ached, and his mouth was a slimy, sour mess. *He* was a slimy mess. He said again, "Even if I wanted to." Which he did not. "All I want is my dog."

"Well, at least he hasn't killed you yet."

"Great vote of confidence. Thanks."

Alex laid his head back against the tree. He caught a glimpse of red and craned his neck. High in the tree trunk, too high to reach, was a dangling square of red.

Chapter 35
Mrs. Lemon's Lemon

They had to get out of there. They had to find Valentine. They started out slowly because Alex's side still hurt. He pushed the red handkerchief from his mind. Of course there would be the red handkerchief. He knew the illness was from ILL. But seeing the cloth there, in his hollowed-out tree, made his side ache as much as the appendicitis.

He showed Penelope his favorite trails and his secret hiding spots. They called and called, "Valentine, Valentine," but heard no responding bark. He told her about his mom and dad and The Fish House. She said it must be cool to have doctors for parents and he said, "Eh." He told her about his school and the kids he'd known since kindergarten who wouldn't look him in the eyes. And Sandy Molloy, the worst of them. "He's allergic to peanuts, like I'm allergic to bees."

"I'm allergic to hazelnuts," Penelope said. "I was the only one in my school with a food allergy."

"School. It seems so unreal."

"We're in the same school. I started yesterday." She paused. "I saw you up there."

"You saw me at school?"

"Yes, on the stage with the principal."

He didn't know what to say to this, so he said, "What are you doing at my school?"

"I live with my aunt now. My mom's sister. She lives near here." Her voice faltered.

"That's nice," was all Alex could think to say.

"My aunt's okay. She's trying hard to help. She lived alone all these years in an apartment, and there's no real place for me. She says we can look for a house, maybe something with a garden. My mom had a big garden in California. We had strawberries and green beans and flowers. And an orange tree and a lemon tree. The blossoms smelled so good I could sit out there all day. When the oranges came, I could pull one off and eat it while it was still warm from the sun."

"Ah...we don't have oranges and lemons here. We do have blackberries. Do you like blackberries?"

"Don't blackberry bushes have pokey thorns and turn your hands all black when you pick them?" Penelope asked.

"Yep, those are blackberries. But they taste good. They're all over here. My mom doesn't cook, but when I was little, Mrs. Lemon used to make blackberry cobbler and homemade ice cream."

Mrs. Lemon. She was the lady who watched him after his dad started back at work. Until she went away.

"She could cook anything—macaroni with three cheeses, shish kabob, chicken teriyaki, meatloaf, homemade pesto." His mouth watered. She was such a good cook, especially compared to his mom. "She showed me how to crack an egg with one hand." Alex remembered going through dozens of eggs before he got it right. They ate a lot of scrambled eggs. She'd taught him to cook.

His mom would cock her head to the side, close her eyes, and inhale. "Mmm, mmm. Simple homemade

143

tomato sauce." He'd been so proud, knowing he had crushed those tomatoes himself.

"Mrs. Lemon showed you this? How would we live without her?" his mom would say.

But they would have to live without Mrs. Lemon. Alex knew before anyone, before Mrs. Lemon herself.

It happened while they made cinnamon buns for a special breakfast treat. Alex wasn't tall, but neither was Mrs. Lemon, and with his hair that spiked up in front, he was as tall as her shoulder. She pointed to his reflection in the shiny silver toaster. His black hair was full of flour, and she tousled it with her floury hands to add more. "Now you look like me." She tilted her gray head so it fit next to his in the toaster.

He remembered them humming, each a different tune, but it sounded pleasant enough. Mrs. Lemon pounded the cinnamon bun dough in time to the music. She pulled off a bit and helped him shape it into tight little spirals.

And he had an awful feeling. He knew something was very wrong. He knew she was sick. He never ate another cinnamon roll.

"Mrs. Lemon had lymphoma, a type of cancer they could treat, but she couldn't take care of me anymore. We went to see her in the hospital where my parents worked, and she came to dinner, an awful dinner my mom cooked. I tried to make ice cream, but it didn't freeze, and it was just vanilla slop. Then she moved to Cleveland to be with her daughter."

Alex's voice broke. He wasn't surprised. He hadn't thought of Mrs. Lemon in a while, but whenever he did, he his stomach ached like it had after the vanilla slop. He had known her forever, and then she was gone. She tucked him in when he was little. She ate dinner with him when his parents worked late at the hospital. She played with him when he had no friends.

After Mrs. Lemon left, they limped along with a series of college girl babysitters who studied on their computers or talked on their phones. When Alex turned eleven, his mom said he was old enough to stay on his own. He loved that, being alone in the Fish House in the woods. But he loved Mrs. Lemon more.

He must not have been talking because Penelope said, "My mom could make ice cream."

Alex kept his eyes down and slowly walked along.

"And sorbet," Penelope said. "With the lemons from the tree. My dad and I would come up with crazy flavors of ice cream like chocolate and chili pepper, and she would make them, or she'd make one, and we'd try to guess what was in it."

Penelope sighed. "My mom and dad really liked each other. They had so much fun together. We all had so much fun." Alex leaned closer to hear her soft voice. "Now it's just the two of us, my aunt and me. It's not a family. It's not fun."

Alex was quiet, too. Not only because of Mrs. Lemon. His family used to be fun. But since he'd found Valentine, since his mom found out he had the curse, since ILL, everyone was all tense and frightened. Everything was different. And now he'd lost Valentine just like he lost Mrs. Lemon.

## Chapter 36
## Still Here

*The Woods*

*What happened? The kid was still here. Not dead. Not using everything he had to save himself.*

*He didn't want him dead. Not yet. But he wanted something. Something only this boy could give him. And give he would.*

Chapter 37
Hot Cocoa

The storm had ended, and the forest was silent and damp. Alex and Penelope were silent and damp. The light was fading quickly. Days were short in the winter in Seattle, and deep in this forest, with the trees blocking the little light there was, darkness came well before five o'clock. Alex shivered and squinted into the dim surroundings. For the first time, the forest looked menacing, with giant branches covered with moss pointing accusing fingers toward him and trees so large they could hide anything behind them. Or anyone. Or ILL.

"Let's go home." He was more uneasy by the moment.

"But we haven't found your dog."

"Maybe he's at home," Alex said, though he doubted it was true. It was just too creepy out here.

They found their way slowly through the dark. Alex's house sat in a clearing, glowing and welcoming. His parents must have switched on every light. He stifled an urge to run toward it.

As they approached, he warned her to keep quiet about the cloud of disease. He had to find his dog, and his mom would never let him out again if she knew ILL was this close.

The door flew open before they made it to the porch steps. His mom spilled out, with his dad close behind. He could see how worried they were. He could see them struggle to pretend they weren't.

"Hi, honey," his mom said in a voice that was too high. "Where have you been? You left hours ago."

Hours ago. Had it only been hours ago?

"This is Penelope." Alex nodded his head toward Penelope.

His parents exchanged a quick glance. They stepped back into the house, and Alex and Penelope followed. "Nice to meet you, Penelope," his mom said, her voice still too high.

"She just moved here from California. She's new at school. I've been showing her our woods," Alex said. Penelope nodded.

He could see his parents relax. His father led them into the living room and sat on the arm of the couch.

"Where's Valentine?" his mom asked.

Tears stung Alex's eyes. He squeezed them shut and turned his head. He tried to sound natural. "Well, that's the thing. We can't find him. He got away from me, and we've been hunting for him in the woods." He took a deep breath. "He's not here, is he?" He peered around hopefully.

His parents glanced at each other again. "No," his mother said. "He isn't here."

The tears stung again. He'd actually allowed himself to think Valentine might have come home.

"He's bound to turn up," his father said. "Though I suppose he may have found his way to his old home."

Alex nodded, dejected. He knew Valentine hadn't gone to any home, this home or his old home.

"You two look wet," his mother said. "I've got some hot cocoa. Would you like some hot cocoa?"

Alex cringed. He couldn't believe his mom was offering them hot cocoa.

"Yes!" Penelope shouted excitedly. "I'd love some!"

His mom jumped up and in no time was back with two mugs of cocoa. Alex knew they were from packets and not the stir-on-the-stove homemade kind Mrs. Lemon used to make. It didn't matter. It tasted delicious.

"I can take you home, Penelope," his father said when they finished the cocoa. "It's dark. Someone must be missing you."

Penelope bit her lip. Tears formed in her eyes.

Alex said, too loudly, "I'm sure missing Valentine. We can look for him on the way."

They climbed into the car and his dad turned on the heat. The windows fogged, and Alex had to keep wiping his off to see out. To look for Valentine. To look for trouble.

Penelope directed them to an apartment building close to the school. "I'll see you tomorrow, I guess," he said.

"I'll see you tomorrow, I guess," she repeated and hopped out. He and his dad watched to make sure she got into the building safely. She pivoted and gave a little wave before she closed the door.

His dad didn't turn the engine back on. He shifted in his seat, his blue eyes dark with concern.

"We were worried, your mom and I. What happened in the woods today?"

Alex sat there miserably. Why bother telling him? He would only worry more, and there was nothing he could do. His father couldn't help him.

"I need to talk to Grandpa," Alex said.

"It's hard to talk to Grandpa," his dad said softly. "It's hard to hear him on the telephone. His voice…it doesn't project across the miles."

"I know. But I need to try."

He'd almost died. He'd almost used the antidote, which he was supposed to save to fight ILL. ILL had Valentine. Alex had nothing.

Chapter 38
Even with Shackles

Alex's father dialed the number and said a few words and handed Alex the phone. Then he left the room, pulling his mom out with him. Alex could see she wanted to stay. They closed the door, so he knew he was safe to talk freely.

He could barely hear his grandpa's voice. It was thin and raspy with long pauses while he caught his breath. The line was crackly anyway, maybe with the storm and all the mountains between them. Alex pressed the phone tighter and tighter against his ear, but the words were faint and nearly inaudible.

He told his grandpa about Valentine and the red handkerchief on the bike rack. And the blue smoke and the appendicitis.

Alex wasn't certain he heard everything correctly. He could tell there was more his grandpa wanted to say, but he didn't have the strength. What he heard was ominous enough.

"ILL wants you dead. This much is clear. You are the last Revelstoke. Without us, he can work unchecked. Even with shackles, he can still harm you. One person at a time, he can hurt. Appendicitis. This is all he can do with the shackles. But appendicitis can be deadly."

Alex already knew it was deadly. He had felt his side explode with pain.

"You fought him off. I don't know how. The shackles. It must be the shackles. But he got to Bea, even with the shackles."

And worse, "You have to act, Alex. You have to find him. You have to destroy that black cloth. Destroy him. Or he will succeed and destroy you first."

Alex set the phone down quietly so that his parents wouldn't know he was finished. He had to think, and he didn't want his parents' anxious faces around when he did.

He had to get Valentine back. He had to cripple ILL's power. He had to get that black cloth.

Chapter 39
Blood

Alex spent the next school day thinking of Valentine and his multicolored fur and his big, fluffy head. How long could a dog live without food? How long could a dog live without water? Alex knew about people. A person could last weeks without food. But water was essential. A person could only last three days without water before they became dehydrated and then the kidneys shut down and then they died. There were stories about people living longer. But most lived three days. Where had ILL taken him? Did Valentine have water?

He stopped by the science classroom after school while Mr. Beaker was at the Friday faculty meeting to borrow something he knew Mr. Beaker would not be happy to loan. He tucked it into his backpack next to the long match box from his grandfather. Penelope waited in the hall. Out of the building without a challenge, they set off toward the lake and the park.

Alex strained his eyes left and right along the way, but he knew in his heart that the dog was in the park. All ILL's danger had been in the park, the bees, the appendicitis.

It was another glorious day, crisp and clear. They came down the hill, and the view opened up. Mount Rainier soared in front of them, massive and majestic.

"Whoa. What's that?" Penelope said, stopping short.

"Mount Rainier. Where have you been?"

"That's Mount Rainier? Wow. Where did it come from? I've passed this corner multiple times, and that mountain has not been there before today."

"It hides," he said. "It hides in the clouds and it looks like there's nothing there, but on a clear day…well…there it is."

"Wow," Penelope said again.

Alex knew what she meant. He had lived there his whole life, and Mount Rainier was still a "wow" to him, too.

"Take a good look because you might not see it again for a while." Alex smiled, despite the awful day.

Alex was glad of the sunshine. Though he didn't mind the rain and the gray, he was a little wary of fog right now, fog that could hide the blue smoke, the clouds of disease.

He told Penelope about what his grandfather had said. Destroy ILL? How could he even find ILL? ILL held all the cards.

"He wants you. It's not a matter of finding him. He will find you. That's just as good," Penelope said.

"Yeah, right," Alex said.

"You don't have any faith. You are stronger than you know. You have something special, someone no one else on earth has. That's why he wants you."

"I'm glad one of us thinks this is a good idea."

They were at the lake now. They headed south toward the park, walking along the sparkling, deep blue lake with Mount Rainier off in the distance in front of them. He showed her the turtle log, the turtles splayed out on top sunning themselves.

"On a day like today, it sure is pretty here," Penelope said.

"It's pretty here every day," Alex said.

"It's not pretty when the sky is low and gray, and the lake is gray, and it's wet and cold."

"Oh, but look." Alex pointed to the pine trees, tall and straight. And the cedar trees, green and fragrant. And the giant ferns, so oversized they were bigger than him. And the grass, green and long from all the rain. "It's pretty. It's just different," he said.

She regarded him for a moment with her black eyes. "You're different."

Whoa. He dropped his head and smiled. He'd never really talked to a girl before, but this girl was very easy to talk to.

ILL could come any time. He was ready.

They were at the edge of the woods. Alex gazed back at Mount Rainier, solid and comforting. They both fell silent as they crossed into the trees. They walked uphill, soundless and watchful. Some of the day's sunshine penetrated the canopy and splashes of light glinted here and there. The light twinkled on the forest floor and made long shadows behind the trees. Dark, ominous shadows that could hide anything. How could the woods look more threatening on a sunny day? But they did.

Alex's confidence faded with the light.

They picked their way gingerly, searching, listening. Alex quashed the urge to call Valentine's name. Every twist in the path brought anxiety, and he stepped around each bend with trepidation.

They looked ahead, they looked behind. They never looked up. That's where it was. Another blue cloud, swooping down on them from the treetops. Falling onto Penelope, falling through Penelope, and then vanishing. She gaped at him, dumbstruck. He waited, knowing any second she would start to hurt.

She shook her head. "I don't feel anything. I feel normal."

They waited a few minutes to see. They took a few slow steps. She insisted she was all right.

They continued along. "My tree fort is just ahead," Alex said. "Let's head for that." It was the tree house on the ground where he hid from the bees.

He showed her the entrance, crawling through the branches of fallen trees into a space the size of a car with a roof of boughs, needles, and leaves completely blocking it from view. They sat there facing each other.

"I really do feel all right. Well, maybe a little queasy." Then Penelope doubled over and vomited into the leaves next to her. "Maybe a lot queasy." Her voice quavered.

Oh, no. Alex's eyes fixed on the vomit on the leaves. Penelope looked down, too. Her eyes widened and hand flew to her mouth. The vomit was red. There was no mistaking what it was, even there on the bigleaf maple leaves. Blood red.

They both stared, horrified. Then she vomited again. Redder. Bloodier.

Alex jerked his eyes back to her. Above her head was a red square cloth, caught on a branch and hanging listlessly.

Her black eyes were fearful. There was a little blood on her chin. "What is it?" she asked.

He gawked at the handkerchief and then at the blood on the ground, maroon liquid, some congealed into clots. She wanted to know what was wrong with her. She didn't know about the cloth.

He concentrated hard, trying to see Penelope's problem. He felt nothing, he saw nothing. "I don't know."

"You don't know?" He heard the fear in her voice.

"How do you feel? Does anything hurt?" he asked.

"No. I'm just queasy. Nothing hurts. But what is it?"

Alex sat there, thinking frantically. What was going on? He knew everything about everybody, even when he didn't want to. Why couldn't he figure this out?

"You're a Revelstoke." She gazed at him from across the shelter. Her voice was still quiet, but now sounded confident, calm. "You will know what to do."

A Revelstoke. Some Revelstoke. She'd put her faith in the wrong guy.

"Oh, oh." She vomited again.

"Okay. Okay. Stay calm. Remember. You can get rid of this. Try deep breaths."

She took a deep gulp of air, went into a coughing fit, then gagged and retched, bringing up a huge amount of blood.

"Okay. Okay. Too deep," Alex said. "Not so deep, just slow and steady, in and out."

He could see her try. Her breaths were shallow and too quick. She was pale from losing blood. Her head lowered, and he thought she was going to faint.

"Put your head down. Lean forward like this." She bent sluggishly. Her expression was dreamy. He didn't have much time before she passed out.

"Stay with me!" he shouted, trying to get his words into her blood-deprived brain. "Breathe slowly!"

She leaned to the side and vomited again. And again. There was blood all around her. Way too much blood.

"You can do this!" He sounded like a maniacal life coach. "Mind over matter, remember?"

She looked at him with those black eyes. "I'm trying."

"Remember what you told me? Stay calm!" he pleaded. He was not calm. He was desperate. "Breathe in, breathe out. You can fight this."

"I am," she said softly. "I'm breathing. I'm doing it."

And she was. She was breathing exactly the way she was supposed to. Her face was composed, peaceful. And pale. So pale.

Why wasn't it working? Where was the pink exhaled mist, like with his appendicitis? Why had it worked for him? Why was she still so sick?

She vomited again, more blood, blood everywhere. Her whole body swayed. She would faint soon if he didn't do something. She would die if she lost too much blood.

Breathing wasn't working. How did he ever think he could defeat ILL with mind over matter and a few deep breaths? He needed to figure out what was wrong with Penelope. Then maybe he could figure out how to stop it.

What had his grandfather told him? Every Revelstoke is different. His grandfather could see disease by looking in your eyes. His great-grandfather looked you up and down like a CT x-ray machine. What did he need to do? He didn't know.

"Penelope! Look at me!" he shouted.

Her eyes were closed. She was concentrating on her breathing, but she lifted her chin and fastened those big black eyes on his. Nothing. No seeing the problem. No diagnosis. Nothing but panic. Her eyes slowly closed again. She turned her head and vomited red again. How much blood did she have left?

The Fish House was only a little farther along the trail. If he could get her home, his parents could help. He would have to tell them everything, all about ILL and Valentine and the clouds of disease. But they could help Penelope.

He couldn't see the leaves from all the blood. She had lost so much blood. What could his parents do? How long would it take to get her to a hospital where they could really treat her? Did she have that much time?

The antidote. He had the vial with the antidote in his pocket. She would bleed to death right in front of him if he didn't do something soon. He grabbed the vial out, his grandfather's words in his ears. "This is all that's left. Saved through the generations. I have never used it. Not even for Bea."

Alex didn't care. He didn't care about Revelstokes or ILL. He couldn't let her die. He was responsible. She was sick because of him. She would die if he didn't save her.

He seized the vial and moved across the shelter, feeling its warmth, watching the liquid in the vial change from purple to gold. The inside of the tree house lighted up in a blaze of brightness, bathing the dark green branches and blood-red leaves in a warm, golden glow.

Alex held the vial in front of her face, but her head was down, her breathing still steady and calm.

"Penelope?" He put his hand on her shoulder to lean her back. "Penelope? I have something to help." He lifted her chin so she could see. An icy sensation of fear ran down his body.

Her eyes were distant, and she could not see the vial. But he could see. Her stomach was laid bare for him, translucent so he could see the small white depression of the ulcer and the blood vessel at the ulcer edge pumping blood into her stomach, filling it with blood. He could feel the bloody fluid fill his own stomach and start to rise in his esophagus. He swallowed hard and the feeling was gone.

Touch! He'd lifted her chin and suddenly he saw everything. He had to touch to see! That's how his Revelstoke gift worked. He was ecstatic and relieved and never so happy to see disease.

"It's an ulcer!" he shouted. "You have a stomach ulcer!"

An ulcer. He'd read an article in the *New England Journal of Medicine*, and he knew all the fancy ways to stop the bleeding with a scope through the mouth to get to the stomach. Useless information. That wouldn't help now.

She focused her eyes on him. She was concentrating so much on her breathing that he wasn't sure she heard. He grabbed her shoulders and she fell forward into him so that his arms circled her whole slim body. She didn't weigh anything. She was so fragile.

How could she fight this? She breathed slowly and counted the breaths like he told her. She was dying and he had her here counting to four. She completed another full cycle, one, two, three, four. Then another. Her words were barely audible. He held her tight and wished he could save her, that the breathing would work, like it had with his appendicitis. A tingle shot down his spine, just remembering the appendicitis.

Penelope stopped counting. Was she even breathing? He pushed her gently back and held the vial in front of her face. His hand trembled as he tried to break the wax seal. The glass stopper was tight. He twisted hard, and it popped off in his hand. He put the vial to her lips.

Pink foam collected at the corner of her mouth, a slight froth. More foam appeared, more and more with each exhalation. He jammed the stopper back on the vial.

"Keep breathing! It's working!" He was giddy. More pink foam formed and dissipated away, like froth from waves rolling onto a beach. Pink came back into her cheeks. Her vomiting stopped.

To beat ILL's diseases, he needed to know what the disease was, and he needed the relaxation breathing. He needed both. But he needed something more. The appendicitis didn't go away when he first started breathing, and he'd known all along it was his appendix. That pain had lasted forever. Penelope was counting her breaths long after he realized she had an ulcer, without anything happening at all. There was another piece.

At least ILL was shackled and his diseases could be overpowered. If Alex only knew how.

Today he was lucky. He saved her. Without him, without the Revelstoke gift of diagnosis, of knowing it was a bleeding ulcer, without that she would have died. She would have bled to death right here in the woods.

He watched her breathing, still steady and slow. Her eyes were closed, her face serene. She had faith in him. She had faith in the Revelstokes.

A Revelstoke. A doctor. A doctor needed to know the diagnosis to start the correct treatment. With his gift, he was halfway there. He thought of Sam. His gift had saved Sam precious time to get the AED before it was too late.

Miracle, Sam said. This gift was a miracle.

ILL. ILL had done this to Penelope. Throughout history, ILL had hurt and harmed and destroyed through sickness and disease. ILL was out there, shackled, weak. Now was the time.

Penelope's breath came stronger and stronger. More mist formed, and then it was gone. Alex still had the vial in his hand. He carefully placed it back in his pocket. He would need this. He would need this to fight ILL.

He couldn't fight his Revelstoke gift. He wanted his Revelstoke gift. He wanted to kill ILL.

Chapter 40
Alive

Penelope slowly moved out of the pool of blood. She used leaves in vain to brush at her shirt and hands.

"Good thing my mom's not here. She would flip out. She was such a Nervous Nelly."

"My mom won't let me go on trampolines," Alex said. "All moms are Nervous Nellies."

"Not like my mom." Penelope leaned against the tree branches. "She makes—made—us wait for the next taxi if it didn't have head rests for the backseat so we wouldn't get whiplash if it stopped too quick. She never let me go on a Ferris wheel because she read an article about someone who fell from the top. She made us wash our fruit with gritty fruit cleaner and a brush in case of pesticides. She and Dad never flew together on an airplane without me in case of plane crash." She shook her head and laughed, a harsh, ugly laugh. "Isn't that ironic? My dad actually does die in a plane crash, like Mom always worried about. But then she drives into a tree. Super cautious, don't go one mile over the speed limit, 'we're not backing out of this driveway without you in your seat belt' Mom drives into a tree."

She wasn't crying. Her little chin was out, and her mouth was set.

"I used to be like that, too. I washed that fruit and wore a helmet on the ice-skating rink and never left the

163

house without my sweater so I wouldn't catch cold. I stayed inside if it was too windy in case a tree branch might crack off and land on me. I skipped a zip-line party last year because it was too dangerous. I was afraid of everything."

She stuck her chin out farther, her black eyes determined, strong. "Not anymore. The absolute worst thing that can happen happened. My mom lived her cautious life and so did I. And look what happened anyway."

He thought she was going to cry then. But she didn't. "Look at me now. In the woods with someone I only just met. Chased by clouds of disease. I even had a bleeding stomach ulcer! I am not afraid. Not anymore. Not even of ILL."

She couldn't see herself, pasty-skinned and covered in blood, Alex thought.

When they finally came out of the tree fort, it was dusk. "I don't think we should look anymore tonight." Alex hated to think of Valentine alone in the woods another night, but look at Penelope. She was still weak, still recovering. "Tomorrow's Saturday. Meet me at the library."

She nodded. She could barely stand. An hour ago she was sitting in the tree house with blood all around. ILL was after Alex. ILL had taken Valentine. She was only there because of Alex. She had almost died. Like Grandma Bea. He had to talk to his grandfather again. Grandpa knew how this felt.

He couldn't drag her along again. They were lucky she wasn't dead. "Actually, you don't need to come. You're not part of this, not a Revelstoke. ILL won't hurt you if you're not with me. And Valentine is not your dog."

Her sad black eyes flashed. She shook her head and laughed, that same harsh, ugly laugh.

She sat on a log to rest. "You don't get it, do you? You don't understand."

"Understand what?"

"My parents died. Everything I knew died." She took a deep breath. "My grandma tried to keep me in California, in the same house, in the same school, thought that would be best. So every day I'd see our kitchen where my mom made me cream cheese and jelly sandwiches, and our piano where my dad played show tunes and sang in his awful, out-of-tune voice. Until one day I couldn't take it and started screaming and couldn't stop. Not for days. So here I am. A change of scene, they said. But it doesn't matter. It still hurts, worse than when I had appendicitis. There is nothing ILL can do that would be worse."

What could he say to that?

"For six months I haven't felt alive. I get up in the morning or I don't, I eat or I don't. I don't feel anything but pain, but sadness. I don't care about anything, don't care about me. This week has been the most alive I've felt since my parents—" She breathed deeply, then lifted her head and straightened her back. "Since my parents died."

She didn't cry. She stood there defiantly. There was no way he was changing her mind. Without thinking, he reached out and gave her hand a quick squeeze.

"Okay," he said. "We'll do it together."

165

Chapter 41
So Close

*The Woods*

*So close. He had been so close.*
*The boy hadn't wavered when it was for himself.*
*But to save the girl... It had been a surefire plan.*
*She was expendable. He only needed the boy.*
*It was time to increase the stakes.*

Chapter 42
The Last Revelstoke

Alex and Penelope picked their way carefully through the dark woods. Alex's foot caught on a tree root, and he hurtled forward, landing hard on his knees. He hauled himself up, using a giant stump for support.

Even if he hadn't stopped, he couldn't have missed it. Penelope stood stock still, mesmerized.

Ahead on the trail, right in front of them, hanging down from a branch like a tree snake searching for prey, was a large square handkerchief. But not red this time. Black. Shimmery, despite the low light, as if it had an aura around it.

They edged nearer, half expecting it to come alive. The handkerchief billowed in the wind, opening up like a sail, but it stayed in place on the tree branch.

Alex hunted wildly around. This was the black cloth! It had to be. Where was ILL? It was supposed to be connected to ILL. All of ILL's power came from this black cloth.

Alex didn't want to touch the thing. It emanated badness, a feeling of dread and hopelessness, even standing away from it on the trail. He fumbled in his backpack for the cylinder of long fireplace matches. He struck one, and it ignited into a flame the size of an orange. He held it out as far from his body as he could. He edged closer to the blackness. His hand trembled.

Don't blow out. Hold still! He touched the fat flame to the cloth. The handkerchief burst into a shower of tiny sparks, crackling and hissing. And just like that, it was gone.

Alex gaped at Penelope, stunned. Was that the black cloth? Was it gone?

They had to get home. Alex wanted to move faster, but Penelope was exhausted. He dragged her along, scanning for ILL, scanning for trouble. The dark woods could hide anything. He could only see a few feet in each direction. The trail straightened and they saw the light at the edge of the forest. Finally they were out.

Alex could see well now, and he saw nothing. The clearing was wide open and empty.

In the light of the clearing, Alex got a good look at Penelope. She was a mess. Blood covered her shirt and skirt. To most people, the crusted brown would look like dirt, but his parents would know dried blood when they saw it. Alex pulled his jacket out of his backpack and helped Penelope put it on. He was broader than she was, and the large jacket hung almost to her knees. Perfect to cover her bloody clothes. They would never make it past his parents without the jacket.

They slowly made their way to the house. Penelope leaned hard on him. What would his parents make of this? A girl wearing his jacket, pushed against him like they were one person? The door opened before they got to the porch steps. Dad had been watching.

"Mom's still at work. I came home early. Expected you a while ago from school."

"I burned the black cloth. It's gone." Alex spoke at the same time.

His dad stared down at them from the porch. "ILL? Was ILL there?" His dad's eyes swept the clearing, the same way Alex's had.

"No, we never saw ILL. Just this shimmery black cloth on a tree branch. I burned it. It's gone."

Alex's father exhaled, deflated.

"There's more. There must be more. This must only have been a small part."

It hadn't looked small, that was for sure. But Alex knew it couldn't be this easy. He shuddered, remembering the shimmery, menacing material.

Penelope needed help up the steps. They shuffled into the house, still silent. Alex settled Penelope in the wooden rocking chair. She was shivering. "Cocoa?" he said, too cheerfully.

She smiled faintly and nodded. Alex's father followed him to the kitchen. Alex tore open the packets and put the kettle on to boil. His father gently put his hand on his shoulder and swiveled him around. Blue eyes to blue eyes.

"What happened in the woods?"

Alex didn't look away. He stood as tall as he could, but he still had to tilt his head to meet his father's searching gaze. How could he explain the clouds of disease? How close Penelope had come to death? He wanted to tell his dad. But if he did, his parents might never let him in the woods again. He had to go back.

"I have to find Valentine. I have to find ILL."

Alex's father didn't say a word.

"You know I have to do this. I am a Revelstoke, just like you, just like Grandpa, just like his dad. I have to finish what your grandfather started."

His father finally shifted his eyes. "I didn't have the Revelstoke gift. I couldn't help." His father paused. "I studied fish to get away from disease and medicine and the constant reminder of all ILL has done to humankind. But the allure is too strong. Even without any diagnostic gift, I can still fight disease as a doctor. I can do something.

"When you were born, I hoped you'd be like me. I hoped you wouldn't have the Revelstoke gift. Then it would be over. It would have ended with my father."

"But ILL?" Alex said. "There would be no one left to fight ILL."

Alex's father nodded miserably.

"Revelstokes have battled ILL for centuries," Alex said. "Your grandfather made him weak. I am the only one who can finally stop him. I have to kill ILL."

His father put his hand on the counter to steady himself. Alex saw a flood of different emotions cross his face. Fear and worry and love and resolve.

"I am a Revelstoke, but I don't have the gift," his father said sadly. "I can't help you. But I understand. You have to do this, to kill this evil. You are the only one who can. You are the last Revelstoke."

Chapter 43
The Other Sign

Alex called his grandfather again that night. His father set him up without his mom even knowing.

This time the line was clear, but he still had trouble hearing his grandpa's weak voice on the phone. Alex told him about Penelope and the blood.

"This is one of the hardest things about this gift," his grandfather said slowly. "Some illness will be directed at you personally. But some will hurt others, innocent others."

The line was so clear that Alex could hear his grandpa's breathing change. Grandpa was thinking about Grandma Bea. Alex wanted to ask what he could do, how he could protect Penelope.

Who was he kidding? His grandpa didn't know. His grandpa couldn't help him.

"You must fight him even with this burden," was all his grandfather could say.

"How?" Alex shouted. This was impossible. "How do I fight him? I can't see him. I can't find him. All I can do is walk into his traps."

"Yes. That is how it is. But those traps expose him. He is near. You will find him because he wants to find you."

This was not what Alex wanted to hear. He did not want to hear any of it.

He had one more thing to ask. Even thinking about it made his hands shake. Something about the shimmery glow, the slow movement of the black cloth in the wind, like a flag on a pirate ship portending doom. He had to know. He forced himself to get the words out.

"I saw the black cloth," he said. "A square of black cloth in the trees, and I burned it, but my dad said there's more."

The line went dead. That's what Alex thought, it was so silent for so long, absolutely silent.

"Grandpa? Are you there?"

Even then his grandpa only grunted. Or groaned.

"Grandpa?"

"It cannot be," his grandpa whispered.

What? Alex's chest heaved and tightened, like Mr. Cylinder's with the heart attack.

"It cannot be," his grandpa said again.

Oh, boy. He knew this black thing would be bad.

"ILL is shackled," his grandpa said finally. "Shackled. It cannot be."

Then it came out. The shackles prevented ILL from creating disease, except for very small efforts, one individual at a time. Nothing infectious. Nothing major. Nothing epidemic.

"Remember when you were here, and I said the only clue that ILL had a new disease was when he started to attack Revelstokes? That was not true. There was one more clue, one I prayed I'd never see in my lifetime. Your father does not know of this. In time past, the black cloth was a foretelling. Of horror to come."

Alex moved the phone a little farther from his ear, but his grandfather's voice now came through loud and clear.

"Revelstoke history tells of this. The black cloth appeared in the time before the plague. And smallpox. God, smallpox. The worst of the worst of disease. And polio. ILL created those. Each one came with this black, shimmery cloth, too late for Revelstokes to stop them. Appearing as the creation was complete, right before it was set upon humanity. A sick reminder of who was in control and who was impotent. ILL cuts a piece of his powerful cloth to prove his strength."

"It's a sign?" Alex licked his dry lips.

"The most dreaded sign a Revelstoke could see. A taunt. I used to be haunted by it, terrified it would happen to me."

The line silenced again. His grandpa finally spoke. Alex could barely make out his words.

"My father's shackles do not allow for disease on this scale. He must have broken free. The shackles must have shattered."

His grandfather's voice was stronger now, loud in his ear. "He has a new creation. A new disease. It is ready. It is imminent. You are the only one who has a hope of stopping him. He knows this. You are the last Revelstoke."

Alex sat there numbly, the phone pushed so hard against his ear it hurt. It took him a while to realize that his grandpa was gone. The phone was dead.

Chapter 44
Worse Than Smallpox

Could it be? The shackles? Gone? What would ILL do to him? He could do anything he wanted. Alex was the last Revelstoke. Kill or be killed.

And not just Alex. ILL could destroy Alex, but now, unshackled, he could also decimate whole populations like he had before.

Was there a new disease? Something worse than polio? Worse than smallpox?

It didn't seem possible. Smallpox was one of the most horrifying diseases ever. Alex knew a lot about smallpox. He had written a paper on it when they studied Native American history. He had seen the pictures in the book.

It started in the early centuries and had been around until the 1980s, finally wiped out by a vaccine. It spread like fire, from person to person to person until everyone had it, whole families, whole towns. There was a time in history when it accounted for ten percent of all deaths. Ten percent of ALL deaths. Due to smallpox. Due to ILL.

The death rate was not the worst of it. The worst of it was the disease itself. The fever, the aches, the vomiting. And the smallpox rash. It started with a few tiny red spots in your mouth. Then it spread. To your face, to your body, to your arms, to your legs. The spots

174

became bumps that became blisters that became pustules. Sores of pus, hundreds of them, thousands of them all over your body. And then you died. Some lived, but most died.

How could anything be worse than smallpox?

Chapter 45
Don't Tell

He didn't know how his father did it, but neither parent balked when he left the next morning. His mother gave him a long hug before she let him go. Her red eyes implored him to stay.

He walked up the hill to the library, slowing as he neared. He scrutinized the bus stop before passing by. No sign of him. No sign of ILL.

He didn't see Penelope, but Ms. Parker was there as usual behind her wide desk. She stared off into space and didn't notice him at first.

"Hi, Ms. Parker," he said.

"Alex," she said.

"How are you?" He scanned the room for Penelope. Ms. Parker didn't answer right away, and he looked back at her. Her eyes seemed a little vacant. And yellow. Even though the computer was switched off, her eyes were definitely yellow.

"Are you all right?" Alex asked.

She looked at Alex. She looked down.

"I have pancreatic cancer," she whispered.

His mouth was open. He closed it. This couldn't be. Not Ms. Parker. Pancreatic cancer was one of the worst cancers. The deadliest. The quickest. His father talked about it because his very first patient when he

176

became a doctor had pancreatic cancer. And was dead in eight months. Less than a school year.

"There. I've said it. You're the first one I've told." She continued, just talking, not really talking to him. "My doctor ran some tests because my eyes are yellow, and he said the CT scan shows pancreatic cancer. He wants me to see a specialist. He said to expect the worst."

The worst. Alex knew what that meant. It meant she was going to die.

"Why now?" she said. "Why now? It would be okay if it was only me. That would be okay. Now I have someone who needs me."

Alex knew Ms. Parker lived alone, wasn't married, had no children. Did she get a dog, too? She'd always been alone and so had Alex. That's how his life was for all those years, just him and his parents. Now he had Valentine. And Penelope.

Ms. Parker regarded Alex, and he knew she was seeing him. "I'm sorry, Alex. I shouldn't be talking about these things to you."

Before he could reply, the door opened and Penelope walked in. She looked fine, normal, black eyes full of life and blue hair pulled into a short ponytail on one side. Her face was only a little bit pale. "Hello, there," she said. "I couldn't find you."

"I thought we were going to meet here," he said.

"You were still asleep when I left," Ms. Parker said.

Penelope laughed. He had never heard her really laugh, but it was a beautiful sound. He looked at her and at Ms. Parker.

"This is my aunt," Penelope said.

"This is my niece," said Ms. Parker at the same time.

That was why Penelope seemed so familiar. Both she and Ms. Parker had the same delicate features, the same tiny chin. Must have been the blue hair that threw him. Seeing them together, they actually looked very much alike.

Ms. Parker peered at Alex, sending him a message. He knew she meant "Don't tell." Don't tell this girl who recently lost her parents that the only other person she had in this world was going to die soon, too.

Chapter 46
Release the Shackles

*The Cave*

*The Revelstoke shackles had been in place long enough. He was powerless. It was time to be set free. This last child was no match for him.*

*He'd laid the bait. He'd set his trap. He'd cut the last precious uncharred bit of cloth and left it in the tree. A tiny piece compared to its full size. The scrap was not enough for any creation. It gave him no power. But it was enough to fool a Revelstoke. The Cloth of Black Doom would tell its tale. The Revelstokes would believe his lie.*

*He was still shackled, but the Revelstokes would believe otherwise.*

*The boy would not hesitate. To save his dog. To save himself. To save the world.*

*Then he would be free of the Revelstokes forever.*

Chapter 47
The Cave

Alex and Penelope headed back to the park. Penelope chattered happily, more chattery and more happy than Alex had seen yet. Alex trudged along glumly. Ms. Parker was her aunt. Ms. Parker, kind, playful Ms. Parker, would make an excellent aunt. But Ms. Parker was going to die of cancer. Penelope would be alone again.

Worse, so much worse, they were all going to die. Humankind. ILL was unshackled. He had a new disease. Worse than polio. Worse than smallpox. It was too late to stop him, if Revelstoke history was correct. The black cloth meant the disease was imminent. Too late.

Alex didn't believe it. He had to try. Just like Revelstokes before him. There had to be some chance.

And Valentine. He had to find his dog.

He told Penelope what his grandfather said about the black cloth. The taunt. The huge new disease about to be unveiled. Penelope listened, her black eyes large. She wasn't chatty anymore.

They arrived at the edge of the park, and Penelope reached her shaking hand for his. Her whole body trembled, but she couldn't be as nervous as Alex. He instinctively patted his pockets to make sure the antidote vial was there, and in the other, the fireplace matches. In his backpack he had the box he'd borrowed from the science lab.

Today was the day. Today he was going to find Valentine. Today he was going to find ILL. This was why ILL took his dog. To lure him in. To get rid of him. Today Alex was going to stop the new disease. Or die trying. Like his great-grandfather.

He knew this park inside and out. He knew the forest trails and the loop road and the stumps and the crags and the nurse logs. He knew the hiding places. There was one place they had not looked.

The cave. He hadn't been there in years. Even before it was cordoned off, he never liked its smelly darkness. The cave was in the center of the park, hiding under a crest of the hill. He led Penelope there, hand in hand, silent.

Heavy links chained off the area, with metal signs that said, "Off Limits." The actual cave wasn't obvious at this point, hidden by the trees and the underbrush. They ducked underneath the chain and paused. The landscape seemed different. He tried to get his bearings. Where was the cave? Where was the entrance?

They circled around as best they could with all the brambles and brush. He knew the opening was under a rock overhang. He couldn't see anything remotely familiar. They moved the brush aside. It was stiff and sharp and strong.

"Ouch!" Penelope held up a finger bleeding from a thorn.

Alex shook his head, discouraged. "We can't uncover the whole area. We'll never get all this stuff off. We need to figure out where the opening is."

He stepped back and surveyed the heap. He closed his eyes and tried to picture it from before. It had just been a cave, easy to climb inside. No brambles, no brush.

Where had the cave been? Think! The entrance had been underneath a large boulder. He could picture the opening. He moved over to that spot.

No wonder he was confused. The place he remembered as the cave entrance was blocked by the thickest of the thicket. So many brambles the opening wasn't apparent at all. Thorny, spiky brambles, worse than blackberry bushes.

He took off his jacket and twisted it into a protective covering over his hands. He also had his fleece if he needed more armor. The sacred vial was zipped inside its pocket. But the jacket was enough. He pushed the brambles aside and moved in sideways with his body, using his shoulder to shove the prickly branches away. He was lost in the brambles. They grabbed him, scratching from all directions. He kept going, and after a foot or two he could see the rock face, then he could touch the rock overhang.

The opening eluded him. It should be right here. He'd been there enough to remember. A bramble broke free and catapulted out. He ducked forward, too late. A thorn gouged his cheek.

From his bent position, he realized the reason he couldn't find the cave. The entrance was lower and smaller than he remembered because he was bigger and taller. The entrance was tiny. But it was big enough. And big enough for Valentine.

Penelope shoved against him, falling through the brambles behind him. She was scratched and bloody, but she stuck out her chin and nodded determinedly.

He lay on his belly, squished between the rock and the brambles. He slithered through the gap, pushing his backpack ahead of him. The cave was as dark and smelly as he remembered. Way more smelly. He couldn't see anything but blackness, but the stench made him gag. He inhaled anyway, filling his lungs. This was more than stinky puddles. He inhaled again. Urine, dog poo, and bad breath. He was never so happy to smell this bad breath! He was here! Valentine was here!

Alex's head was all the way inside. His eyes adjusted slowly. The cave was big, with a few short side tunnels and a large central room. It was hard to see everything. The cave was silent and shadowy.

But the dog was there. Alex saw his glistening eyes first, two tiny beacons of light, then the dark shape of his Valentine.

The big dog was as far from the cave entrance as he could be. He backed further against the rocky side of the cave. In the dirt underneath him, Alex spied a red square of cloth.

"Valentine," Alex whispered.

The dog growled, a low, scary noise that filled the cave.

In the murky light, Alex could see white foam at his jowls, frothy, slimy. Then the dog lunged at him, barking, all teeth and foul breath and foam.

Alex jolted out of the cave, bashing his head on the rock. He peered up at Penelope, waiting outside.

"He's sick," Alex said, anguished. "ILL did this."

Penelope peeked her head through the opening. It was easier for her because she was slimmer. A barrage of barks and yelps erupted in the cave. Penelope pulled out immediately.

"Yikes. Are you sure that's your dog?"

"Yes," he said miserably. That breath was unmistakable. "That's Valentine. But it's not really him. ILL made him sick. He's frothing like he has rabies or something."

He started back in, to touch him, pet him, see what ILL had done. To help him.

Penelope grabbed his arm. "Wait," she whispered. "You might be right. I know about rabies. We had an outbreak in my town last year. Two kids got bit by a rabid dog. It was pretty awful. They thought the dog got it from a bat or a raccoon. They never figured it out. The dog was just like this. Foaming and crazy. The kids had to get painful shots, and they had to put down the dog. My mom never liked me being around dogs anyway, but after that she said I couldn't go near any dogs at all. And I didn't. Do you believe that? I was scared of dogs."

Alex shook his head, forlorn. He started forward again.

Penelope held him back. "You can't go near him. If he bites you, you'll get rabies, too."

The dog growled again, low and menacing.

"I have to help him," Alex said.

"You can't. He'll bite you. Dogs with rabies are mean."

"If I can get him to breathe calmly, he can get rid of it, like we did."

184

"Breathe calmly?" she whispered. "Did you see him? How are you going to get him to breathe calmly? He doesn't know what he's doing. My mom said that dog was out of his mind."

And what if the breathing didn't work? Alex thought he could heal Valentine by diagnosing the problem and then getting him to breathe slow and deep. Which was ridiculous and impossible. Plus, there was some other piece of the puzzle he hadn't figured out. How had he gotten rid of the appendicitis and the ulcer? He had no idea. What if he couldn't heal Valentine?

And all that was when he thought ILL was shackled. Now he knew he was not. ILL could do anything. His powers were full.

Rabies was a horrible disease, and once the symptoms started, it was untreatable, fatal. It usually took a few weeks to get sick after the bite, but then it moved quickly with muscle pain and uncontrollable, violent movements and agitation and too much saliva and no way to swallow. Plus a really bizarre thing called hydrophobia where the person was afraid of water. It happened because every time the victim tried to swallow, the throat muscles contracted into painful spasms. Hydrophobia meant water fear. The picture he'd seen in the *NEJM* was scary enough. After that came hallucinations and paranoia and terror. And finally death.

His dog was clearly very far along.

Chapter 48
The Super Disease

Growling and barking continued from the other side of the rock. His Valentine. Alex remembered finding him and his mom taking out the glass. How Alex rubbed his tummy and Valentine calmed down and let his mom work. Could he do that again? Could he even get to his belly?

He felt his pocket again for the antidote. The lump reassured him, though he couldn't fathom a way of pouring the liquid into the dog's fang-filled mouth.

His blue eyes searched Penelope's black ones. He said the same words he'd said to his dad. "I have to do this."

She finally said, "I wish I could stop you. But, Alex..."

He waited for her to talk. She bent down, and when she stood she had a large rock in her hands, the size of a basketball. "In case, in case he attacks you..."

Alex nodded wretchedly. Oh, boy. He pushed the rock gently through the gap with his foot. Then he took his jacket and covered his head like a turban. He hitched the backpack up around his neck. He started in again. As soon as his head was through, the dog was on him, barking and gnashing his teeth, foam flying everywhere. Pressure closed on Alex's head. His dog was actually biting him. But the jacket held in place, and the teeth didn't sink in.

He quickly pulled his body through and stood. He unfurled the jacket from his head and held it in front of him to ward off attack. The dog paced, breathing fast, shaking his big head, still frothy.

"Valentine," Alex whispered. "Valentine." The dog barked again, then bowed down on his front legs and bared his teeth. Alex's dog, his sweet, trusting dog, was unrecognizable. This gnarling beast, this spuming menace, was not his dog. Not his Valentine. This was ILL's work. This was ILL's doing.

Still softly calling his name, Alex tried to advance without looking the dog in the eyes. Alex covered his hand with the jacket and reached out slowly. Valentine backed away toward the far side of the cave, barking. He couldn't go any further, and Alex crept toward him until he was close. He stretched his covered hand toward the dog, aiming for his belly.

Valentine pounced forward and sank his teeth into Alex's unprotected arm. Alex lurched backwards and landed in a rank puddle, sending water flying. The dog stopped in his tracks and yelped as if the water was boiling.

He was afraid of the water! He had hydrophobia! Alex whipped his hand free of the jacket and splashed it in the water. The dog backed away, whining and yipping. Stretching toward the dog, keeping one hand splashing, Alex thrust the other toward Valentine's underside, speaking quietly. The pain from the bite on his arm made him want to scream. He found the soft fur and stroked. He sang as softly and calmly as he could. "Tummy rub, tummy rub, tummy rub."

Alex's stomach and throat muscles tightened painfully, and his leg jerked once. His mouth filled with saliva. It came so fast it made him choke. The icicle of terror gripped his chest. This was how rabies felt. How Valentine felt. Plus petrified of his only source of drinking water.

Though the light was dim, Alex saw Valentine's scared eyes. They were huge, frightened orbs in a skull, no skin, no fur, only eyes and bone and teeth. His brain was there, and his stringy spinal cord arching over his skeletal back. Both were swollen and red. Infected and inflamed by the rabies virus. By ILL.

Alex closed his eyes. He couldn't bear to see his dog this way. He sang quietly, over and over. "Tummy rub, tummy rub, tummy rub." Then he opened his eyes, and the fur was back, the beautiful brown and black and tan fur. He stopped splashing the water. Valentine snarled and barked. His dog was no better.

Alex quickly slapped his hand in the water again, sprayed it on the dog. He slowly drew the vial with the antidote out of his pocket. Its warmth dried his wet hand. Maybe he could get the dog to drink it after all.

What was he thinking? This was the Revelstoke antidote. He loved his dog. He would do anything for him. But he could not use the antidote. He would need this antidote to fight ILL.

He held the health of the world in his hands.

Alex sadly placed the vial back into his pocket.

He slapped his hand into the water to send up a large spray. He wrapped his arms around Valentine, circling his body and the long, wet, smelly fur. A final good-bye. He wished with all his heart he could make him better, take him home. He would have to leave him here in this dark cave alone.

How could he do that?

He felt the soft fur of Valentine's tummy. He couldn't help himself. He stroked his tummy one more time, singing the song again. "Tummy rub, tummy rub, tummy rub."

The dog stopped struggling then, stopped snarling. Alex's back tingled. Valentine's rapid breathing slowed, and his muscles relaxed.

The dog's saliva turned pink, still lathery and rabid, but pink. It was happening again! He'd done it! How, Alex did not know, but it was working. Alex held Valentine tight and kept petting. He tried not to look at the bite on his arm, deep and ragged and bloody.

Rabies. What if Valentine had given him rabies?

"It's rabies."

Alex wrenched his head up, but the dog didn't move. The cool voice went on. "My own special kind of rabies. Quick acting. In a few hours you will look like him."

He was here. ILL was here. It was him. Right above him. Black tee shirt and blue jeans, immaculate, though who knew how long he'd waited in the cave.

"You gave my dog rabies," Alex spat out.

"Spare me your sorry tale of woe. Yes, I gave your dog rabies. And now he has given it to you."

Valentine squirmed, and the pink mist stopped. Alex held tighter and continued the petting, murmuring low, "Tummy rub, tummy rub, tummy rub," until Valentine quieted and the pink foam returned. He kept petting and singing, trying to hear ILL at the same time.

"I will be done with you. Done with the Revelstokes. Your grandfather is no threat to me. You are the last. The last."

"Tummy rub, tummy rub, tummy rub." Think, think, think! He had to get closer. He had to get his backpack. ILL was too far away. Alex couldn't move. He was trapped here with a dog that needed a tummy rub to survive.

"Your dog might survive this, but you will not. I will be here to watch you die."

ILL! Stay focused! Get him! Get out! ILL was out of reach but stood between Alex and the opening. There was no way for Alex to escape, let alone escape with Valentine.

"Tummy rub, tummy rub, tummy rub," Alex sang. It was laughable.

Valentine put his big front paws out and lay down and rolled on his side, belly fully exposed, like with the hurt paw. The foam around his jowls disappeared into a pink mist.

Concentrate! Was ILL still talking?

"Mount Rainier National Park. Most beautiful place on earth. Two million visitors a year, from all over the world."

Was he hallucinating? Did he have rabies already? What was this man saying?

"No continent will be spared. And no Revelstoke will get in my way."

ILL's voice was booming inside the cave, reverberating off its stone sides, penetrating Alex's mind.

"Blisters, the worst sunburn you've ever had, then burn it more and more, until bubbles form all over your

190

body and your skin starts to slough. The delicate skin underneath, so delicate it bleeds when you touch it. Ripe for infection. The same thing inside your body, your mouth, the lining of the intestines, just like your skin, blisters and bubbles and sloughing. So painful to eat, so painful to drink. Oozing, bleeding, raw. And then you die."

ILL reached in his pocket and brought out a cloth, large and black. Most of it was charred, and a smoky smell wafted over. An edge broke off and fell in ashes to the ground.

There it was! The black cloth! Alex had to get it!

ILL folded it carefully and placed it in his back pocket. Alex knelt next to the dog, stroking his underside. He was powerless, stuck here with the dog.

"You haven't heard the best part." ILL's voice was a whisper now, but still easy to hear in the cave.

"Mount Rainier, pure Mount Rainier. Its air will be pure no more. Breathe it in! Breathe in my creation. Two million people may not seem like much. But I can wait. I am a patient man. These things take time, but if the outbreak is obvious, if the first cases are obvious, these modern medical detectives will be on it, finding the cause, finding a cure. Like you Revelstokes used to do. This is much better. My disease will spread on the wind, across the oceans. And it will spread with visitors from all over the world. Breathing on others from all over the world. Looking normal, looking healthy, going about their puny, little lives, but passing on my creation. A long, long incubation period, long enough to infect the world, long enough to never figure out where it started. A silent incubation period of months.

By the time they are sick, everyone will be sick. Very, very sick."

ILL was sick. Alex felt sick. Tingly. Headache. Weak. The rabies vaccine only worked if you took it before the symptoms started. If this headache was due to rabies, it was too late for the shots. Too late for Alex.

Stop thinking about rabies! You're just hyperventilating! Concentrate! Take a deep breath yourself!

What a ridiculous situation. ILL was talking about world destruction, and Alex was singing to a dog that had given him rabies. Every time he stopped, the pink mist faded and the dog twitched. If nothing else, he had to save his dog. "Tummy rub, tummy rub, tummy rub."

ILL stared right at him, his eyes boring into Alex's.

"You will die here. Your dog has bitten you. My rabies will kill you within hours. You will be gone. You cannot kill me. You cannot stop my disease."

ILL was shouting again, his voice so loud Alex couldn't hear his own singing. Think! What happened to his plan? He'd been ready for ILL. Alex's mind faded in and out. His mouth was full of saliva and he spat it out, spat it at ILL.

"The Revelstokes are finished," ILL spat back. "There is nothing you can do."

Revelstokes! The antidote! He had forgotten it was right here in his hand. Alex shifted his eyes to see if the vial was visible under the dog's fur. He couldn't see a thing and he hoped ILL couldn't, either.

He could save himself. He had to live to stop ILL's disease. He had to live to beat this monster.

He kept his free hand moving over Valentine's fur. He had to somehow get the vial open and to his mouth and drink it. All before ILL stopped him. Then maybe he could get to his backpack.

He stole a quick glance at ILL.

And Penelope. Penelope stood right behind him, with the rock in two hands over her head. She brought it down onto ILL's head with a crash, cracking his skull with a splintering, awful sound that no one could survive. No man could survive. But ILL was not a man.

Penelope turned her head and covered her eyes. Alex stared at the crumpled lump, the bright red blood seeping into the dirt. ILL did not move.

Alex was still singing, automatically now, he didn't even notice. "Tummy rub, tummy rub, tummy rub."

He tore his eyes off the blood and back to Valentine. He was sleeping. Normal. Well.

Alex slumped his body against the dog. He held up his arm to examine, hoping, praying the bite would be gone. Normal and well like the dog. But the wound was still there, the blood congealed, the skin purple at the edge.

He had rabies. ILL's special superfast rabies. Without the vaccine, he would die. Even with the vaccine, if the virus had already taken hold, he would die.

Alex held up the antidote vial so he could see its swirling contents. He tilted it and the dark fluid turned golden, its warm glow lighting up the gloom of the cave for an instant and illuminating the body on the ground.

It was such a tiny amount of fluid. Almost nothing. Alex zipped the vial back into his pocket.

He squinted at the still mound and the blood. ILL's head was shattered. Blood still flowed, more blood even than with Penelope's ulcer.

"Don't look," Alex said.

"Don't worry," Penelope replied.

She dashed back through the hole without saying a word, her head turned away from ILL's body. Alex, too, averted his eyes as he maneuvered the dog around ILL's form, sweet-talking a skittish Valentine over to the small opening.

Getting him out was another matter. Penelope knelt outside and coaxed, and Alex squatted inside and pushed, trying to get that enormous rump through that little opening. The huge dog got stuck, and his back feet splayed out flat for a moment. Then Valentine wriggled and shifted, and one hip popped through. Then the other, and from inside the cave Alex watched him spring over Penelope and through the brambles in one leap.

Alex wished he could follow. Instead, he turned back to ILL. Alex unzipped his backpack and removed the cardboard box he'd stolen from the science classroom. One of their portable Bunsen burners with the butane canister and its striker lighter.

Was he going to be able to do this?

ILL lay face down in a bloody heap, unconscious, maybe dead. Trying not to look at the misshapen head, Alex crouched next to him. There it was! The black cloth protruded from ILL's pocket and draped on the ground, more charred fringe than actual material.

Alex let out a sigh of relief. He shoved the Bunsen burner box back in the backpack and took the matches out of his pocket. He didn't have to touch ILL to get to the cloth. He didn't have to touch his flame to a man, even though the man was dead and was not even a man to begin with.

Alex struck a match and the large flame appeared. He touched it to the black cloth. It caught fire instantly, filling the cave with acrid smoke.

Alex jumped back, holding his breath. The fire grew huge. He fled from the cave with his backpack, blue flames shooting in all directions behind him.

Chapter 49
Over

Alex and Penelope picked their way back through the bramble patch, thorns jabbing them and piercing their clothes. Once out, both had rips and tears, sometimes through to the skin underneath. Their faces were scratched and bleeding. Alex's cheek had a deep gouge. Dog teeth and thorns had shredded his jacket. His arm throbbed.

He breathed deeply. The smoky smell could not penetrate the brambles and the air was fresh. The three of them ducked under the chain and out of the "Off Limits" area. Alex jumped into the air. He felt light, free. It was over.

They were out. He had his dog. He had destroyed the black cloth. ILL was dead.

He knelt and put his good arm around Valentine's neck and clung on.

Penelope shivered. She zipped her jacket, but she still shivered and her teeth chattered together. "Did you hear what he said?" She knelt next to him.

"I heard."

"A new disease! He was going to release it at Mount Rainier. Thank goodness, thank goodness he's dead! All those innocent people. From all over the world. What a terrible disease. Blisters and pain and blood. But not for a while. You feel fine, you look fine.

For months, he said. The whole time you're contagious, breathing on people, infecting people, your family, your friends. No one knows, and then they breathe on people and infect people, and by the time the symptoms start months later, you've infected everyone you know, everyone you love, and everyone they know and love."

Alex shuddered. "He's pure evil. *Was* pure evil. But not anymore."

"We should keep moving. It's getting dark. We have to do something about your arm."

Oh, yeah. That. He forgot for a moment. He forgot he was going to die.

He let go of the dog, and Valentine raced around, first here, then there, then in a circle, full of energy, full of life. At least one of them was feeling well. Valentine trotted back to them and fell in line, walking so near Alex could rest his hand on his back as they moved along.

His father greeted them at the door again. Alex ran when he saw him, taking the stairs in one leap and throwing himself into his father's arms. "We killed ILL!" he shouted, and he wanted to shout it again and again, but instead he buried his head against his father's shoulder. They killed him, but at what price?

By the time Penelope and Valentine reached the porch he was upright, and she nodded to his dad that it was true. Her face was serious, though, and Alex stuck out his arm and whispered the word. "Rabies."

His father grabbed the dog's collar, but Alex shook his head. "It's only me. Valentine is fine."

"ILL is shackled. Your dog can't spread the rabies to you. ILL can only hurt one person"—his dad nodded at Valentine—"or one dog, at a time."

"He wasn't shackled." Alex's stomach hurt just saying it. "He somehow broke free. He gave Valentine rabies, and Valentine gave it to me."

His father sat them down, and Alex told him what happened in the cave. His father cleaned the wound, washing deep and painfully. He cleaned their scratches and cuts.

His dad was remarkably calm, even when Alex told him it was an "ILL special" rabies, souped-up and speedy, ready to kill within hours. His mom wouldn't be this calm. Did his father know about the antidote? Did he think he should use it, the very last of the Revelstoke fighting power? Was now the time?

"I think this time we've got ILL beat," his dad said. "Rabies is preventable. A few shots are all it takes. If we give them before you get symptoms, you should be fine."

"But all that takes time. ILL said it was quick. And the hospital will want to know where I got it. About Valentine. They'll take him away." Alex's voice rose in panic.

Did he have the symptoms already? Did still have his headache? He had forgotten about it with all the excitement. Was he weak? Tingly? He didn't feel any of these things now.

"Yes, well…I happen to have the vaccine right here."

"You have the rabies shots?" Alex couldn't believe it. The antidote was safe.

"I have the rabies shots. A few months ago, your mother found a bat in your room. You weren't here, and your mom didn't want you to know. Poor thing had wandered in through an open window and couldn't get out. Most bats are safe, they almost never carry rabies, but your mother, being the careful person that she is, was worried. Even though rabies in bats is rare, we do have a lot of bats in these woods. She wanted to keep the vaccine on hand just in case. So good for Mom."

Alex was never so thankful for his worrywart mom. And for his dad, calm and stable and always standing by him, here now to fix him up. Alex was so thankful for his family, Revelstoke weirdness and all.

Dad was still talking. "In addition to rabies, we have to watch out for infection. Dog's mouths are cesspools of disease. You'll need antibiotics, too."

The dog panted happily, his smelly breath wafting all around them.

His dad drew up the shots, first one then a second, one injected right around the bite on his forearm to prevent the rabies from infecting him and the second deep into his upper arm muscle, the actual vaccine to fight the virus in case it had already spread. He said there would be three more shots over the next two weeks. But, according to Dad, it should work, so Alex sat there and let him poke all he wanted.

His dad mixed the obligatory prepackaged cocoa, which actually tasted quite good. Penelope drank two cups. Valentine drank two bowls of water. Then his dad fed the dog, and Alex fed him again. Valentine let out a satisfied, stinky belch and nestled on the floor at Alex's feet.

They called his grandfather, and Alex told him the news. The line was so noisy with static and his grandpa's voice was so soft. Alex told him what they'd done, split ILL's head open and burned the black cloth, burned ILL.

"I cannot believe it," his grandfather said. "Revelstokes throughout time have never accomplished this feat."

Alex strained to hear his words. "What you did took courage. What you did took wits."

Finally he heard the words he'd been waiting for, his grandfather's voice a whisper on the crackly line. "It's over."

Chapter 50
The World is Full of Chocolate Dingaloos

When Alex's mother walked in the door at dinner time, Penelope was safely home and Alex's ragged clothes hidden away. His mom clucked over his scratched face but never saw his arm, bandaged and under a new shirt. After a warning look from his father, she didn't even ask a lot of questions.

Alex told her ILL was dead. "It's over," he said. His mother dropped her veggie burger and started to cry. Valentine ate it, and she made another but said she was too happy to eat and sat feeding that one to Valentine, too.

"Why do you like this dog so much?" Alex asked her.

His mom fixed her eyes on Valentine and gently petted his back. "He needs a bath. We'll have to put him in the shower."

"He eats everything in sight, he smells, his breath is the worst, and he vomited on your Oriental carpet. Why are you so nice to him?" Alex persisted.

"Come here." She pulled Alex to her and stroked his hair the same way she petted the dog. "We always thought we'd have another child. A little brother or sister for you. We never wanted you to be an only child." She paused and gazed at the dog. "It didn't happen. It didn't work out. We couldn't have another baby." She bit her lip.

"You didn't have anyone to play with when you were little." She paused again and then said quickly, "You don't have a lot of friends." She tousled his hair some more. "But a dog is a friend. I could see by the way you soothed him that first day. You were good for him, and he was good for you. A boy needs a dog."

Embarrassing, but a good explanation. And Alex got a dog because of it.

Right after dinner, Alex and Valentine took a shower together, water squirting all over the place as it hit the dog's broad back. Alex lathered him with dog shampoo, then used it on his own hair to see if it would tame its stiffness better than people shampoo. He stood under the hot shower. The filthy water swirled down the drain, and he hoped all the darkness and evil from the cave would swirl down along with it.

Alex rinsed the dog and rinsed some more, trying to get the water under his belly. The dog refused to turn around in the shower and never put his head anywhere near the spray, so Alex had to use a plastic cup to pour over his head and face. Eventually, Valentine was clean and every part of him smelled good except his breath. Despite extra breath mints from Alex, plus a few more his mother slipped in.

"I have something for you." His mom fished a crisp plastic package out of her briefcase, a multicolored packet so recognizable that his mouth started watering even though he'd never eaten one. A Chocolate Dingaloo.

"The vending machine gave me this yesterday instead of mints. I was going to throw it away, but I'm glad I kept it. Today's the day for a special treat."

Alex had never had anything remotely like a Chocolate Dingaloo. A square cake of chocolate covered in a hard, thin layer of chocolate with a squishy chocolate center. Delicious and a little disgusting at the same time. His mouth had a slimy feeling afterwards. Still, too bad she didn't have another one tucked in her briefcase. Maybe a third.

Alex fell into bed, tired, elated, expecting to fall right asleep. The dog was asleep, breathing deep and slow on the floor by Alex's head. As soon as his eyes closed, though, his exhilaration vanished. He'd survived ILL's clouds of disease. He found his dog. He endured shots against rabies. He tried not to think about the dark mound left back in the cave. And the splintering noise and the flames leaping around ILL's body. ILL was dead, that was the important thing. His super disease was finished.

But… Alex's stomach churned. Not from rabies, he was sure of that. It was the Chocolate Dingaloo. Even his mother had succumbed and couldn't throw away a Chocolate Dingaloo. The world was full of Chocolate Dingaloos and cigarettes and pork rinds and chips. Which led to diabetes and cancer and heart disease and obesity. It was so depressing.

Then there was Penelope. Ms. Parker had pancreatic cancer. He had seen her yellow eyes. Yellow eyes meant jaundice, and jaundice meant bile duct blockage, and bile duct blockage meant cancer. Pancreatic cancer. His dad told him this. Deadly. Ms. Parker, Penelope's aunt, was going to die. Poor Ms.

Parker. Poor Penelope. What good was the Revelstoke gift now?

ILL created clouds of disease. Well, this was a cloud of dread. ILL. Chocolate Dingaloos. Ms. Parker. Penelope.

Wait a minute. He still had the vial. The antidote against ILL's ill. ILL was gone. Alex could use it now. He could cure the cancer. He could save Ms. Parker.

Once. He could use it once. He had not used it when he was in agony with appendicitis. He had not used it when Penelope almost bled to death from an ulcer. Or for Valentine or for the rabies Valentine gave him. His great-grandfather had not used it to save himself. His grandfather had not used it for Bea. He saved it for Alex. To use once.

Chapter 51
Red Death-Signal

Alex didn't dream about Valentine that night. Or Ms. Parker or Penelope. He dreamed about ILL and the rock's crashing noise and the flames. Mrs. Lemon had dropped a cantaloupe once on their tile kitchen floor. The sound was the same, sickening. The cantaloupe had split open in three places. ILL's skull had split in two.

He also dreamed about Mount Rainier National Park and people from all over the world. In his dream they wore shirts with the flags of their home countries, like in the Olympics. He tried to keep track of all the countries, but there were too many to count.

ILL stood in an alpine meadow full of wildflowers, the huge, glacier-covered mountain behind him, hikers all around, children running on the paths, families pouring out of the visitor center below. ILL sifted a powder from one hand to another, losing some with each pass, a gentle breeze blowing it away. Blowing it this way and that, around the hikers, around the children, around the visitor center, around the whole mountain. When his hands were empty, ILL took his red handkerchief from his pocket and dusted them off. He lifted the handkerchief until it, too, caught the breeze and drifted away, a red death-signal floating in the sky.

Alex was wide awake when his dad came in early to check on him. Dad inspected the bite for infection and asked questions to make sure the rabies was gone. Except for an extremely painful arm, Alex felt fine. His mother made a big breakfast with soy sausages and spinach omelets, the best she could do with the ingredients in the kitchen. Alex cracked the eggs one-handed, the way Mrs. Lemon showed him.

"You are full of talents." His mom laughed and rumpled his spiky hair like he was six.

He couldn't have cracked them two-handed. His arm was that sore, but his mom didn't need to know.

Valentine sat next to him while he ate, solid, panting in happy anticipation. His Valentine. When Alex stood, the dog nuzzled this way and that, so excited he bounced. Alex took his big head in his hands and knelt down. The dog's bad breath washed over him. It didn't matter. He breathed that breath in deeper, but the stench made him cough, so he threw his good arm around Valentine's great neck and buried his head in the soft fur. His dog was back.

He attached the leash to his collar and they set out, the dog full of energy and pleased to be going anywhere Alex led him. Which was the long way, around the loop road. No way Alex was going in the woods today. Not with what was in that cave.

Once out of the park, Alex and Valentine jogged along the lake, then up the hill to the library. Penelope was there, like he thought. She came outside to greet him and oohed and aahed over the dog.

"He looks so different," she exclaimed. "All I knew yesterday was that he was big and smelly. Today he looks so soft and cuddly."

She hesitated, then she took a step closer to Valentine.

"I haven't petted a dog in a year." She put her hands all over his back, her fingers hiding in his long fur. She put her face near his, then jumped back. "Ewww, bad breath, though."

"I know, I know." Alex laughed. Poor dog, always getting this reaction.

Penelope leaned against the bike rack. "How are you feeling? Is it over?"

What could he tell her? ILL was dead. Valentine was back. That was over. He didn't have rabies. But ILL's presence was still out there, always would be. He'd set up a system of temptation and bad habits. Alex glanced at the bus stop with its advertisements of soda and cheese goo. He'd never view these signs the same again.

"Is it over?" Penelope said again.

"Yes. It's over." He thought of her aunt and the vial and the last thing he had to do. Tomorrow. Today he had something else in mind.

Alex didn't tell her what it was. They circled back to his house to drop off the dog, then caught the bus downtown and walked down the hill to the water. Seattle sat between two large bodies of water, Lake Washington, where he lived, to the east and the Puget Sound to the west. A man-made channel connected them, with locks for the boats and a fish ladder for the fish. The salmon that started and ended their lives in his park clambered up the fish ladder to get to Lake Washington and home before spawning.

The sun was bright, and they squinted out at the Sound and the Olympic Mountains covered in snow. A ferry horn sounded, and the sea birds scattered.

Alex led her to the next pier. An enormous white Ferris wheel rose above the water. He hoped she'd like this. The sun was high, and the mountains were lighted up. The water was a silver, shimmery sea.

Penelope peered up at the towering wheel and bit her lip. "I've never been on a Ferris wheel. My mother was afraid of them."

"I know."

They climbed in the car and started the ascent, slowly, smoothly. The water was far below, and the skyscrapers shrank in size. The sky was a clear blue. Penelope moved all around the car, looking down, looking up, looking at the spokes and the gears and the lights. The grin never left her face. The car stopped at the top, and Penelope laughed her beautiful laugh. "I could stay up here forever." She liked it, all right.

Back on the pier, they watched a seagull float on a wind gust offshore. A white and green ferry glided across the sparkling water.

Penelope smiled at him. "Thank you for that. And…this week…thank you for all of it."

Chapter 52
Hideous, Wonderful, Glorious Breath

"Is pancreatic cancer always bad?" Alex knew the answer, but he asked his dad anyway.

"Oh, pancreatic cancer. It's awful. One of the worst. I hope I never get that when I'm older. Why?"

"I know someone who has it. But she's not old."

"Hmm. Well, there are different kinds. The most common is adenocarcinoma, which is the deadly kind, but you usually get it when you're older. There's a slower growing kind, but that doesn't usually have any symptoms, you find it by accident, like if you're getting a CT scan for another reason."

"This person has symptoms."

Alex's dad raised his eyebrows and twitched the corner of his mouth like he did when he was enjoying himself. "And there's a mimic."

"A mimic?"

"Yep. A disease that looks like pancreatic cancer and has symptoms like pancreatic cancer, but it's not cancer."

"How can that be?" A mimic!

"It's called autoimmune pancreatitis. Autoimmune diseases are strange diseases where the body's immune system gets out of whack. In this case, the immune system attacks the pancreas and causes inflammation and swelling and scarring and even something that can look like a mass, like cancer. But it's not cancer. Best of all, it can be easily treated."

"How can you tell the difference?" Alex could hardly contain himself.

"Sometimes it's hard. A CT scan can look identical in both cases. Sometimes you need a biopsy, a sample of the pancreas taken with a needle. Unfortunately, if the biopsy says it's cancer, it's cancer."

Had Ms. Parker had a biopsy? Had she mentioned that? Was it possible that she didn't have cancer?

"This dog sure is handsome, but, boy, his breath still stinks." Alex's mom stood in the door waving her hand in front of her nose. Valentine crammed in the doorway next to her.

"That's exactly what Penelope said," Alex said, laughing.

He stopped abruptly. Why hadn't he thought of this earlier?

"Maybe I could see if there is such a thing as a doggie dentist. He'd need sedation, but they might be able to give him a thorough teeth cleaning, much better than we can do," his mom said.

"He'd be the perfect dog if it weren't for his breath," his dad said.

"What did you do today? You were gone a long time," his mom said. "Dinner will be ready soon."

"Wait! No! I have to go back to the library," Alex said.

His parents exchanged smiles, and his dad shrugged. His mom sat down and mindlessly scratched the dog's ears.

Bad breath. Had Ms. Parker ever smelled Valentine's breath? He couldn't remember her ever meeting the dog. Could she walk away from him or would he chase her? Lean on her?

Alex raced back to the library as fast as the dog would let him. Ms. Parker was leaving, and she stood in the doorway with her key.

"Alex, hello," she said. "I'm so glad you found your dog." She turned the key and came out to join him. Valentine stayed where he was at Alex's side. "Penelope told me he was missing. He looks like a wonderful dog."

Ms. Parker bent to pet him. Alex held his breath. Valentine looked elated. Ms. Parker drew back in surprise. "Wow, he's got some bad breath." She said it smiling, but she stood up and shied away from the dog. Valentine stayed sitting next to Alex.

Ms. Parker could smell his breath! Valentine didn't lean or pay any more attention to her than anyone else, not more than Penelope or his mom or his dad.

Ms. Parker did not have cancer! She must have this other thing, this autoimmune pancreatitis. She couldn't have cancer, or his dog would have known.

Alex let out a whoop, and Valentine jumped up and tackled him, ready to play. Ms. Parker's bemused expression vanished when Alex told her what he thought. She started to cry and said she'd better get home to Penelope.

Ms. Parker had already had a biopsy and it came back "inconclusive," meaning "we can't tell if it's cancer or not," but her doctor told her that was often the case with cancer. He said the specialty center might want to take a second biopsy.

When she went to the specialty center two days later, they did a special stain on her biopsy sample and confirmed what Alex already knew. Autoimmune pancreatitis. No cancer.

Alex didn't need a special stain. Not just because of Valentine. Ms. Parker had brushed his hand when they looked up autoimmune pancreatitis on the library computer together, and her skin disappeared, and he saw her pancreas lying between her stomach and her intestines. He saw the scarring, the inflammation, but not a hard mass of cancer. He didn't tell Ms. Parker he'd seen her pancreas. He knew from experience she would not find that fascinating.

Alex had seen Ms. Parker smile before, she was always smiling, but she'd never smiled as big and as happy as the day she told him the news about her pancreas. Penelope was shelving books. She never knew anything about it.

Valentine waited for him outside the library. Alex ran around in circles and the dog ran around in circles, and then they collapsed in a heap. Valentine stood over him and his big mouth dripped drool on Alex's face, the hideous breath blasting down like a blow drier, the hideous, wonderful, glorious breath.

Chapter 53
Green Eyes

The school year was almost over. Three months since they left ILL dead in the cave. School was so mundane. But so comforting. Hot-Dog Boy soccer player gave him a thumbs-up when he saw him in the hall, calling out "Dude!" as he passed. Sam made a point of coming up to him and clapping his shoulder. The first time, right after the rabies shots, it really hurt, but the shots were long forgotten, and Alex looked forward to seeing Sam. He looked forward to school.

Alex sat in science gazing out at the bright June day. It was seventy degrees, but Mr. Beaker jabbered on about glaciers. "How do glaciers move?" he asked. Alex shot up his hand and said glaciers move because of their own weight, deforming and flowing and cracking into crevasses, something he knew from all the trips to Mount Rainier he'd taken with his parents. He winked at Penelope, who cracked a sly smile.

As he left the classroom, Isabel Matthews stopped him with a gentle touch on his arm. She had never approached him before, certainly had never spoken directly to him. Here she was, right in front of him. She said she loved Mount Rainier, too. She stood there looking up at him with her beautiful green eyes. His heart gave a little lurch.

"It's a real volcano, you know," she said. "We go hiking there every summer when the wildflowers are out. My dad and brother hiked all the way to Camp Muir."

She was talking to *him*. Isabel Matthews had noticed *him*. His mind raced to think of something undorky to say. He had been to Camp Muir, too, the place that was as far as you could go without ropes and crampons. And experience. Above that, the mountain was riddled with ice crevasses and snow bridges that could cave in. He was lucky his mom let them even go to Camp Muir. Don't say that. That was not the thing to say to Isabel.

Isabel was still talking. "We saw two girls from Japan in shorts and flip-flops start out on that hike." She shook her head and laughed. "They turned back before they even got to the snow."

Isabel was talking about flip-flops while his heart did flip-flops. He didn't have to come up with anything to say at all. He just nodded, and she twirled around to go. He was tongue-tied, but she didn't even know. She waved as she left, and he gave her a tiny salute like he'd seen James Bond do once. He skipped and grinned as if he were on top of Mount Rainier itself.

Alex knew what she meant about the flip-flops. All kinds of people went to Mount Rainier. Babies in strollers and old people. Serious mountaineers with sixty-pound packs heading for the top. Families with moms in shorts and sneakers or moms in saris and woven slippers on the paved trails outside the visitor center. And all kinds of tourists, like Isabel had seen.

ILL was right. People from all over the world visited Mt. Rainier. When Alex's family signed the

214

visitor book last year, they signed under a man from Ethiopia and a couple from Australia. It would be the perfect place for ILL's super disease. All Alex's happiness left him. ILL.

He hadn't thought of him in ages. ILL and his evil, all the diseases he'd caused throughout time. ILL was dead. Because of Penelope, because of him. ILL would never harm again.

He thought of Penelope standing behind ILL with the large rock over her head and the splintering noise and the flames and how scared Penelope had been.

Alex turned to find her. Penelope was gone.

Chapter 54
Fish Boy

Where was Penelope? Had she seen the whole thing? What was it about Isabel Matthews and her green-eyed, curly-headed charm that made him forget everything else? This conversation was the most he'd spoken to her in his entire life. And he hadn't actually said a word.

He remembered something about Isabel from fourth grade, something he'd shoved to the back of his mind long ago.

He'd come in during recess to get a book from his desk. Some of the desks had little orange envelopes on them. He knew they were invitations to Katie Mitchell's annual Halloween party. He wasn't invited, but he was never invited. He was used to it.

Back out on the playground, Katie and Isabel played a complicated jump rope game in the courtyard. Sebastian and Wolfgang goofed off as usual, chasing each other around. Wolfgang got tangled in their jump rope and fell hard on his knees, and he started to cry. Isabel whispered to Katie, and they erupted into giggles. Just like them.

The class filed in after recess. The orange envelopes were still there. Except Sebastian's and Wolfgang's. Their desks flanked Alex's. They had had invitations earlier.

He always blamed Katie. But he knew these girls, had known them since kindergarten. Isabel wielded all the influence in their friendship. In his heart of hearts, he knew Isabel was responsible.

Then he thought of Penelope. He had never hidden anything from her. She knew his darkest, strangest secrets. Yet she treated him like he was just another Joe. When he was with her, he felt like a normal kid. He had never, ever felt normal until he met Penelope.

He walked into the cafeteria and there she was, Penelope with her blue hair and her pale face. What had he been thinking? He wasn't thinking, not when it came to Isabel. That was the problem.

Penelope smirked at him, stuck out her tongue, and laughed.

He laughed back and stuck out his tongue and gave her the James Bond salute. She rolled her eyes, but she was still laughing.

He sat down next to her at his usual table. He ate lunch with the same two guys, Tom with the limp and the gassy kid, Ed, whose name he never knew until Penelope showed up. She had a class with Wolfgang and Sebastian Nguyen, and they ate there now, too.

Soon after they all started eating together, Sam stopped by their table and punched Alex in his sore arm and said, "You guys have a winner here, I'm sure you know."

Wolfgang had punched him again, and said, "Winner."

The guys at the table all greeted him with that now, not silence anymore, just a bunch of good-natured punches. The whole spring had been like this, talking and eating together, instead of scarfing the food down without a word to each other and racing out separately to the library.

It was because of Penelope. She was like a whole new girl, not at all the person he'd first met behind the library shelves. He thought of her throwing a squishy ball for Valentine and laughing when he brought it back all wet and drooly. And all the time they spent in the woods. She was so easy to talk to. They had talked about everything there was to talk about in life.

The only thing they hadn't talked about was what they left back there in the cave. They'd never spoken about that again in all these months. About the crunching sound, ILL's head splitting open, the blood, the fire.

There was Penelope now, laughing at the twins, who set down their identical food trays at the exact same time. He'd known Wolfgang and Sebastian from elementary school. She'd only known them a few months, but you wouldn't know that. She looked totally comfortable, and Alex was comfortable, too. He examined the group at the table. They all looked comfortable.

Alex felt normal. This is what it was like to be normal.

Wolfgang and Sebastian sat next to each other, two short, skinny boys with the same haircut and voices that sounded alike. They finished each other's sentences or sometimes they didn't, letting the half sentence hang there, with only the two of them knowing what they meant. Today was no different.

"Could you believe Triangle?" Sebastian was referring to the substitute music teacher.

"I know." Wolfgang took up the story. "She didn't know an aria from—" They both laughed, leaving Alex shaking his head.

Tom loved card tricks and could shuffle a deck with one hand. He did it now, and Ed belched in approval. Tom's fingers gripped the red deck of cards, divided the pack, and flicked. The cards whished and fell into place, settling in perfectly. Like a magician could do. Which made Alex think of ILL and his oversized red handkerchief. Red, like all the blood in the cave.

Alex shook his head. Everything reminded him of ILL today.

A shadow fell across the table, and he sensed a presence behind him.

"If it isn't Fish Boy! Asclepius Fish Boy!"

Sandy Molloy stood over him, an enormous cookie crumbling in his fist, bits dropping into Alex's hair. "Katie's birthday." Sandy motioned with his head toward the table where Katie and Isabel sat. "Triple chocolate chip." He passed the cookie under Alex's nose. He stood so close their bodies were touching, and the cookie smell was a welcome relief from his sweaty shirt. "You guys missed out."

With that he raised his cookie to his lips, sneering at Alex. "Fish Boy doesn't care. Fish Boy only eats fish, anyway. Right, Asclepius?"

Alex's mind emptied. He was in kindergarten again, with Miss Teeter and his spiky hair and Sandy pushing his birthday treats to the floor.

Well, Sandy wasn't going to eat this cookie. That's all Alex knew. He jumped up, striking out against Sandy's arms. The cookie crashed to the floor.

"You little weasel!" Sandy shouted. He hauled his fist back to punch.

"Sandy! Sandy!" Katie ran toward them, waving her arms. She must have seen the whole thing. Isabel must have seen the whole thing, too, that Alex was about to get pummeled by Sandy Molloy. He didn't care.

Katie was out of breath when she reached them. She grabbed Sandy's hands in hers.

"Did you eat it? Did you eat the cookie?"

Sandy and Alex gawked at her.

Katie pointed to the cookie on the floor. "The cookies have peanut butter chips in them! Did you eat any?"

Sandy shook his head. Katie let out a huge breath. "I completely forgot about your allergy. I'm so, so sorry."

Sandy looked bewildered.

"Sam told me," Katie said. "Thank God he told me in time. Thank God for Sam."

Sandy crushed the cookie with his shoe and ground it into the floor. He raised his eyes to Alex, but he didn't say a word.

Chapter 55
Friends

Alex dropped into his chair. A lethal cookie. That could have been a lethal cookie.

"Wow," Tom said. "That was close. He had to go to the hospital once. His reaction to peanuts is that bad."

"You saved him," Penelope said. Then she chuckled. "Fish Boy?"

The twins were on to another subject, talking about an upcoming concert, urging them all to go. "You can sit in front with us," Sebastian said.

"They don't want to sit in front," Wolfgang said. "Then they'll have to—" Laughter again from the two of them. Tom caught Alex's eye and winked.

"Seriously, though, would you all like to come? My dad has extra tickets." Sebastian turned to Alex. "Alex, would you come?"

What? What had Sebastian said? In all Alex's time at school, had anyone ever invited him to anything besides a birthday party? No. Never.

He must have looked funny because Wolfgang and Sebastian were staring at him. Penelope jumped in. "I'd like to come. It sounds like fun. Can I come?"

Wolfgang smiled. "Absolutely. You can all come. Just don't sit in the front row." Laughter again, this time from the whole table.

Alex sat back, grinning. Everyone was chattering, laughing, joking, and he was a part of it. For the first time in his life.

"Can I have your water?"

"What?" Alex hadn't been paying attention.

"Can I have your water?" Sebastian grabbed his plastic water bottle.

"You already drank mine," Wolfgang said. "How much water do you need?"

"As much as you did last year on that hike when you—" More laughter.

Alex knew this story from fifth grade. The whole class knew. The twins had gone on a hike in the North Cascade Mountains and Wolfgang dropped his water bottle and got really thirsty, and before his parents caught up with him, he'd drunk out of a delicious, cold stream. His father told him he'd get *Giardia*, an infection common in streams because of the animals that pooed nearby. One week later he had nausea and diarrhea and terrible abdominal cramps. He came up with a song sung to the tune of "Old MacDonald." "Gi-Ar-Di-A lives in streams, Ouch, ouch, ouch, ouch, ouch, Do not drink it or you'll scream, Ouch, ouch, ouch, ouch, ouch."

The twins sang it now at the top of their lungs, and the table joined in for the "ouch, ouch, ouch" part.

For such small boys they had pretty big voices. They looked alike, and Alex couldn't tell them apart for certain until third grade. Sebastian had an asymmetric eye on the right. That was the only difference. They were both short and skinny and had straight black hair. Their voices were similar, so you had to look to see which one was talking.

Alex studied them carefully now so he could be sure. Sebastian was talking again, saying he was going back to get seconds.

"Seconds?" Ed said. "It was terrible the first time. Who puts spinach in lasagna?"

"I thought it was pretty good," Penelope said.

"It wasn't great, but I'm hungry," Sebastian said. "And look how skinny I am." He thrust out a scrawny arm. "I have to get some meat on these bones."

"I don't think there's any meat in that lasagna," Ed said.

Alex looked at Sebastian's arm. It was really thin. Wolfgang's was more substantial though still slim. But not like Sebastian's.

He watched Sebastian make a detour to the bathroom, then get in line for seconds. Sebastian was thirsty. He was losing weight. He was hungry. This was a triad, a constellation of three symptoms that went together. Alex just had to think what.

Stop it, he told himself. No more *NEJM*. Be normal. None of these kids read *NEJM*. If he kept this up, he'd think all his friends had some disease or other. He knew from a story his father told that it was common for first-year medical students to diagnose themselves with every new disease they read about in their medical texts. They read the descriptions, then realized they had all the symptoms and thought they had the disease. Medical Student Disease of the Week, Dad called it.

But it didn't work like that. Many symptoms are common things that everyone has, like being thirsty or tired. None of the medical students had any disease. It was all in their heads. Overdiagnosis.

When they first met in medical school, his dad thought his mom had rheumatoid arthritis, a disease that caused swelling and pain in the joints, especially the hands, but also made you tired and sick. His mom was always tired, and she was losing weight. She said it was because she was a medical student and she stayed up late to study and didn't have time to eat. Dad was sure she had some terrible disease. Then she developed a swollen, painful knuckle, and he was certain it was rheumatoid arthritis. They were studying arthritis that particular week in class. He was so positive—she had all the symptoms. Fatigue, weight loss, a swollen joint. He'd read about it the night before.

His mom knew then that he liked her, that he cared enough to worry about her. She told him it wasn't arthritis, that she'd bashed her finger trying to hammer in a nail over her desk to hang a picture. Dad hammered in the nail himself, and they had their first kiss right there, Dad with the hammer in his hand.

All because of Medical Student Disease of the Week.

So he'd better stop this, or he would be diagnosing rheumatoid arthritis or some such in all his friends.

All his friends. He looked around the table. These were his friends.

The end of school was approaching. For the first time it did not mean a summer of endless days alone. He had a dog. He had Penelope. He had friends.

Chapter 56
Medical Student Disease of the Week

Alex couldn't stop thinking about Sebastian. He'd eaten lunch every day for months with the twins, and before this week Sebastian had never had seconds. He never drank much water. He hadn't been any skinnier than Wolfgang. Now he spent all his time in the bathroom. He even got a tardy because of it.

When he got home, Alex slipped into his parents' study and pulled their old medical textbook off the shelf. *Harrison's Principles of Internal Medicine.* Now *Harrison's* was online, but his parents had this old one, too. They couldn't bear to throw away a book.

It was a huge book, the thickest Alex had ever seen, and heavy. He had to place it on the desk to flip to the index. Hungry. No, wasn't there. There was probably a medical term for hungry, but he didn't know it. Weight loss. He looked that up. Too many options, too many possibilities. What about thirst? Under thirst, the index showed "diabetes insipidus" and also "hypothalamic regulation." He didn't know what any of that meant. But he knew one word. Diabetes.

He flipped the heavy book to the chapter on diabetes. Diabetes mellitus. It had its own chapter, that's how significant a disease it was. Diabetes was a problem with blood sugar control. Over time the high sugars damage the organs, almost every organ in the body. Diabetes caused heart disease and stroke and kidney disease and eye problems. And lots more. It made Alex's head spin to read about it because it led to so much trouble.

He read about the two types. Type 2 diabetes was the one his mother always warned against, due to obesity and sugary foods. Ninety percent of diabetes was Type 2, and it was growing by leaps and bounds because obesity was growing. Thanks a lot, ILL.

Then there was Type 1 diabetes, which had nothing to do with obesity and was more common in young people. This would be the one Sebastian might have.

Alex was interested in the initial symptoms. And there it was. He hadn't remembered it quite right. The triad was thirst, excessive urination, and hunger. There was a medical term for that. Polydipsia, polyuria, polyphagia meaning too much thirst, too much pee, too much hunger.

Sebastian had all the symptoms. Could he have Type 1 diabetes?

Alex knew how to tell. All he had to do was touch him.

The book said it was important to diagnose and start treatment promptly because good blood sugar control prevented the organ damage, but also prevented the sugar from getting too high and causing a person to get really sick really quickly. It only happened with Type 1 diabetes, but it could be deadly.

You had to treat diabetes with a shot of insulin under the skin every day or through a pump. Not a deep shot like the rabies or other vaccinations, just a little "prick" to give the medicine. The patient gave it himself. Sebastian would have to learn to do it himself.

This was ridiculous. Sebastian didn't have diabetes. It was the Medical Student Disease of the Week. Alex could probably flip to any other disease in the book and think of someone who fit the symptoms, some perfectly healthy person who had nothing at all.

He turned the pages. Rickets. Hmm. Not enough vitamin D caused the bones to weaken and grow funny and get fractures. Nope. No one he knew had rickets.

He flipped more pages. Epilepsy. Abnormal electrical activity in the brain causing episodes of muscle contractions and loss of consciousness. No, he didn't know anyone who had epilepsy, either.

Okay. Maybe not any disease. But Sebastian did not have diabetes. And he was going to prove it.

This would be the first time he had ever done this. The first time he used his Revelstoke gift to diagnose someone on purpose and not by accident.

Chapter 57
The Red Handkerchief

Sebastian and Wolfgang weren't at lunch the next day because of a special orchestra practice. But they were in gym. Alex rushed to try to change as fast as he could, but the twins were faster, and they were in the gym by the time he finished. Mr. Sphere had already started making teams, and he had the twins on the far side of the gym ready for armless ball tag. It was a crazy game to play in the gym, it was a crazy game to play anywhere, but Mr. Sphere loved it because no one touched anyone and there was no chance of coming to blows. With their hands and arms stuffed in their shorts so they waddled like penguins, they kicked fluffy balls filled with stuffing that floated through the air and barely registered when they landed. It was impossible to tell if anyone was out because the balls were so light. And the balls didn't go where the boys kicked them, they blew up into the air and landed wherever. Mr. Sphere didn't allow talking during armless ball tag. Tom said he should have called it armless, mouthless ball tag.

The boys only put up with it because Mr. Sphere gave everyone an "A" for the semester if they participated and a "D" if they didn't. Two grades, "A" and "D." So everyone played every game every day.

The only sound in the gym was the squeak of their sneakers, a few grunts, and a yell if someone fell over and hit the floor. Which hurt because their hands were stuffed in their shorts and couldn't break their fall. Mr. Sphere took his usual place on the bottom bleacher. Alex maneuvered close to Sebastian to touch him illegally, but every time Alex eyed Mr. Sphere, he was watching the game, not staring off into space like he usually did. So Alex kept his hands stuffed in his shorts.

Finally, dressed in the locker room, Alex approached Sebastian. Sebastian was hogging the drinking fountain, and there was a line behind him. Alex sauntered up and casually put a hand on his sweaty shoulder. Sebastian lifted his head, then continued gulping.

That one touch was all it took. The familiar icicle of fear chilled Alex's core. His tongue stuck to the roof of his dry mouth as he felt Sebastian's thirst, so thirsty no amount of trickle from the fountain was going to quench it. He wanted to eat anything in sight, even a few stray pretzels he spied on the bench by the water fountain. His eyesight was blurry, and he couldn't see very far across the locker room.

Sebastian became a boy made of blood vessels, no skin, no bones, just a maze of vessels, four limbs and a trunk dangling off his head. One arm came up to wipe his mouth, thin red ropes moving together up and back down to his side.

Then the blood vessel linings fell away, and now Sebastian was held up by tiny cells flowing in lines like cars in traffic, red blood cells, white blood cells. And tiny white sugar crystals, so many tiny white crystals, far too many for his body to use. All that glucose would injure the blood vessel, and all the other organs as well. Sebastian's superhighway of blood cells straightened from the drinking fountain and stepped away.

Fear seized Alex. The fear was familiar now. That didn't make it any less scary. Alex gritted his teeth and clenched his hands.

Grandpa Asclepius said he felt the fear when he saw a disease ILL caused because he didn't know if he could get rid of the disease, rid of ILL. Part of ILL was in him for a second.

ILL was scary. But ILL was gone. ILL was dead.

Why did he feel afraid?

Sebastian had diabetes. Alex was certain. Sebastian, back to normal, blood vessels under wraps and sweatshirt back in place, gave up his place at the fountain only to head to the back of the line to wait for another turn. Poor Sebastian would need insulin for the rest of his life.

Alex's blurred vision cleared, and he was able to see now. He was able to see Sebastian's gym locker, see the colorful cloth hanging from it. See the red handkerchief.

Chapter 58
Back to the Cave

Though Alex could see the handkerchief perfectly well, he ran over and yanked it off the locker. It was the same overly large, bizarre red handkerchief. ILL's handkerchief.

The bell rang as he reeled out of the locker room, handkerchief clasped in his hand. He sprinted down the hall toward Penelope's locker, teachers shouting "Walk, don't run" as he flew by. He ran up to her, waving the handkerchief like a flag in a windstorm. She took one look and dropped her books. She shoved them back in the locker and slammed it shut.

They ran from the building and much of the way down the hill. At the lake, they collapsed against a tree, gasping and wheezing. They started off again down the lake. Neither one said anything, but they both knew where they were going.

They stopped at the park edge. Who wanted to go in there? They stood together, but they didn't meet each other's eyes, and they certainly didn't speak.

Finally Alex said, "I have to go up there. Back to the cave. I have to find him."

"I'll go with you, but I can't go in that cave," Penelope said. "If that body is there, that body that I killed, that's horrible. I haven't been able to think about it at all. I don't want to see it."

Alex remembered the terrible cracking sound, the sickening sight of ILL's head splitting, the blood, the flames. The body should be nothing but ashes. How could ILL be alive? But he was. He had to be.

Alex took her hand and led her along. Into the woods and up the hill.

The overgrowth was just as thick. The opening to the cave was again unrecognizable. There was no sign that they had ever been there. Alex got his bearings from the crest of the hill, then scrabbled through the branches and thorns. He could just see Penelope through the thicket, but she shook her head. She was crying. He forged on alone.

He crouched down at the entrance. His stomach churned. He didn't know what he would find. A dead body? Ashes and bone fragments? ILL? Nothing?

He lay flat on his stomach and slowly crept through. It was so dark. He couldn't see anything yet, but the close air reeked of rank puddles, urine, and acrid, smoky char. He pulled himself fully into the cave and let his eyes adjust before he slowly stood.

Nothing. There was nothing there. He sunk to his hands and knees and inched his way around the cave in case he had missed something. The putrid puddles were cool and disgusting, but there was no solid mound of a body of evil. No ashes or bones or rags. He could see the whole cave. Even so, he felt along the rock walls and the short side tunnels, seeking some hiding place, some secret way in and out. He scrambled faster and faster. ILL had to be there. He had to be.

The cave was empty. ILL was gone. ILL and his super disease were gone.

Chapter 59
Useful to be Dead

*Fighting had taken up energy, precious energy.
The shackles were too strong. Making those ridiculous
little diseases took its toll. As it had with the elder
Revelstoke and his wife all those years ago. So much
work. He couldn't even create a rabies to spread from
the dog to the kid. But the kid didn't know that.*

*Still, he had not gotten what he wanted. All that
effort. The cave had an opening in the roof of a side
tunnel, but it was not ideal for movement. The rabies
for the dog was not easy. All that exertion. Wasted.*

*Sometimes it was useful to be dead.*

*He needed to conserve his strength, store it up. He
had just enough power for one final play. But one final
play was all he needed.*

Chapter 60
Still Time

Alex backed out of the cave as slowly as he had crept in. Penelope was there, still crying. He shook his head.

"Empty," he said.

Penelope dropped to the ground and sat there with her hands covering her face, her shoulders heaving.

"I thought it was over. I put it completely out of my mind. I thought he was dead," she cried.

He knelt next to her and put his hand on her shoulder.

"What do we do now?" Her voice quavered.

He lifted his face toward the blue June sky. He thought of the red handkerchief floating away in his dream. He remembered the day he first met ILL and first saw that repulsive cloth.

"We keep looking," he said. "And I know where."

She shook her head. "I can't. I can't go with you." She took a deep, ragged breath. "I thought I was fearless now. But I'm not."

He didn't say anything for a minute, then he gazed into her black eyes. "You have something to live for now." Alex thought of her laughing on the Ferris wheel, laughing at the lunch table with their friends, laughing with Valentine, laughing with her aunt, always laughing.

She wiped her nose on a tissue from her pocket. She wasn't laughing now.

"I have to do this alone anyway," he said. She nodded, and he left her there, crying near the cave.

He retraced his steps, down the hill to the edge of the lake. Mount Rainier was partially hidden even on this warm day. Fluffy clouds like cotton candy covered its base, but the rounded peak rose above, majestic and beckoning. Alex stared at it, feeling nothing but dread.

It was all there, hiding under the surface of his mind, the horror, the cataclysm. It was going to happen. ILL was alive. ILL had a super disease. A painful, blistering disease with an excruciatingly long incubation period. To be unleashed at Mount Rainier National Park.

But he wasn't there yet. Alex was certain. ILL was luring him, reeling him in with his disease and his bait, the red handkerchief. ILL was not done with him. And Alex was not done with ILL. He knew where to go, where it all started.

Alex could still stop him. He was the last Revelstoke.

Chapter 61
Waiting Forever

*Without the shackles, the rock would have been no match for him. Without the shackles, he could have crushed this boy from the beginning.*

*His powers were weakened. His powers were fading. Recovery was slow.*

*His super disease was real. But in his head, not yet created. In its cocoon stage. So long, decades long in the planning. Everything was ready, enough components painstakingly collected over the years for one small batch. But large enough. Waiting for the shackles to release. Waiting for his cloth's power to be restored so he could burst the cocoon open. Waiting forever. With the shackles, there could be no creation, no disease, no death. With the shackles, he was useless.*

*He would wait no more.*

Chapter 62
The Bus Stop

Alex left the park and trekked back along the lake and up the hill. A few blocks from the library, he slowed. The bus stop came into view. Alex stopped. There was someone there, all right. His back was to Alex, and he had a satchel over his shoulder. Fit man, black tee shirt, blue jeans. ILL.

Okay. Go on. Don't just stand there. Go on. But... This superhuman creature had survived his head splitting open and leaping flames. Had triumphed despite the Revelstoke shackles. Had almost killed Alex with appendicitis and rabies. Alex's legs wobbled.

Think of Penelope and the bleeding ulcer. Of Sebastian with diabetes. Of Grandma Bea. Of all the innocent visitors to Mount Rainier.

He approached cautiously, silently, but it didn't matter. He knew ILL was waiting for him.

ILL pivoted as Alex reached the edge of the bus stop. His head was a hideous mass of raw scars, red and raised, a long one slanting across his face and a second over the top and down his forehead. Alex stood transfixed, eyes riveted on the scars.

"I am here, you see. You cannot kill me. I am forever protected." ILL pulled from his pocket his red handkerchief, the one he always carried. "Did you think I could do this without protection myself? This is my protection. I will never fall ill." He wiped his hands three times, then reached up and delicately touched a scar with the handkerchief's edge. "Though it is not perfect."

This red handkerchief had protected ILL from the fire? Had healed his head? What were they up against?

ILL drew a glass container from the satchel. "But this is. This is perfect." He stroked it reverently, slowly. The vessel was small and round, the size of a peach, with a glass stopper and half filled with a black powder.

ILL held it in his hand and caressed it like it was a living thing.

Alex pulled his eyes from the scars and the red handkerchief to the glass container. He knew what it was. The super disease.

"I have worked many years on this. You are my last obstacle. You Revelstoke. You will not stop me." ILL raised the handkerchief and waved it in a quick circle. A whiff of blue smoke swirled and instantly disappeared into the air.

At first, Alex didn't understand. He expected to feel something, like the day he shot across the bus stop or when one of ILL's diseases attacked him. But nothing happened.

A soft murmur resonated around the bus stop. A humming, a buzzing, a sound that chilled him. First one bee, flying in a circle around ILL's hand, then another, then a swarm, with ILL in the middle laughing maniacally.

Bees. Alex was allergic to bees. Face-swells-up allergic. Can't-breathe allergic. Could-die allergic. ILL was surrounded by bees.

"Come and get me," ILL said. "Come and die."

Alex focused on the glass container, barely visible now amongst the teeming horde of bees. The din was deafening. He had trouble thinking. His mouth was dry, his heart raced. He was terrified of bees.

"I could be a patient man." ILL gestured to the advertisements on the bus stop. "Humankind will destroy itself in time."

ILL held the container up, looking at it lovingly. "But I can speed things up."

Could Alex get to the container? Could he knock it out of his hand?

ILL regarded him. "Of course, if you make me drop this, the glass will shatter and it will release here. Seattle. Not what I'd planned, but…" He paused and caressed the container again. "Acceptable."

"You can die two deaths. If not from the bees, then from this. Two deaths for the last Revelstoke." He held the container out, so it was just a few feet from Alex. Tantalizingly close. But in a throng of orbiting balls of death.

Could he grab it? Could he get it without the container dropping, smashing, sending the black powder into the air, into Seattle?

Alex took a tentative step closer. The bees surged toward him. He rushed back, tripping and almost falling. He floundered for a second and then caught himself. His arms dropped with a thud to his side.

His hand banged against something hard in his pocket. The vial. The antidote. The antidote against ILL's ill.

ILL's ill was right in front of him. ILL's ill was this super disease, this container of black slow death.

"Some Revelstoke. Even your coward of a grandfather had more guts than you. I am right here." ILL took a step toward him, the bees following along. One or two brushed against Alex's cheek.

Alex didn't move. He kept his hands where they were. He had to keep calm. He took a deep breath in, his abdomen pushing out and his lungs filling with air. Breathe in, breathe out, one. His eyes were on the glass container.

ILL moved closer, slowly, the bees all around now, surrounding both of them.

Breathe in, breathe out, two.

He knew what he had to do. He was a Revelstoke. He had no choice. He knew he would die.

The whine of the bees drowned out any other sound. Alex struggled to concentrate, but the bees were in his face, in his hair, flitting, landing.

The sting came quick and sharp, not nearly as painful as he imagined. Not as painful as it should be. A prick, really. A prick that would kill him.

And then another, more painful this time. And another. His throat tightened. He had to act. Now or never. Soon he would be dead.

He could see ILL watching, mesmerized.

Alex lunged forward. In a single move, he brought out his vial and cracked it against the bus stop edge with one hand the way he cracked open eggs with Mrs. Lemon. He seized the glass container and knocked off the stopper, poured in the antidote, and swirled.

The black powder changed into a purple and gold slurry, then burst into a giant rush of blindingly bright golden glittery smoke. Alex blinked against the light.

The black powder was gone, along with the antidote. The glass container was empty.

Alex had vanquished ILL's super disease.

The glass fell from Alex's hand, crashed to the ground and shattered. Alex saw it but he didn't hear anything over the roar of the bees. The whole mass was upon him now, stinging and stinging so that he couldn't feel the individual jabs anymore.

Alex's legs buckled. He sank to the sidewalk. He stared up at ILL, who appeared to be dancing in the yellow smoke that illuminated the roof of the bus stop. ILL's hand reached out, clutching the immense red handkerchief. ILL unfolded his hand and the entire handkerchief spread open, not just a red square, but a red square with a charred black fringe of material on one edge.

ILL waved the handkerchief high in the air where the bright yellow smoke accumulated at the top of the bus stop, around and around in the haze. ILL, too, circled around, his distorted face uplifted into the smoke. He took in huge breaths with his mouth open, breathing it in like it was the last oxygen on earth.

Alex's breathing was tight, shallow, not enough.

The smoke was gone. ILL stopped his slow dance and glared down at him. He seemed taller, bigger, from where Alex lay.

ILL threw open his hands, and the red handkerchief sprang out. ILL gripped one end and held it up like a flag, hanging there in all its glory for Alex to see. ILL held the red half and the other half floated in the air, a shimmery, shiny black cloth, enormous, restored. The two handkerchiefs were the same, each half of a whole, two ends of one cloth.

The black half held the power to create disease, the red half held the power to protect ILL.

"The last Revelstoke," ILL spat it out. Alex could barely hear him over the buzzing and a wheezing coming from Alex's own throat.

Then ILL grew even larger, his body, his head. His head was no longer a mass of scars. They were gone and his face was whole, unblemished, looming over Alex from the height of a giant.

"Look at me!" ILL's voice boomed, reverberating around the bus stop. "I am here. I am back. You used your precious antidote for me! I am healed of your Revelstoke shackles."

Alex's mouth tingled. His mind wandered.

"There was no disease. Not yet. I was shackled. But your antidote has solved that. I am whole now. I am ready. You will die here, you and all of Revelstoke history. I am free of you."

ILL stood directly over him, his voice so loud there was no way Alex couldn't hear.

"I have waited decades, preparing for this day. Everything is ready. With my powers back, the final step is at hand. By this time tomorrow, my disease will be complete. You will be dead in a few breath's time. The Revelstokes will be dead. I would love to stay and watch you die. But there is work to do. No one can stop me now."

Chapter 63
Free

*Finally free. His own figure, not that puny, weak form he'd embodied all these years. His own powers, not the paltry stunts forced by the Revelstoke shackles.*

*Those Revelstokes had only known half the story. They only knew of his black magic, his black handkerchief of creation. They did not know the cloth from the old leper was split in half with two colors, bright red and deep black, two squares meeting at the center to form a large rectangle. Deep black, the side that captured and created disease. Bright red, the side that protected him from all disease. Just as it had protected the leper for centuries before it left his hands. The red side had been unblemished, and he could pull it into an endless sheet and cut square after square to leave behind. With the cloth in his possession, he was invincible.*

*This Revelstoke's great-grandfather almost destroyed his black creative power. Only a small portion remained, shackling him for all these decades.*

*This puny Revelstoke almost finished the deed. But the neophyte did not know of the red half, the protection, protecting him through time from any threat to his survival.*

*When the flame in the cave reached the red, it extinguished immediately, leaving a tiny fringe of singed black material. Enough to create the bees in the bus stop. That fringe had been his final salvation.*

*The fringe and the Revelstoke antidote. Created to do good, to heal. He used it to heal, all right. To heal his cloth. To release the Revelstoke shackles.*

*Those Revelstokes had made it impossible for him to steal their precious antidote outright. Its power required a Revelstoke. A Revelstoke had to release it.*

*He needed it in the air.*

*That trifling child had finally cracked. Not for himself. Not for his friend or his dog. Only for humanity. The Revelstokes were all alike. Humanity.*

*Now* he *controlled humanity.*

Chapter 64
The Trap

Alex lay flat on the ground, eyes transfixed on the square of red cloth that flapped against the bus stop glass. The square transformed into a line as his face puffed up and his eyes became little slits from the allergic reaction.

Breathing was impossible through his swollen throat. He was dizzy and he couldn't move, couldn't even lift his hand. His blood pressure must be low, dangerously low, close to shock, soon not enough to keep the blood moving through his body. He had anaphylaxis, a full-blown reaction to the bee stings. He would die here. In this bus stop.

There was no point in trying to breathe, so little air was coming in. Alex pictured Valentine and his big head and his soft fur. It was peaceful lying here. So peaceful.

Bright light filled his mind, and his dog faded away. Very peaceful.

"Ow!" he howled. He'd been stung again, the sharpest and biggest bee sting ever. His leg was on fire. His heart raced. It beat so strongly in his chest he could hear it in his ears, faster and stronger than ever. He heard his breathing, wheezy and faint. But he was breathing!

He could see, too, and the first thing he saw was the advertisement. "24 oz for the price of 12." Then he saw Penelope, brandishing a spent epinephrine pen, its one-inch needle exposed. It was Penelope and not a bee. Penelope had an epinephrine pen, and she had jabbed him in the leg.

"I'm allergic to hazelnuts." She waved the pen. "Nothing ever happened to me except a scratchy throat. But my mom wouldn't let me go anywhere without epinephrine. I carry it with me always."

"You saved me," he said.

"It wasn't me," she cried. "It was my wonderfully overprotective mom. She saved you."

Alex's heart was still racing from the epinephrine medicine in the pen. He felt ready to take on the world.

"Where is he?" He sat, too quickly, and he dropped to the sidewalk again.

"ILL? He's not here. Just you."

What? Where was ILL?

"I didn't know where you went, so I came to the library. And here you were. Your face was all swollen, and you were hardly breathing. I figured it out, my mom had told me about it so many times."

She helped him to sit, and they leaned against the bus stop.

Now Alex's head hurt from his thudding pulse. ILL's words flooded back. What had he done? ILL had tricked him. It had all been a trap. The clouds of disease, the rabies. ILL tempted him over and over. He hadn't wanted to kill him. That's why Alex was still alive. ILL wanted the antidote. To use for himself. To heal his black cloth. ILL had used the Revelstoke antidote to rid himself of the Revelstoke shackles.

Alex's whole body shook, sick with dread. He rested his head back. High above him, the red cloth tapped against the glass, mocking him. He splayed his hands against the bus stop for support, rubbing against the advertisement. The huge red cup of soda leered at him.

How could he have been so stupid?

Alex grabbed the poster and ripped and shredded until it fluttered around him in useless pieces. He shoved them in his jeans pocket, he ground them under his foot, he threw them wildly around the bus stop.

The red handkerchief swirled from his breeze. He was out of breath. His burst of energy vanished. He looked around at the mess of paper scraps. What a mess he'd made of everything. Some Revelstoke.

ILL needed the antidote. Alex had handed it right to him, delivered in a round glass container of harmless dust.

Chapter 65
Disease

*Mount Rainier would explode with his disease. The volcano would be felt worldwide.*

*Not literally, of course. He couldn't produce natural disasters. Not that he wouldn't enjoy making an earthquake swallow a town or churn a seaside village into rubble. But he had his own methods, his own powers. At long last, they were intact.*

*Mount Rainier was waiting.*

*There were other places to consider. Flashier places. Football stadiums, the Olympic Games. It wasn't that he was old-fashioned. Those places were too much. Too big. Too obvious. That had never been his style. He was subtle. Clever. This was not biological warfare. This was disease. To be set free in his own way. Slowly. Spreading insidiously. Undetected. Unnoticed long enough that the medical detectives would always be behind. Playing catch up. Disease was the natural way of the world. Of his world.*

*He needed international travelers and he needed wind. He cared not where. He had seen the Revelstokes travel yearly to Mt. Rainier. He had seen the boy pause every time the mountain peeked from the clouds. He would set his creation free on that mountain. A little symbolism. His own personal dig at the last of the Revelstokes.*

*The winds would blow, this way and that. From the mountain the boy admired so. His special microdust would not dissipate, would not dilute. The most infinitesimal particles were infectious. His contagion would float forever, across the oceans, across the continents. Sightseers would hasten its spread, breathing the infection in and then out into the air, on airplanes and ships and trains. Breathing it on others. Family members, coworkers, people at the gym, at the grocery store, on the subway, in the parks, on the street. Indoors, outdoors. There was no escape.*

*With its long, long incubation period, his blistering disease would go unnoticed until the whole world breathed it in over months and months. Until the whole world was infected.*

Chapter 66
The Mountain

There was one bus a day to Mount Rainier, going up in the morning and returning at night. Alex and Penelope planned it the night before, walking home from the bus stop. They left that morning with their backpacks as if they were going to school, but they met near the library and made their way downtown to the Mount Rainier bus instead. It was a tourist bus, intended for visitors to see the glorious mountain up close. Not for fighting ILL. Not for saving humanity.

Excited tourists packed the bus, with backpacks and cameras and picnics. The bus pulled onto the highway, and the mountain came into full view. Passengers erupted in oohs and aahs even though they were two hours away. Alex slumped in his seat.

"All this time, I thought I was fighting him. I thought I could do it. But I wasn't fighting anything. ILL had no power. It was all a ruse, all to get the antidote. Now the antidote's gone, and ILL's at one hundred percent, and I have nothing."

"You are a Revelstoke," Penelope said. "That's not nothing."

"You have too much faith in me."

"I don't think so. Do you know your name, Alexander, means defender of man, protector of humanity?"

"What?"

"I looked it up."

She looked so hopeful, so confident. Alex was not. Protector of humanity? He couldn't even protect the Revelstoke antidote.

"I can't stop him," Alex said. "ILL is the one protected, protected forever by his red handkerchief. He can create whatever evil he wants with the black handkerchief. I lost the one thing that might save us, the Revelstoke antidote."

"You don't need the Revelstoke antidote. You *are* a Revelstoke. You will think of something."

Penelope laid her head back. Her face was serene. He'd seen her like this before, in the tree fort when she was bleeding from the ulcer. Great. At least one of them thought this would work.

Green pine trees sped by as the bus rolled on, off the highway now and on the road to the mountain. Huge trees, huge like ILL was huge now. Bigger than life. At full power. With a fury stored up and waiting for this moment that Alex had given him.

The handkerchief. One side for disease, one side for protection. Not just one black cloth. How could Alex possibly destroy the entire handkerchief?

The bus slowed at the national park entrance. Alex wanted it to stop, turn around, go back to Seattle, take them away from here. He remembered the bee stings, the chest tightness, the peaceful light. He'd been dying. If not for Penelope, he would be dead.

Like all the people in ILL's plan. Dead. A painful, blistering, oozing, bleeding disease. Alex had to stop it. Somehow, he had to stop ILL.

But he didn't have to do it alone. He had a friend. He had Penelope. She had faith in him. Like the Penelope in *The Odyssey*, waiting for Odysseus to come home.

The bus started on its way again. They would be there soon. Alex contemplated Penelope's calm, unwavering expression. He wished he had that much faith.

Chapter 67
Up

The bus came to an abrupt stop. They were there. Alex and Penelope tightened the laces of their hiking boots and gathered their backpacks, which were filled with waterproof jackets and the "ten essentials of hiking," not books. And trail mix. That was Penelope's contribution.

There were two more items in Alex's backpack, the long fireplace matches and the pilfered Bunsen burner, and he checked now to make sure they were near the top. Ready when he needed them. Even if he couldn't destroy the entire handkerchief, he could at least try to do what his great-grandfather had done, destroy the black part that gave ILL power to create disease.

"Bus leaves at six," the driver told them as they stepped off. Alex looked at his watch. Ten o'clock. Eight hours. Eight hours to find ILL. Kill or be killed.

A sickening idea struck him. In all his previous encounters with ILL, the deck had been stacked in Alex's favor. ILL had been shackled. ILL had needed something from him. As long as Alex had the antidote, ILL needed Alex alive. Now ILL had what he wanted. He was at full power. Alex was dispensable.

Full power. What was ILL capable of?

Alex and Penelope stood in the Paradise parking lot and looked out at Mount Rainier. Up close, the mountain was impossibly big. The visitor center faced an alpine meadow with the enormous glacier-covered dome towering behind. It was so early in the season that snow still covered many of the paths. Tiny white flowers grew in the sodden grass where the snow had recently melted.

The day was glorious, with a bright blue sky and no clouds in sight. Alex knew that could change at any moment. The mountain made its own weather. A stiff breeze blew the trees, which made a whispery sound.

Just as the bus had been crowded, the mountain teemed with people. Alex tripped over a little girl before he was out of the parking lot. The lot was already full, and rangers directed new cars to the overflow area.

For an instant, Alex toyed with the idea of asking a ranger for help. The rangers looked capable, strong, responsible. Right now, Alex felt none of those things.

He imagined the conversation. "Sir, I need your help to track down and thwart an ancient evil being who is going to use Mount Rainier to launch a new disease that will engulf the world in its terror."

Alex was twelve. Penelope had blue hair. He looked at the rangers again. No. He and Penelope were on their own.

Alex hoisted his pack on his back. Penelope stood there gawking. He followed her gaze and remembered the first time he'd seen Mount Rainier up close. Easily one of the most beautiful sights ever.

Today was different. Up there, somewhere, was ILL.

They started up the trail. Several trails left the visitor center, but they all headed the same way. Up.

They chose the most direct, the steepest. The meadow spread out before them. Trees grew in groups, but not so many that they couldn't see most of the hillside climbing to the edge of the snowfields.

Even this steep path was crowded, and they hiked slowly. They crested a hill, and Alex pulled Penelope over to a viewpoint.

"The higher we go, the more we can see." Alex was breathing hard from the steep climb. He scanned up and scanned down.

"There are so many people," Penelope said, her hands on her knees to catch her breath. "How are we ever going to find him?"

"Believe me, he will stand out." ILL was tall now. Enormous. He had filled the bus stop. "And there won't be as many people farther up."

"This wind isn't good." Penelope's hair flew around her head like a tornado. "His disease…"

"It's always windy up here. His disease will fly everywhere." Alex pointed high on the mountain. "It will be even windier up there. That's where the snowfield starts. It's all glacier. It never melts."

"It looks like there's a line of ants up there."

"That's where we're going," Alex said. "They're hiking up snow stairs. That's why they're all in a line. That's the way to Camp Muir. The last place before you have to rope up. Then they climb to the top of the mountain."

They started out again, falling in behind climbers with ice axes and crampons dangling from their heavy packs.

"Should we have all that stuff?" Penelope whispered.

"I don't even know what half that stuff is," Alex whispered back.

"Well, at least I brought trail mix," Penelope said.

"And we're better off than them." Alex pointed to a dad with a barefoot toddler on his shoulders and a mom with a baby in a sling on her hip. The dad stopped and inhaled deeply, taking in the view, a huge grin on his face. The mom leaned against him, and they chattered away in some foreign language, maybe French.

They had to stop ILL. They had to get going.

Alex took Penelope's hand, and they moved forward in front of the family. They pulled over at every viewpoint, scouring the mountain to try to see ILL's massive form. The wind picked up and Penelope's hair whipped around until it was a tangled mess.

Snow covered the path now, and they plodded on, slower. Eventually they reached Pebble Creek.

"Once we cross this, we're on the snowfields." Alex helped Penelope across the slippery boulders. The mountain was much steeper here. Tiny icy crystals lashed his face. They climbed a snowy hill and rounded a corner, and the whole mountain opened up before them, a mass of white laid out as far as they could see.

And there he was.

The climbers were all in a line, ascending the snow stairs, slowly, carefully, one climber behind another in a steady line all the way up in the direction of Camp Muir. A few groups made their way separately, twos and threes here and there near the main line. Way off to the side, on the edge of what they could see, was a large form in black. Also moving steadily. The climbers kept to the center of the snowfield for safety. The edges were hard to see completely and ended in cliffs on either side. If visibility changed, you could easily walk off the edge and die in a free fall. Few people ventured away from the middle. There was no doubt it was him.

As if to make the point, the large man stopped, brought out a red cloth from his pocket, and wiped his forehead.

Alex and Penelope tried to blend in with the other hikers, but ILL never glanced back.

"Here are the snow stairs," Alex said as they came to a much steeper part of the mountain. The stairs didn't look like much, just indentations where countless boots had hacked into the snow on the mountainside. But climbing them was far easier than slogging up the snow, which was ankle deep on top of the packed layers underneath.

For such a large man, ILL moved surprisingly fast. He wasn't even on the snow stairs but making his way through the snow drifts on his own.

Alex and Penelope kept no distance between themselves and the climbers in front of them in case ILL turned around. It wasn't easy. The group was in better condition than two middle-school kids. The stairs were steep, and the air was thinner than lower down. But most of the climbers had large packs and extra gear to go all the way to the summit, and Alex was glad he was traveling light.

He kept his eyes on ILL. ILL kept moving, up, up, up. His gaze never veered right or left. Then Alex realized why. ILL thought he was dead, killed by the swarm of bees. ILL had what he wanted. He was free of the shackles. He'd left Alex for dead and set off to unleash his disease without any Revelstokes to interfere.

ILL was at Camp Muir, still far above Alex and Penelope. He was off to the side, not at the main camp, with its wood cabin and stone hut shaped like a little castle and flat space with tents. The climbers rested here, then set out again at midnight to make the ascent to the summit. The climbers wanted to get up and down before the sun came out and made the snow at the top softer and more dangerous.

Alex had never gone beyond this point. Hiking to Camp Muir was hard enough, four and a half miles from the parking lot, more than half of it on snowfields and snow stairs. Alex's lungs burned and his legs wobbled. His head ached from the thin air. His heart was already pounding from the exertion. Now it beat faster. Beyond Camp Muir lay danger.

When they'd started at the bottom, he hadn't considered how high they might go. Where they might finally meet ILL. The snowfields were one thing. They were dangerous enough, if a sudden storm caused a whiteout with zero visibility and you walked off the edge, or you hunkered down and froze to death, both of which happened on a regular basis to hikers just like them.

At least he knew these dangers, had had them drilled into him over the years by his parents. His mom kept a constant watch on the sky and made them turn back if any wisp of a cloud appeared. Like the ones forming now, he saw. Don't think about that. Pretend you didn't notice the clouds.

Beyond Camp Muir, without helmets and crampons and ropes and the skill to use them, they were at the mercy of the mountain. Rock falls. Avalanches. Crevasses, endlessly deep cracks in the glacier that would swallow you with no chance of escape. ILL was going on. He was past Camp Muir.

Alex could only speak in short sentences. He was that out of breath. He tried to convey to Penelope what lay beyond, but she was dazzled by the view, the exhilaration of being so high. She didn't even look scared. She didn't know to be scared.

They finally arrived at Camp Muir, huffing and coughing and trying to get their breath. Alex pulled Penelope past the hut and cabin and toward the tents. A single trail headed off the back of the camp, the only way ILL could have gone. The area wasn't crowded, but a few climbers were repacking their backpacks.

Alex paused. They'd be challenged if they were seen because they didn't have any gear and they didn't belong past this spot. They ducked behind a tent to get past the group, then fled down the path and around the corner.

Alex had never been past Camp Muir and didn't know what to expect. The path led to another open area with a main trail carved into the snow. In front of them was a sheer wall of snow, going up as high as he could see. The trail headed in that direction. Off to the side was nothingness, an edge. The wind whipped through the area, loud and strong, blowing small ice pieces through the air as if they were feathers.

Far off the trail, near the edge, they saw ILL. He was higher and farther, but he was stopped, gazing out over the vast view. His back was to them.

Alex looked at the view, too. They were so high, he should be able to see forever, mountains and valleys.

He couldn't see anything. A wall of white, a huge puffy cloud moved in quickly. Penelope waved her arm and pointed, her words lost in the wind except "cloud of disease."

It wasn't a cloud of disease. It wasn't created by ILL. This was the mountain's own weather. A huge storm loomed. Alex could hear his mother's voice from all their Camp Muir hikes. "Turn back at the first sign of weather. Turn back if you see any clouds." He'd been purposefully ignoring the weather the entire time. Now it was here.

Alex pulled Penelope close and shouted in her ear. "Hold on to me! We won't be able to see much soon." He opened his backpack and fished around for the flashlight and the compass and the whistle. Thank you, Mom and Dad, for this always-packed bag of "hiking ten essentials," easy for him to slip into his school backpack unnoticed.

He fixed the compass on ILL, setting his course in case the storm blocked his vision. He could still see him now. ILL reached into the satchel slung over his shoulder and brought out the black handkerchief. Alex grabbed Penelope's hand and tried to run forward. The snow off the trail was deep. He stumbled and she tumbled into him, and they both went down.

ILL unfolded the handkerchief and held up a glass orb, much bigger than the one at the bus stop, but still unmistakably filled with black. ILL's super disease.

Alex sprang to his feet and plowed through the snow again. Penelope was right behind him. ILL was close, but Alex could barely make him out in the storm. Snow fell now, sharp, biting crystals on their faces.

Alex tripped again, and Penelope fell over him. The compass flew out of his hand.

Even over the wind, Alex heard an ominous sound. Instead of nothing, or a soft cushiony sound of the compass landing in the snow, he heard a slapping and a tinkling. Then, long, long after that, the compass clinked deep beneath them.

Penelope tried to move, but he pushed her shoulder back down on the snow. He put his mouth to her ear and shouted. "Crevasse."

It was dark, and the snowfall was heavy. He couldn't see far. He pointed his flashlight toward the ground in front of them and switched it on. Snow glittered back at them. But only for a foot. Beyond Penelope, nothing glittered but the swirling snow in the air.

Where the ground should be was only blackness. Vast blackness. More than ten feet of blackness before the snow picked up on the other side of the crevasse.

Alex swept his light around them. The snowfall lightened and he could see more. Penelope was splayed out in the snow. Most of her body was not on firm ground but on a little lip of snow and ice that spanned the pit. A snow bridge.

On the other side, clearly illuminated now by Alex's light, stood ILL.

Chapter 68
The Crevasse

Alex shined his flashlight on ILL. Surprise and shock spread across that massive face.

"You!" ILL bellowed, his voice carrying even in the wind. "I killed you! You are no more!"

Alex lay still in the snow. Up close, ILL was enormous, his face twisted into hatred and his huge hands cradling the glass sphere.

"It is of no matter," ILL continued. "You are there and I am here."

He was right. Ten feet across the chasm. The bottomless chasm. Some of these crevasses were a hundred feet deep. There was no way to get to him.

A flash of color caught Alex's eye. Penelope had been close, but now she was halfway out on the snow bridge, crawling on all fours. She didn't know it was a snow bridge, an unsupported span of snow and ice. To her, the ground would appear normal. Until it gave way. Some snow bridges were solid. But most were delicate and weak.

She shouted, but he couldn't hear her over the wind.

ILL took two quick steps toward the snow bridge and stomped with his foot.

Penelope froze. She thought ILL was coming for her. Alex's flashlight showed the confusion and fear on her face. Then her expression relaxed. ILL didn't move. It seemed as if nothing had happened.

Then they saw the cracks. The wind was so loud that all the other sounds were silenced. The bridge near ILL gave way, ice pieces and snow chunks falling over the side into the crevasse. Then the whole bridge gave way, and Penelope fell with a scream that carried over the wind.

"Nooo!" Alex screamed, and his scream and Penelope's scream and one other all melded together. Alex whipped his flashlight around toward ILL. His footing was loose from the collapse of the snow bridge. He staggered back, his glass globe leaping from hand to hand as if he were juggling. Then it shot from of his grasp and out over the crevasse and in.

ILL was upright, to the edge of the crevasse quickly. Alex was still down. Take it slow, go inch by inch, hands and knees, or he'd end up in the crevasse with Penelope. The wind howled, but something else howled as well.

It wasn't ILL. His face was set, grim, in Alex's light. Alex reached the edge, leaned his head carefully over, and shined his flashlight in.

There she was. Penelope hung from an ice ledge about ten feet down, arms over its slippery top, her foot wedged into the side of the crevasse for extra support, her other leg dangling. She was absolutely still as she stared up at him, eyes wide. The low howling noise was hers.

Farther below her, resting on another ice ledge, sat the dark glass globe of the super disease, sparkling in the light.

Alex trained his flashlight back on ILL. ILL had tied the black half of the handkerchief around the handles of his sack. The handkerchief, initially a large rectangle in his hands, half red, half black, grew as ILL pulled. The black side stretched longer and longer until it was deep into the crevasse, the sack at its end far deeper.

Was he was going to rescue Penelope? Not a chance. Absurd. The makeshift rope was not five feet from her, but ILL was not going after Penelope. He was aiming for his super disease.

Even if Penelope could let go with one hand, there was no way for her to reach the black rope. There was too much space between them.

Alex furiously unzipped the backpack, the noise lost in the wind. He grabbed the match cylinder and lighted one, and it burst into a large glowing flame. He touched the cardboard cylinder with the flame and the tip became a flare of fire.

ILL glanced up from his task but only briefly. Alex hesitated, eyes flitting from Penelope to the black rope. Was there was enough space? There had to be. He hurled the torch into the pit, aiming for the cloth, aiming for IILL's magical power.

He underestimated the force of the wind.

His fire sailed past the cloth like a bright orange streamer and into the crevasse where it immediately went black. His grandfather's matches were gone.

Alex sank his head in the snow. He lifted the flashlight again and shined it into the crevasse.

ILL was surprisingly skillful. Alex watched, mesmerized. ILL maneuvered the sack onto the ice ledge and right up next to the orb. Getting the round container into the bag proved harder. A false step would send his prize off the ledge and into obscurity, buried deep in the never-ending crevasse. After several painstaking tries, he still was no closer.

Alex had to do something. But he was stuck. A slight shift of his hand sent a trickle of snow into the crevasse. Penelope gave out a louder howl as it landed on her face. If he startled her and she moved, she would fall to the bottom and die.

ILL yelped, too, and paused.

Any small movement could cause snow and ice chunks to fall. The sides of the crevasse could cave in. Along with Penelope. Along with the super disease. Alex knew it. ILL knew it. Penelope knew it.

"Let it go, ILL. I can send this side down and bury your disease. It's over," Alex bluffed, shouting as loud as he could. The wind had died, but even to him, his voice sounded thin and uncertain.

"You wouldn't dare, Revelstoke," ILL boomed, his voice strong and full. "You can't stop my disease. Or the girl dies, too. Save the world but lose the girl. A classic dilemma that has plagued humanity throughout time. You are not up to the task."

ILL turned back to his rope, moving it gently to and fro, wiggling the sack into just the right spot.

"You will perish with the rest," ILL went on. "I took what I needed from you. The Revelstokes are through."

Chapter 69
The Train

ILL had it now, had the super-disease orb at the edge of the sack, slowly, carefully sliding the sack around it. Alex's fingers sifted through the silty snow and ice bits at the edge of the crevasse. With one kick he had the power to send the sides crashing in.

He couldn't do it. ILL was right. He couldn't hurtle Penelope to her death as well. All he could do was watch. He moved the flashlight from the orb to Penelope to the orb.

He could see ILL concentrating, already a look of triumph on his face. No! Alex had to at least try.

He flung his arm back and threw the flashlight with all his might at ILL's hand. ILL's arm jerked. The sack collided into the super disease globe. The glass orb slipped off its ledge and fell, hitting off the walls and finally landing with a thunk far, far below.

An inhuman wail filled the heavy air. ILL ran along the edge of the crevasse, head down, searching for a way to the bottom. He covered the length of the crevasse remarkably easily despite the newly fallen snow, and he scaled the steep hill at the far end, still trying to see his treasure. Snow thrust out from under his feet, and for a few moments he didn't make any upward movement. He dug in with his hands and legs,

266

the black handkerchief trailing behind. Snow spewed everywhere. He clambered higher.

Alex kept his eyes on Penelope, still holding strong on the ledge, and on ILL, finally higher on the hill.

"Hold on!" Alex yelled to her. "Don't move! These things are unstable!"

ILL stopped, quite a way up the steep slope now. He would have a view of the entire crevasse. If he could see his orb, he would still try to reach it. Alex scanned the bottom from where he was, but all he saw was ice and the deepest pit he could imagine. Penelope had her eyes on him, thankfully. If she looked down, she'd freak.

"I see it, Revelstoke," ILL's voice carried over the distance. "You will not stop me."

Alex looked from ILL, standing tall on the mountain, determined, arms raised in victory, to Penelope, wedged in with one foot, hands and arms locked onto the ice ledge, determination on her face, too.

Her hands wobbled. No, not her hands, the whole ledge, a split-second movement. The snow vibrated and sound exploded above them.

A train. A deafening train on the mountain bearing down on them.

That's exactly what it sounded like. But Alex could see what it was. Not a train. An avalanche.

The snow beneath ILL gave way. The entire slab below him disintegrated, crumbling away like a sandcastle. ILL was at the center, then he disappeared in the snow. The cloud of white swept toward Alex and Penelope, so loud and so cold. In an instant the avalanche would be on them.

Alex pressed his body flat on the ground with his hands over his nose and mouth to make a tiny air space. He shouted to Penelope, but he couldn't hear his own words over the thunderous booming. The frozen blast took his breath away. He couldn't hear, he couldn't see, he couldn't breathe.

Then it was over. He hadn't moved. He was still there on the side of the crevasse. He wasn't covered in snow, just a dusting. He hadn't tossed and tumbled in the avalanche. He lifted his head and peered into the crevasse and there was Penelope, still holding on, blinking her eyes, snow in her hair.

What? Alex slowly stood. The air was misty and silent. The entire landscape had changed. The slope ILL had climbed was gone, the snow beneath sheared off in an avalanche ILL set off with his own body weight. Across the void of the crevasse was another void. A jagged new hole had opened in the snowfield, and steam seeped out mixing with the light snowfall. Alex gagged from the noxious burnt egg smell.

The avalanche had stopped short of them. The crevasse itself was partially filled in, heavy snow and ice burying everything in its depths.

The super disease. Buried deep in Mount Rainier's cavities, hidden forever, encased in its glass sphere and ice.

Screaming pierced the air. It was Alex's own voice. They'd done it.

"Hey!" Penelope shouted. "What's happening?"

"It's gone! The super disease! It's buried!"

"Get me out of here before I'm buried! Where's ILL?"

Alex peered through the mist. He saw endless white. No black figure. No red and black cloth. Was ILL in the crevasse with his super disease?

A crunching noise broke the still air. A black arm emerged from a white snow pile, the fist opening up toward the sky. Then the entirety of ILL broke free, standing in one motion.

Snow fell from ILL's large figure as he swayed left and right, then homed in on Alex. Uh-oh.

ILL was still distant but advancing steadily. Nothing separated them now.

The avalanche had thrown ILL to Alex's side of the crevasse, or what was left of the crevasse.

This was not good. Alex leaned over the edge. "He's here. He's coming."

## Chapter 70
## Black and Red

The wind gusted out of nowhere, strong enough to blow Alex into the void. He leaped backward to safer ground. The wind raged, then quieted. He swiveled his head toward a faint flapping noise. Caught in the snow right next to him, fluttering now in the wind, was the black handkerchief.

Alex jerked back. The handkerchief fluttered, and nothing more. The avalanche had thrown it, too, to his side of the crevasse. ILL and the magical cloth were separated!

Alex whipped his head around to see ILL. ILL was nearer but moving slowly.

Alex bent to seize the handkerchief, thankful he had mittens on and didn't have to feel the mystical material. He pulled on the black cloth, more and more of it, longer and longer.

ILL was closer but fighting the deep snow and strong wind. Alex worked frantically to free the handkerchief from the wet, heavy snow. The piece of cloth was strong, with more than enough length to reach Penelope. He could get her out. Then he had to destroy it. Or destroy it now and rescue Penelope some other way. Save Penelope. Save humanity. The classic dilemma, ILL said.

270

Alex heaved, and the black became red and soared into the air. The cloth drifted down and lay on the snow, a long black snake with a red tip. His grandfather's matches were gone, but Alex still had the Bunsen burner. He could destroy the cloth in an instant, destroy ILL's powers.

But what about Penelope? Alex had no other way to get her out. Without further thought, he lifted the snake off the snow.

Shuddering as if it would bite, Alex wrapped the cloth around his waist. He hoisted the free end over and lowered it into the crevasse. Penelope slowly, carefully wrapped it twice around her forearm, most of her weight supported by one arm. She clenched the cloth tight. Alex walked backward, leaning against her weight. He struggled and lurched, but he stayed on his feet. Her head appeared above the lip of the crevasse. Alex's strength seemed to multiply in his excitement. He surged backward, pulling her whole body out.

Penelope fell into the new snow and lay staring up at the dark sky. Icicles hung from her hair. Alex ran over to her, his end of the sash gripped in his hand. ILL was almost on them. Alex hoisted Penelope to her feet and unwound the rope from her arm. He held the entire mass of cloth in his arms.

There were two of them, but Alex felt small compared to ILL's gigantic figure. He felt a lump in his throat he couldn't swallow down. His strength, so immense a moment before, left him like the avalanche took the slope. His knees shook in their effort to hold him up.

Alex held all ILL's power in his hand. He tried to tell himself this. He could destroy ILL right now.

Somehow, it didn't feel that way, seeing ILL this close, so massive.

"Stay where you are," Alex shouted. He didn't know if ILL could hear, but in any case, ILL did not stop.

Alex wriggled out of the backpack and ripped open the zipper. The cloth was so large he had to drop it in the snow to pull the Bunsen burner out. He threw his mittens down and twisted the knob to start the butane flowing. He flicked the striker. A flame shot out, bigger than any they'd used in class.

ILL stopped, just a few feet away, his eyes fixated on his handkerchief. Alex's eyes were stuck there, too, and they both realized the same thing in the same moment.

The cloth was wet from being buried in the avalanche. Alex crouched and touched the flame to the handkerchief, and it sizzled but it did not catch. Come on, come on! He tried another spot, then another, but the cloth would not burn.

Alex faced ILL and held the Bunsen burner out in front of him as if he were warding off a vampire with a crucifix.

ILL cocked his head, then laughed, a huge, menacing noise that filled the small space between them.

"A lighter?" ILL boomed. "You think you can hurt me with a lighter?"

In one swift movement, ILL dove forward, snatched the bundle off the ground and stuffed it under his cloak. Alex lunged as well, catching ILL in the chest with the Bunsen burner's huge flame.

The flame fizzled against ILL's cloak.

Alex's Bunsen burner flame was out, too, blown by a gust of wind. He had dropped the striker and lost it in the snow. He couldn't even see an indentation.

What were they going to do? How could they fight this monster?

ILL bent and lifted the striker from near his boot. Penelope slipped next to Alex and pulled him several steps back as ILL stood, his full height unfolding before them. ILL threw the striker far out of reach. He brought out the red part of the handkerchief and wiped his hands three times.

"It is over, Revelstoke," he boomed. "You have lost, and I have won. You will be part of this mountain forever, and, in time, I will be back with my disease."

What had Alex done? He'd had the cloth, all ILL's powers, in his hand. Now he had nothing. He and Penelope would die here. ILL would live on forever. This was a mission of futility.

Keep calm. He took a deep breath. Breathe in, breathe out. He coughed, the pungent smell of sulfur stronger now from the gaping hole on the other side of the crevasse.

He knew what this was. A fumarole. An opening in the snowy surface emitting superheated steam and volcanic gas, a crack leading deep into the volcano, to magma. Hot, bubbling magma. Fire.

ILL was less than ten feet away. He towered over them, his healed face still hideous with its expression of hate, his cloak rippling as the wind picked up.

"You, Revelstoke, you had to come. Decades of planning. My creation. Gone because of you." ILL's voice thundered above the wind. He advanced toward them, drawing out the black handkerchief, showing them his power. "But I can make more. It will take time, but I will return."

A memory flashed into Alex's brain of the first time he met ILL and the force that sent him flying across the bus stop. The force between centuries of good and the gift of seeing disease coming up against all that dark sickness inside of ILL. Ancient evil itself. Alex had been no match for it.

Penelope inched closer behind Alex. He could feel her shaking, but her voice was strong in his ear. "You are a Revelstoke."

A Revelstoke. Able to see disease and help people. Like the boy with the hot dog stuck in his windpipe. Like Sam and his heart. Like Penelope and her ulcer.

Good versus evil. ILL reached out his arm, almost close enough to touch them. Alex steeled himself. He leaped forward, shoved his hand out, and grasped ILL's outstretched arm.

ILL's expression of hatred quickly turned to surprise, then melted away to blandness like a stocking covering his face before the skin itself disappeared. ILL dissolved into black swirls, black flames, a churning sea of blackness. So much evil that Alex thought his head might explode.

Alarm surged through Alex's body, along with a freeze so deep his bones felt like they would snap. Not an icicle of fear, but a glacier of terror. His muscles quivered. His teeth chattered. His mind screamed, "Let go! Let go!"

"You don't know if you can get rid of him, rid of his disease." His grandfather's voice echoed in his head. "You embody the disease. Part of ILL is in you for a second in time."

The roiling blackness melted away. Alex didn't know there was a color deeper than black. But there was. Emptiness, nothingness, a void as deep as the fumarole.

Alex wanted to let go, to purge the horror from his eyes. The pressure of the blackness closed around him, pushing against him. He had to fight back.

The wind lashed his body from all directions. He kept his hand in place, the place where ILL had been a moment before. Where he would materialize soon enough.

He could see his grandfather, hear his words. "You have to use your power. More power than any recent Revelstoke."

ILL's form began to take shape again. The churning sea of blackness solidified into a man, his arm in Alex's hand, his eyes glued on Alex's.

This all took a split second. ILL's skin had melted away to reveal the black vapor and then reappeared, and no time had gone by. But everything had changed. Alex was a Revelstoke, with centuries of Revelstoke power behind him.

Alex tightened his grip. His spine tingled. He'd felt this before, when he overcame appendicitis and Penelope's ulcer and Valentine's rabies. The tingle grew into a coursing vibration along his nerves, stronger and stronger. He let it build until he thought his body would fly apart. The current shot through Alex's body and out his fingers. He released his hand.

ILL jolted into the air, rocketing across the crevasse to the snowfield beyond, landing on his feet at the edge of the fumarole. Penelope screamed and jumped back, taking Alex down into the snow with her.

ILL staggered on the edge of the precipice, his black and red handkerchief whirling in the air as he tried to get his balance in the strong wind. His arm flailed. The wind blew the cloth out of his grip, upward, where it wavered for a second before plummeting into the hole. Even the shrieking wind couldn't drown out the anguished scream.

Sparks shot from the fumarole like a volcano erupting, with a crackly, popping noise that lasted far longer than the sparks, like the finale of a Fourth of July fireworks show.

ILL stood at the edge of the fumarole, arms outstretched, his large face expressionless. His scars returned, Penelope's scars from hitting him with the rock, first along his forehead and then down his face. White foam appeared at the corner of his mouth like Valentine with his rabies. ILL recoiled and vomited red blood, like Penelope's ulcer. ILL clutched his side and bent forward with the appendicitis pain that tormented Alex.

Alex realized what was happening. All of ILL's diseases, everything he'd created, were still part of him. He'd absorbed every disease known to man. His red handkerchief of protection was entombed in the magma. Without it, the diseases took over.

ILL knelt in the snow facing them. Tiny red measles spots appeared, one, then another, then so many they couldn't see his features. ILL coughed from the Spanish flu and hacked red sputum into the snow around him. He started to vomit again, vomiting and vomiting, and when they saw his face, it was a mass of blisters, pustules, an oozing mess of smallpox. ILL coughed and raised his hands so they could see his blackened plague fingers.

He threw back his head and let out a wail. The cloak around his body swirled in the wind and ILL swirled. He burst into a puff of blue smoke.

The scream faded, and there was just the wind. The blue smoke lingered for an instant as an eerie haze, then vanished in a gust.

ILL was gone. Nothing but snow lay where he had writhed.

Alex gaped at Penelope. A huge smile slowly split her face. She fell back in the snow, her arms spread wide. Red splotches covered the ground next to her. Fear seized Alex again. Blood.

But Penelope laughed her beautiful laugh. She wasn't injured. He leaned over and peered at the little pieces of red. He grinned, too. He jammed his hand in his pocket and brought out a fistful of red paper. The remnants of the "24 oz for the price of 12" advertisement from the bus stop. It seemed like an eternity ago, but it was only yesterday. He had released ILL's shackles with the Revelstoke antidote. Now he had destroyed ILL with the Revelstoke power.

The super disease was buried forever in a crevasse under an avalanche. The magical cloth was burned in magma, fire inside ice. ILL was gone, ravaged by his diseases and evaporated into smoke.

It was over.

Alex opened his palm and lifted the paper pieces into the wind. They floated into the dark sky like ILL's red handkerchief in his dream, not a death-signal, but a new life.

Chapter 71
A Flip

Tomorrow was the last day of school. Alex and Penelope and Valentine sat in the tree house on the ground, the air growing stinkier by the minute with Valentine's panting. Alex closed his book. *The Odyssey*. Penelope had her own copy. Valentine rolled over on his back, hoping for a tummy rub. Alex obliged, happy to be here with his dog. And Penelope.

"Wolfgang and Sebastian's party is tomorrow," he said, remembering Smooth Jack asking Isabel to the Valentine Dance. "Go together?"

"Of course," she said. "I assumed we would. Why do you ask?"

"No reason," Alex said, smiling. He didn't have to ask her anything. She always already knew.

At lunch the next day, Wolfgang and Sebastian talked nonstop about blowing up water balloons and making homemade ice cream for the party. Penelope's mom made homemade ice cream. Alex glanced at Penelope, but she was smiling and laughing and gave no hint that she missed her parents and her old life. He knew she did, but she was happy now, too.

"This lasagna is awful. Save your appetite for our ice cream," Sebastian said, pushing his half-eaten plate away.

Alex had cured him. He'd gone back through every step and figured out that with an encompassing hug, fingers clasped, plus a wish, once he felt his spine tingle, the pink foam would appear to counter the diseases ILL set upon them with his blue smoke. Sebastian never knew he had any problem other than a few days of hunger and thirst.

Alex felt a gentle punch in the arm. "Any plans for the summer?" Sam stood next to him. "Maybe we can shoot some hoops," Sam said. "And I mean that literally. That's about all I can do, shoot hoops, no running or anything, but I bet I can beat you at HORSE." Sam looked around the table. "Any of you want to join us? Think you can beat this winner?"

As Sam walked away, each of the guys punched Alex's arm, saying "Winner," "Winner," "Winner," "Winner." Four guys, four punches. Penelope just laughed.

That afternoon, Alex waited for Penelope outside the library. Ms. Parker waved from the door and smiled her dazzling smile. Penelope ran up to him and he took her hand in his.

Alex led her toward the bus stop, which sported a new advertisement. "Avocados. Why Not?"

"I heard Wolfgang and Sebastian have a trampoline," she said. "I've never in my life been on a trampoline."

"Me neither," he said. "They promised they'd show me how to do a flip."

## Catalog of Infectious Diseases

COVID-19

This book was written before the COVID-19 pandemic. ILL's super disease and COVID-19 are not the same, though pandemics and infectious diseases through time share similarities. Understanding of COVID-19 is ongoing. Some of the following information may change.

COVID-19 is caused by a virus, coronavirus, and was first detected in late 2019. It spread worldwide, creating a pandemic (a disease that spreads over a wide area, like multiple countries or continents and affects a lot of people). Coronavirus is transmitted (spread or passed from) person to person by inhaling small droplets in the air after someone coughs, sneezes, or talks. It might also spread by touching something that was recently touched by someone with the virus and then touching one's eyes, mouth, nose, etc. Wearing a mask and washing hands are two important ways to decrease the spread.

The incubation period (the time between getting infected and showing symptoms) is variable, but about three to fourteen days. People can spread coronavirus before they have symptoms and even if they never get symptoms. While some who are infected might have no symptoms, others get very sick and can even die. The most common symptoms are fever, cough, muscle aches, headache, trouble breathing, sore throat, diarrhea, abdominal pain, nausea, and loss of smell or taste. People with COVID-19 can get pneumonia (lung infection with chest pain, cough, trouble breathing), blood clots (which can cause a stroke or trouble breathing), heart troubles, and many other problems.

The disease is more serious in older people or in people with other health problems, but even healthy people can get sick. The current vaccines (man-made preparations typically using killed, weakened, living, or pieces of infectious organisms to provide immunity (protection)) will hopefully prevent COVID-19 in the future.

Plague

Plague is a disease caused by a bacterium, *Yersinia pestis*. Plague has been around for thousands of years, with three major pandemics, including the "Black Death" in Europe in the fourteenth century that killed one-third of the population. It is transmitted (spread or passed) by fleas, and the fleas are carried on rodents like rats, or very rarely, cats and dogs. Humans get the disease most commonly through flea bites, but also by inhaling respiratory secretions (the breath) of infected rodents. The disease can also spread from person to person through inhaled respiratory secretions from someone with pneumonia due to plague. Plague is very rarely caused by scratches or bites from infected cats or dogs.

People with plague are very sick, and symptoms can include fever, painful, swollen lymph nodes, weakness, headaches, necrotic tissue (dead skin and tissue that can turn black, especially the fingers, feet, and nose), pneumonia (lung infection with chest pain, cough, trouble breathing), shock (sudden drop in blood pressure/flow, so low that blood and oxygen are not pumped adequately to the organs of the body), and often death.

It is treated now with antibiotics but remains a very dangerous disease. Plague is very rare.

Cholera

Cholera is a disease caused by a bacterium, *Vibrio cholerae*. Cholera was a common cause of death of the pioneers on the Oregon Trail, and cholera still causes death worldwide today. It is a waterborne disease and outbreaks occur when people have unsafe drinking water. People can get cholera by drinking or eating contaminated (infected or tainted) water or food (especially undercooked shellfish) or by being exposed to a person with cholera, touching what they touched, especially after going to the bathroom, which is why hand washing is so important.

*V. cholerae* causes abdominal cramps, vomiting, and diarrhea and in some cases can cause profuse diarrhea that leads to severe dehydration (fluid and electrolyte loss) and even death. Death can occur very rapidly, in less than a day.

Treatment involves rehydration (giving water and electrolytes like sugars and salts), either by mouth or in an IV (intravenous line, a tiny tube inserted into a blood vessel to give fluids or medication). Antibiotics are also given.

Spanish flu

The Spanish flu was a serious worldwide pandemic (a disease that spreads over a wide area, like multiple countries or continents and affects a lot of people) of an especially deadly influenza (flu) in 1918 and 1919. It infected one-third of the world's population, killing fifty million people including 675,000 Americans. In the United States, it quickly spread after first sickening military soldiers fighting in World War I and returning to the States. More soldiers died of the Spanish flu than in WWI battles.

It was called the Spanish flu not because it started in Spain but because Spain was neutral during World War I, and its free press reported on the illness. Other countries, fighting in the war, did not want media to cover news of this deadly illness affecting its troops and citizens.

Influenza is caused by a virus and is spread from person to person through droplets with sneezing, coughing, talking, etc.

Symptoms of the Spanish flu included fever, chills, and tiredness like the standard flu, but Spanish flu also caused pneumonia (lung infection with chest pain, cough, trouble breathing), fluid-filled lungs making it hard to breathe, bleeding, blue or black skin due to lack of oxygen in the blood, and sometimes even necrosis (dead tissue, especially the feet). Death could occur in a matter of hours due to trouble breathing.

As is still true today, prevention of spread included hand washing, wearing masks, covering coughs and sneezes, and staying away from infected people. Isolation and quarantine were common with many schools and businesses closed. A yearly flu vaccine (a man-made preparation typically using killed, weakened, living or pieces of infectious organisms to provide immunity (protection)) significantly decreases the risk of getting the flu.

Measles

Measles, also called rubeola, is a disease caused by the measles virus and is extremely contagious. Prior to vaccination beginning in the 1960s, millions throughout the world died from measles every year. In the first half of the twentieth century, measles caused thousands of deaths each year in the United States. Even in the 1960s in the US, measles caused tens of thousands of hospitalizations yearly, hundreds of deaths, plus countless other complications. Measles is spread by being near someone with measles and breathing in virus.

Symptoms include high fever, cough, runny nose, red eyes, and a red, bumpy skin rash starting on the face and spreading over the whole body. Measles can lead to diarrhea, pneumonia (lung infection causing trouble breathing, chest pain, and cough), ear infection (which can cause hearing loss or deafness), neurologic problems (seizures, muscle problems, brain problems), and death, especially in children younger than five.

There is no specific treatment for measles. Because it spreads so easily, prior to the vaccine (a man-made preparation typically using killed, weakened, living, or pieces of infectious organisms to provide immunity (protection)), almost every single child got measles by age fifteen. Measles is now prevented by a vaccine, but the disease has not been eliminated or eradicated yet. With higher numbers of people vaccinated, eradication may happen in the future.

Polio

Poliomyelitis is a disease caused by the poliovirus, which damages nerves in the spinal cord and brainstem. In the United States, outbreaks increased in the 1940s, seeming to peak in the summer months. To minimize spread, children were kept inside, pools and other gathering places were closed, and travel was restricted. 21,000 cases of paralytic polio were reported in the United States in 1952.

In severe cases, polio causes meningitis (brain and spinal cord infection with stiff neck, headache, fever, vomiting), muscle pain, muscle weakness, and paralysis, including problems with the muscles for swallowing and breathing. President Franklin Roosevelt survived polio but was paralyzed from the waist down, using a wheelchair and walking short distances with a leg braces and a cane.

The method of transmission was found to be through the mouth by touching something the sick person touched (especially after using the bathroom) and then touching the mouth, or by inhaling contaminated droplets.

Polio was prevalent worldwide prior to the vaccine (a man-made preparation typically using killed, weakened, living or pieces of infectious organisms to provide immunity (protection)), which was developed in the 1950s by Dr. Jonas Salk. Cases rapidly declined after vaccination programs were begun. Polio is rare today, though it is still found in some countries.

Leprosy
Leprosy, also known as Hansen's disease, has been around since ancient times and was spread along migration routes or with armies. It is caused by the bacteria *Mycobacterium lepra* and *Mycobacterium lepromatosis*. How the disease is transmitted (passed) is not clear, maybe by inhaling droplets, maybe through broken skin or other contact. Most people who are

exposed do not develop leprosy, so the disease is not very contagious.

The bacteria infect the nerves and cause damage to multiple organs, but especially the eyes, hands, and feet. It causes skin changes (light patches or red patches) and nodules (lumps and bumps). Leprosy causes weakness of the hands and feet leading to a misshapen hand, trouble walking, and even paralysis. It causes numbness so pain in the hands and feet cannot be felt, and any injury in these areas worsens, so much so that the severely injured finger or toe can be reabsorbed by the body, resulting in loss of fingers and toes. The eyes dry out, the eyelids do not fully close, and corneal ulcers (a sore on the outer covering of the eyeball, usually painful) can lead to blindness.

In modern time, leprosy is treatable if caught early, but in the past, it was feared as a deforming, disfiguring, devastating disease that was mistakenly thought to spread easily. At some points in history, it was even thought to be hereditary (passed down from one's parents), so whole families were shunned. People with leprosy were isolated and stigmatized, including in the United States, which had several places people suffering from leprosy were sent. The most famous was a leper colony on the Hawaiian island Molokai.

Smallpox

Smallpox is a highly infectious disease caused by variola virus. Smallpox has been around for thousands of years, spread from one area of the world to another, for instance throughout Europe during the Crusades in the eleventh century, or to the Americas by European settlers in the seventeenth century. Large numbers of Native Americans died of smallpox.

Smallpox causes fever, blisters in the mouth, a severe skin rash with painful blisters and sores, and often death. Symptoms also include fever, headache, and vomiting, and smallpox could lead to corneal ulcers (a sore on the outer covering of the eyeball, usually painful) and blindness, joint pain, pneumonia (lung infection with chest pain, cough, trouble breathing), and encephalitis (brain infection).

Smallpox is spread very easily, but only by humans (not animals), by breathing in droplets from sneezing or coughing or by touching the fluid from the skin sores.

Since 1979, because of a vaccination (man-made preparation typically using killed, weakened, living, or pieces of infectious organisms to provide immunity (protection)) program, smallpox has been completely eradicated worldwide.

Rabies

Rabies is a virus that is spread through saliva through a bite from an infected animal. Worldwide, approximately 60,000 people still die from rabies each year, mostly from rabid dogs in developing countries. Some countries, especially island nations, have no rabies at all. Rabies is rare in the United States, where it is found mostly in bats, raccoons, skunks, and foxes, though any mammal can be infected. Even so, very few bats in the United States have rabies.

Symptoms begin days to months after the bite, and include fever and chills, muscle aches, headache, then nerve symptoms like pain, tingling, burning, numbness, and then often throat muscle spasm (making it difficult to swallow saliva, leading to foaming at the mouth, coughing, vomiting, and choking), which causes fear of water, especially drinking water. Rabies can also cause agitation, combativeness, muscle paralysis, coma, and death.

There is no good treatment once the symptoms have begun, so suspected bites are treated with preventative shots so the rabies does not take hold. The first vaccine (a man-made preparation typically using killed, weakened, living or pieces of infectious organisms to provide immunity (protection)) was developed in 1885 by Louis Pasteur. Dogs and cats in the United States are required to have rabies vaccinations.

References

UpToDate, Post, TW (Ed), Waltham, MA, https://www.uptodate.com, accessed 2021

Centers for Disease Control and Prevention, https://www.cdc.gov, accessed 2021

## A word about the author...

Susan McCormick is a writer and doctor who lives in Seattle. She graduated from Smith College and George Washington University School of Medicine and served as a doctor for nine years in the US Army before moving to the Pacific Northwest and civilian practice. She is married with two boys, neither of whom have any special powers. She loves giant dogs and has had St. Bernards, an English mastiff, Earl, and two Newfoundlands, Edward and Albert. None of them had any special powers, either, except the ability to shake drool onto the ceiling.

https://susanmccormickbooks.com